Liam

A Walker Brothers Novel

Seven Sons Ranch in Three Rivers Romance™
Book 3

Liz Isaacson

ISBN-13: 978-1-63876-364-2

1

Callie Foster sat on the edge of her bed, the magic of Christmas hardly touching her heart. She normally loved the holidays, especially since the Walker brothers had moved in next door and started sprucing this lane up. They put up garlands and hung Christmas balls on their fences. And the giant oak tree Callie had always coveted in front of their house was filled with lights, tinsel, balls, and even a popcorn string.

That had been added quite last minute for Oliver Osburn, Ivory's son. Ivory was married to Tripp Walker, and Callie couldn't think about the Walker brothers or the ranch next door without thinking about Liam Walker.

"Oh, Liam." She sighed as she ran her hands through her dirty blonde hair. She hadn't showered in a couple of days, but she had plenty of time before the big Christmas dinner at Seven Sons Ranch.

Liz Isaacson

Callie normally loved going next door and eating a meal she hadn't had to think about or cook. Or clean up after. Not only that, but Jeremiah Walker was a fantastic cook, and Callie's mouth was already watering for some of the ham candy he'd serve for lunch.

But it wasn't Miah that made Callie's pulse skip around, and it wasn't Miah she dreamed about at night, and it wasn't Miah who'd asked her out or offered to buy her ranch or actually proposed a crazy idea to help her and Simone keep the Shining Star.

"Actually proposed," she said aloud to herself, the sight of Liam down on both knees, holding that giant diamond out to her, so much hope on his face.

Callie had said no, of course. At the time, she was not going to take Liam Walker's money, even if her ranch was only a month away from getting foreclosed on. She was not going to marry him for his money either, though she'd been all for the idea when it was Evelyn walking down the aisle.

"That was different," she told herself as she padded down the hall to the kitchen. Everything around the ranch was just on the wrong side of shabby-chic, with more shabby than anyone would like.

She set the coffee to brew, no sign of Simone yet. Her sister loved to sleep late, and they had no reason to get up early even if it was Christmas morning. If Callie wanted to get Simone out of bed, she'd make a bacon quiche, the saltiness of the bacon a scent her sister couldn't resist.

Callie had no room to talk, as her brands of kryptonite included ice cream and potato chips. She'd had to go up a size the last time she bought jeans, and the stress of keeping the ranch afloat hadn't helped her ease up on her comfort foods.

So she didn't tempt her sister with bacon, and she went back down the hall to shower while the coffee brewed. She took a long time in the hot spray, first spritzing her eucalyptus mist and inhaling the clear, clean scent to clear her mind, and then reaching for her purple shampoo.

Her hair was naturally blonde, but her stylist had told her to use the brassy-reducing shampoo a few times a month, and Callie was a little bit protective of her hair. At this time, this was all she had in her life.

She hadn't been out with anyone in several years, as she spent all of her time, energy, talent, and money on the ranch. In quiet moments while she stood in the shower, Callie wondered what it would be like without the Shining Star.

What should I do? she prayed, tilting her head back as if that would allow the prayer easier access to God's ears. He hadn't answered any of her previous prayers about the ranch, and though she felt a bit abandoned by Him, she still went to church every week. But she hadn't felt anything there either. She wondered if she was completely past feeling and should just give up.

On everything.

She and Simone could sell the ranch and get a house in town. Simone could still do her antique restoration, and her craft fairs, and Callie would...be completely unhappy.

Completely.

She loved the ranch with everything inside her, and she couldn't imagine her life without it.

You've gotta do something then, she thought and she reached for the lemongrass soap, the scent another of her favorites.

By the time she'd dried, dressed, curled, combed, painted, and plaited her hair, she could smell the evidence that Simone had beaten her to making breakfast. Thankfully.

"Merry Christmas," her sister said from her spot in front of the stove. She grinned like she was thirty years younger and Santa had brought them dozens of toys.

"Merry Christmas," Callie said, getting down a mug for her coffee. "What are you making?"

"French toast," Simone said. "And Mom's hash brown hash."

"Mm." Callie smiled at her sister and opened the fridge to get out some cream for her coffee. She couldn't find it, and she straightened, remembering that she hadn't bought more cream when she'd gone grocery shopping last time.

Because they couldn't afford it.

She turned back to the island and set her coffee down, sighing.

4

"Why don't you just tell Liam you'll marry him?" Simone asked.

"Because," Callie said.

"Because why?"

"Because I'm not taking charity from any of those Walker men."

"Because you're prideful," Simone said. "If one of them was proposing to me, I'd not only say yes, I'd say *heck yes*." She smiled and flipped the French toast. "I mean, what's not to like? Liam is super good-looking, he—"

"You said hot last night," Callie said, cocking her eyebrows and adding too much sugar to her coffee. But she had to do something to make it palatable without cream.

"Fine, he is hot," Simone said. "They all are, and if you can't admit it, you're blind."

"I can admit it," Callie said.

"Good." Simone flipped the three pieces of French toast onto a plate from the pan and set it on the counter next to Callie. "And he's rich, and he wants to help, and he's liked you for a very, very long time."

Callie thought of something Tripp had said to her months ago. *You have to know he really likes you.*

Callie knew, and she felt really bad for keeping Liam at arm's length. Especially because her own feelings for the "super good-looking" cowboy next door were too high and too advanced for her to ignore. If she went out with Liam, she just knew she'd end up kissing him, and telling him that things were actually worse than she'd let on, and then she wouldn't have any choice but to walk down the aisle with him.

And that scared her more than almost anything.

More than losing the ranch?

That was the million-dollar question, and if Callie could just answer it....

"Morning," Evelyn trilled as she came through the front door, her own cowboy billionaire husband right behind her. Rhett had helped a ton on the ranch over the past year, and Callie was extremely grateful for him. But one cowboy's work wasn't enough to save the Shining Star, and Callie had hidden everything from her sister and her brother-in-law. Because Rhett had plenty of money too, and Evelyn knew how to login to the mortgage company and pay the bills.

"Merry Christmas," Simone said gleefully. "Did you bring the syrup?"

"Right here," Rhett said, setting it down on the countertop before kissing Simone's cheek and then Callie's. "Whoa, what's wrong here?"

"Nothing," she said, putting a smile on her made-up face.

"You look nice." Evelyn sat at the bar, her eyes sharp and all-seeing. "What's going on? You gonna try to win over Liam?"

Rhett chuckled. "She already has, like a year ago." He slung his arm around Evelyn and grinned at Callie. "All you have to do is say the right word."

Callie's misery knew no bounds, and she nodded. "I'll be right back."

———

"Cal," Evelyn called after her, but she couldn't stay in the kitchen for another second. She was going to cry, and nobody needed to see her mascara mask. Frustration and anger combined with her misery, and she barely made it behind a closed door before the first sob pulled through her throat. ENTERED the homestead at Seven Sons Ranch last, automatically looking around for Liam. He wasn't in the room yet, and Callie relaxed a little bit.

"Hey, Cal," Miah said as he came in behind her. "Wow, you look nice. Merry Christmas." He smiled at her and squeezed her hand as he moved past her. "Liam's right behind me, and he's pretending to be happy."

Join the club, Callie thought, but she just turned around and saw Liam coming toward her. The butterflies that lived perpetually in her stomach intensified, and she tucked her hair behind her ear.

She went to step back outside, her thoughts tangled. But maybe she could tell him she'd reconsidered the proposal. Maybe....

Her foot caught on the edge of the sliding glass door, and Callie stumbled. A cry came from her mouth, and everything started to move so, so fast.

"Whoa," she heard Liam say as if she was a horse.

Humiliation filled her as her knees hit the deck just outside the door. Her hands landed next, and then Liam was there, one of his warm hands on her back, the other on her arm.

"Hey, it's okay," he said as if he knew she was only a breath away from crying for the second time that day.

She looked up at him through her lashes, feeling stupid for so many things. This latest fall was just one of them. Liam was downright gorgeous, no "super good-looking" or "hot" about it. He'd always made her heart flutter as if it had grown wings, and she couldn't believe he liked her.

She wondered if he liked her for her, or because he felt some sense of duty to help her. She'd never asked him that. Never mentioned it to anyone. And she wasn't ever going to.

Liam certainly looked at her like he liked her, but Callie wasn't sure why. She carried too much weight, and her greatest asset was kindness. Well, that, and her perfectly non-brassy hair.

"Are you okay?" he asked. "You wanna try getting up?"

"Yes, please," she said, accepting his help for this. Why couldn't she accept it when it came to taking thousands and thousands of dollars from the man?

She got to her feet, the steadiness of Liam's hand in hers so comforting. It was starting to get colder in Texas, and she felt a shiver run down her spine. "Merry Christmas, Liam," she said.

"Yeah," he said. "It could be." He grinned at her and reached out and tucked her hair. "Have you—?" He cut off the sentence and held up his hands, backing up. "Never mind. Of course you have."

Callie didn't know what to say. She needed more time to think. To talk to Evelyn and Simone again.

A general wave of hellos went up, and Liam nodded toward the house behind her. "Tripp and Ivory are here."

And Callie wanted to talk to Ivory. Thankfully, Oliver came skipping out to the deck. "Liam, can we go see Pretzel real quick?"

"Sure thing, bud," he said, glancing at Callie. "But we have to be quick, okay? Jeremiah will have dinner on soon, and he doesn't like it when things start late."

"We'll be so fast." Oliver zoomed away from them, making race car noises with his mouth. Liam chuckled, nodded at Callie, that edge of hope in his eyes, and turned to follow the boy.

Callie let him go without even saying thank you for helping her stand up. Pure humiliation filled her, and she turned back to the homestead. It was almost time for lunch, and she wanted to talk to Ivory. She knew Tripp had married her to help her catch up with her bills and help her keep full custody of her son.

And Callie needed to know how Ivory did that,

because then maybe she would be able to do the same thing with Liam.

2

L iam Walker grinned at Oliver Osburn, the boy's enthusiasm exactly what Liam needed to get through this day.

And of course, the very first person he'd seen upon coming in from the ranch was Callie Foster. The very scent of her perfume had met his nose before he'd come out of the barn, and he hated that his pulse still pumped out too many beats at the thought of seeing her. But it did. He liked her a whole lot, despite the last few rocky months.

Very rocky months.

And "few" wasn't the right number. Ever since Rhett and Evelyn's wedding, which was nine months old now, Liam and Callie had been fighting over whether or not he could help her keep the Shining Star Ranch in the Foster family.

Every month, he watched the desperation in her eyes grow. Every month, he watched her dig her heels in harder. He'd suggested everything he could think of, and Callie had done some of them. But the Historical Society of Texas had denied her application for historical status at the ranch. That would've at least prevented the land sharks from circling.

Liam had seen another fancy town car drive down the lane just last week. He hadn't left his office and gone next-door to comfort Callie. She knew where to find him, and she hadn't come to his office.

In fact, Callie very rarely came to Liam, not that he was keeping track.

"Liam, hurry *up*," Ollie called, and Liam pulled himself out of his thoughts. He joined the little boy at the fence that kept the horses in their pasture, laughing at the squirrelly child. "You got any peppermints?"

"It's have," Liam said. "Do you *have* any peppermints?"

Oliver bent down and ripped out a handful of grass without saying anything. He held his palm out flat for Pretzel to take the fresh grass, which the horse did.

Liam put his hand in his pocket, the faint crinkling of the wrapper enough to bring over another couple of horses.

"Liam," Oliver whined. "You got 'im all riled up."

He chuckled and took the candy out of his pocket. "It's fine," he said. "I have plenty." He handed the treat to

Oliver, who struggled to open it, almost tossing it on the ground once the wrapper gave against his grip.

Pretzel pulled back his lips and gave a disgruntled noise, which made Oliver laugh. "He wants the candy."

"He sure does, bud. You better hurry up and feed them. Jeremiah—"

"I know, I know," Oliver said. "He doesn't like it when we're late." He held out the red-and-white striped candy, and Pretzel sucked it right into his rubbery lips. Oliver giggled and giggled, and Liam kept giving him peppermints for each horse.

"All right," he said, once they'd each had one. "That was their Christmas gift. Now, let's get inside so we're not the last ones there."

"All right." Oliver skipped away, and Liam followed him, taking in a deep breath of the Texas Christmas air.

"Is today a good day, Lord?" he asked. Maybe today would be a good day for him to talk to Callie, though he sort of already had.

When he entered the homestead, he swept the large room for Callie, his stomach plummeting when he saw her sitting on the couch in the family room, her sisters and Ivory gathered around. Their heads were all bent together, and he could only imagine what they were talking about.

Nothing good, he knew that. Probably him and his insane marriage proposal. His face burned, and he wanted to leave. Surely there was a restaurant or church group serving Christmas dinner today. The only thing that kept him there was Jeremiah. Oh, and his mother and father, who'd come all the way from Grand Cayman.

Everyone seemed to be talking, and with the number of people who'd come to celebrate the holiday, the noise level was off the charts. Liam stood by the back door and watched for a moment, usually not one to sit on the sidelines. He'd just stepped over to Tripp and Rhett when Jeremiah yelled, "Dinner's ready. Let's gather over here."

He stood between the island and the stove, various dishes on the counter in front of him, with more pots and pans on the burners behind him. He wore a black apron, and while Liam had some skills in the kitchen, he never minded when Jeremiah put food in front of him.

Jeremiah surveyed the group, and Liam remembered what he'd said at one of their family meetings. It was more of an intervention for Tripp, a few weeks ago when he'd been so miserable about Ivory breaking up with him.

I feel nothing. Absolutely nothing.

Liam was starting to understand how his brother felt, and he wished he'd honored the no-women rule the brothers had established for themselves when they'd first arrived in Three Rivers.

"We're so glad to be here," Jeremiah said. "Merry Christmas, everyone. Wyatt, Skyler, Liam, and I put together a gift for all of our guests."

Liam jumped into motion as Jeremiah nodded at him. He took a handful of tickets from Wyatt and started passing them out while Jeremiah continued.

"These are for the New Year's light celebration down-town. We'd love to go together as a family."

Liam handed his last ticket to Ivory, glad someone else had to pass one to Callie and her sisters. Yes, he thought of the Foster women as family, but not in the sisterly way. Well, Simone and Evelyn. But Callie had always acceler-ated his heartbeat, from the very moment he'd met her.

He retreated back to Tripp's side, because his twin was a safe zone for him. "I love the fireworks on New Year's Eve," Tripp said, grinning at his ticket.

"Yeah," Liam said. "And this year, Jeremiah donated a bunch of money to the celebration, and we have a reserved spot."

"Wow," Tripp said. "Jeremiah's a smart one. Fighting the crowd is half of the problem."

"You just don't like crowds," Liam teased.

"And you do?" Tripp nudged him and laughed, and Liam was glad his brother was here. He sure was going to miss him in the office with him, though he'd had a few months alone and done okay. But Tripp and Ivory had just bought a new home out in the eastern estates of Three Rivers, and Liam knew his brother wouldn't be coming back to Seven Sons permanently.

"And now, announcements," Skyler said. "I'll go first." He adjusted his cowboy hat, and Liam could feel his nerves from several feet away.

"What's goin' on with him?"

"He'll say," Tripp said.

"I'm not going to be the mechanic here on the ranch," Skyler said. "I'm going back to school in business and accounting, so I can run the ranch's affairs." He looked so happy, and while surprise moved through Liam, he clapped along with everyone else.

"Wow, college," he said. "I'd rather die than go back to that life."

"Right?" Tripp laughed again. "But it'll be good for him. He never really went."

"All right, all right," Skyler finally said, raising both hands in the air to get everyone to be quiet. "Anyone else with any announcements?"

Liam hated with the fire of a thousand suns that Skyler's gaze landed on him. He pressed his lips together in a tight line and practically willed his brother to look somewhere else.

How humiliating. Of course, everyone at the homestead knew he'd asked Callie to marry him. Jeremiah hadn't even been upset. Well, he'd been a little bit upset, but he'd stayed in the room, so Liam thought he was making real progress.

"We have one," Rhett said, stepping out from behind Liam. "Evelyn is expecting a baby this summer."

A shriek went up from Evelyn's sisters, and Liam sure did like watching the joy as it crossed Callie's face. Liam loved kids, and he grabbed Rhett and hugged him, saying, "Wow, congrats, brother."

He wanted to congratulate Evelyn too, but she stood

too close to Callie, and Liam actually stepped out of the way so everyone could hug Rhett. The din died down, though Mama was actually weeping, and Skyler retook his role as announcement-giver.

"Anyone else?" he asked.

No one said anything, and Jeremiah said, "All right. Let's pray and eat. This ham isn't getting any more candied." That caused more noise as everyone moved over to the table, where Daddy stood at the head of it and grinned around at everyone.

"I know I don't live here," he said. "But we have a tradition in the Walker family to go around the table and say one thing we're looking forward to in the New Year. Sort of a reflection time. Anyone who wants to participate, can. Anyone who doesn't, can simply say they don't want to." He looked at Mama. "Are you in, Penny?"

"Yes, of course," she said, and Grand Cayman hadn't beat the Southern accent out of her, that was for sure. "I'm looking forward to a new grandbaby."

Liam almost rolled his eyes. When it was just the nine Walkers, this tradition was great. But with the additions to the guest list, Liam felt his attention wandering. He perked up when it was Callie's turn, but he refused to lean forward to see her. He'd deliberately sat on the same side of the table as her, so he wouldn't have to look at her or talk to her.

He was interested in what she'd like this upcoming

year to be for her, but she just waved her hand and said, "Merry Christmas, everyone."

Liam's heart filled his throat as Simone said she was looking forward to new opportunities, and Micah said, "I'm looking forward to coming to the ranch... permanently."

That only made everyone roar with questions, Liam included. "What?" he demanded. "When? You're coming?"

Micah smiled around at everyone and said, "Jeremiah said he needs me, and I've...met a wall in Temple."

Met a wall.

Liam had run into a few of those himself, right here in Three Rivers.

"I'll be moving here as soon as I can get things tied up in Temple," Micah said, turning to look at Liam. His eyes begged Liam to move the conversation to something else.

He'd never passed in this tradition before, but today, Liam didn't want to speak.

"Liam?" Daddy asked.

"I'm looking forward to seeing my CGI in theaters this year," he said. His family cheered for him too, and Liam ducked his head. He hadn't meant to brag, but he had worked hard to get the four-year contract, and he worked almost full-time at the computer now, despite the constant wearing of his cowboy hat.

The tradition finally finished, and Jeremiah got up to get the ham out of the oven. "Let's eat."

Relief filled Liam, because maybe he could just stuff himself and go take a nap. Even as he thought that, he knew he wouldn't. They'd done their Christmas Eve gift-exchange last night, but that was one gift per person. Liam had opened a pocketknife from Rhett, and he expected other gifts from his brothers.

From Callie?

He banished the idea from his mind, though she'd given every Walker brother a gift last Christmas. And the one before that. But Liam knew she had no money, and honestly, if she gave him anything of any worth, he'd give it right back.

He talked to Micah on his left and Wyatt on his right, and Liam managed to make it through dinner without wanting to take too big of a bite of ham just to choke himself. He honestly wasn't sure how much longer he could continue in the manner he'd been these past few months.

As he sat there at the dinner table, the holiday merriment around him, he made a decision. If Callie turned him down and gave back the diamond he'd bought her, he'd pack up his bedroom and his huge computer station, and he'd leave town.

He could work from anywhere, and it might actually be easier to be in LA as he worked on the Marvel project. He'd be lost without his cowboy hat, but he could wear it in the privacy of his apartment.

"Let's do presents in a little bit," Rhett said, blowing

out his breath. "I'm stuffed and need a few minutes to recover."

"You didn't have to have seconds of literally everything," Evelyn teased him, and Liam thought they were a perfect match for each other. Of course, he thought that about him and Callie too, and she just couldn't see it.

He got up and picked up his plate, along with Wyatt's, who said, "Thanks, Liam." He took them over to the kitchen sink, where he leaned into his palms and wondered if he could make a hasty escape down the hall and out the front door. The air was so scented and so noisy that Liam was having a hard time breathing in here.

"Hey." Callie appeared at his side. She looked up at him, and Liam lost himself in the depth of her brown eyes. "I was, um, wondering if you'd like to go for a walk with me." She put her dishes in the sink too and brought her gaze back to his.

"Right now?" he asked.

"Yes," she said. "Right now."

3

E very cell in Callie's body vibrated, and she felt like everyone in the room was staring at her and Liam as they stood at the sink.

"Yeah, all right," he drawled, lifting his cowboy hat and running his hand through his hair. Callie still wasn't sure what she was going to say to him, but she couldn't keep avoiding him. She could feel his misery, and she didn't like the choices he made about where he went and where he sat and what he said.

When I learned to accept help from who God put into my life, everything got better.

Ivory's words would not leave Callie's mind. And God had absolutely led the Walker's to this panhandle of Texas, to this ranch right next door.

He turned away from the sink and looked at the people still sitting at the table. Callie did too, noting that

Rhett and Evelyn had moved with Liam's mother and father into the family room. She met Simone's eyes, who nodded resolutely at her.

Be brave, she told herself. She'd had to do hard things before, like learn to make dinner for herself and her family when she was only nine years old. She'd learned how to do hard ranch chores not long after that. And she'd been working her fingers to the bone for decades now.

Maybe it wouldn't be such a bad thing to let Liam take care of her. *Anyone* taking care of her would be a welcome change, though she knew she didn't want just anyone.

Liam walked out of the kitchen, and instead of going toward the back door, which would lead them right past everyone still at the table, he turned left and headed for the front door.

Smart man, Callie thought, slipping away from the crowd with him. He held the door open for her and then joined her on the porch. They stood at the top of the steps, and Callie smiled at the oak tree decorated so beautifully.

She reached over and threaded her fingers through Liam's, who flinched at her touch. The weight of his eyes landed on the side of her face, and Callie almost burst into tears.

"I've been thinking a lot," she said, her voice hoarse. "And I'd like to talk more about what a marriage between us might look like."

A beat of silence passed. "Are you kidding me right

now?" Liam whispered. "Because if you are, this is a very cruel joke."

"Not even a little bit." She turned and met his eyes. "Not a joke."

"You're serious."

"You're the one who showed up at my front door a week ago with a diamond ring," she said. "Remember how I thought that was a joke too?" She managed a shaky smile, and Liam returned it. But his was strong and steady, with a hint of mischief in those gorgeous eyes.

"Let's walk," he said, and he started down the steps. Callie went with him, because she didn't need anyone overhearing this discussion. In her mind, it was more of a negotiation. A time they could set some ground rules. "What are you thinking?" he asked.

"I'm thinking...." Callie paused. "Why don't you tell me what you're thinking?"

"Well," he said, also pausing. So this discussion wasn't easy for him either, despite how calmly he'd done every-thing else over the past several months. "I want to help you, Callie, because that's what friends do. But, I think it's pretty dang obvious that I want to be more than friends."

"You don't love me," she whispered. "Do you?"

"No," he said slowly. "Which sounds so ridiculous, I know. But I think, if you'd let me into your life, we could fall in love."

"So...until that time, I'm imagining us living together at my ranch. *Our* ranch." She shook her head, confused already. "And I feel like *such* an idiot, but I need more help. I just have no way to pay cowboys." The Shining Star used to employ half a dozen ranch hands, and they hadn't truly fallen behind until Callie had started shouldering the workload herself.

"I can pay them," Liam said. "And catch up anything that needs catching up. And I can live at your place. I just need space for my office."

"We have space," Callie said, turning with Liam when he reached the road that passed in front of the ranch. To the left sat the highway that went back to Three Rivers, and to the right waited her ranch. Her run-down homestead. Her desolate fields. Her empty cowboy cabins. Her hollow life.

She pulled back the tears threatening to stain her face. Everything inside her felt so tight. "Once the ranch is up and running again, I'll pay you back," she said.

"Nope," Liam said. He stopped in the middle of the road and stepped in front of her. "Let's be clear about that, Callie. I just saw Tripp and Ivory go through this very thing. She wanted to pay him back for what he'd done to help her too, and it wasn't healthy. So if you say yes to this, and I say yes to this, no one is paying anything back to anyone."

She watched the fire in his eyes burn, and she really wanted it to singe her. Surprisingly.

"When a man and woman get married, they share

their lives," he continued. "And their resources, and that's what I want for us."

For us.

"What if we don't fall in love?" she asked, needing to know what he'd do then. Would there be a debt to pay then?

Liam's features hardened. "I think it's impossible to address every 'what if.'"

"Is it, though?" Callie asked. "What if—?"

"Yes," Liam said over her. "I'd rather just talk about what's troubling you, so we can move past it than worry about what *might* happen."

"The ranch stays in my family," she said.

"I know that."

"Simone gets to live there."

"Of course."

"You have to know that I...." Her mouth felt so sticky and her throat so tight. "I'm not sleeping with you unless we're in love." She drew in a deep breath, and added, "And you should know that I can't have kids. I know you love kids, and you shouldn't have to feel obligated to marry me and try to, I don't even know what." She exhaled heavily. "Fall in love with me? Because you feel bad I can't pay my bills and I might lose the ranch."

There was no *might* about it. If Callie didn't come up with a sizable amount of money by January second, the ranch would go into foreclosure. She hadn't told anyone that yet, and those blasted tears burned in her eyes.

Liam reached up and wiped her face, the gesture so loving and so kind that Callie didn't even care that more tears spilled down her cheeks.

"Are those all of your stipulations?" he asked.

"Repeat them to me," she said swiping at her face as they started walking again.

"You own the ranch, even if I'm paying the bills. Simone gets to live in the homestead. I get an office space and a bedroom, and we're not sleeping together until we're in love."

"And I can't have children," she said, the fact making her heart quiver again. She'd known for years that she wouldn't be able to carry a child, but sometimes the sadness hit her at odd times.

"Why's that?" he asked quietly. "If you don't mind me asking."

"I had a lot of issues," she said. "Tons of scarring in my uterus. It was causing a ton of pain during my, you know. That time of the month. They found cysts on my ovaries too, so they just took everything out."

"I'm so sorry," Liam said. "Because you sound like you would've liked to have children."

"I would have, yes. It's...hard sometimes," she said. "I went through some deep mourning when it first happened, but." She shrugged, though there was nothing to cast aside here. "You should also know that I haven't dated anyone in eleven years. So at the time, the possibility of children was remote. Now I know it's impossible." She gathered her strength and squeezed his hand. "You should too."

"Yes, well, that's not a huge concern for me."

"You love children."

"I do," he said. "And I want kids. And you do too, so we'll have them."

"You want to adopt?"

"Or foster, or whatever," he said. "There are ways to have children if we want them."

They continued down the road, her house getting closer and closer. "What's a huge concern for you?" she finally asked. "You must have some stipulations and rules too."

"I do," he said.

"Let's hear them."

He took a few steps before breathing in deeply. "I don't want you to fight with me about what I spend money on and what I don't."

Callie didn't know how to respond. "What are you planning to pay for?"

"Whatever I need to," he said. "From the ranch buildings, to equipment, to appliances in the homestead. Whatever will make your—*our* lives easier. I have to live there too, you know."

"Whatever you need to," she repeated, thinking of the threadbare carpet in the family room. She'd seen the complete renovation that had happened once the Walker brothers had bought and renamed Seven Sons Ranch. She could not let Liam finance a similar transformation at the Shining Star.

"We can't talk about what you buy or replace?" she asked.

"We can," he said. "But you won't be paying me back, and ultimately, it's my money."

"Your money?" She laughed, the sound not entirely happy. "You just said that when a man and a woman get married, they share their lives and resources."

He chuckled and shook his head.

"Works both ways, Liam," Callie said.

"You're right." He gave her a look out of the corner of his eye. "We can talk about it, but you have to promise to try to see reason."

"I can try," she said.

"Great." He squeezed her hand. "I have just one more thing."

Callie straightened her shoulders and took in the pitiful state of the yard in front of the homestead. "Say it."

He cleared his throat, and a tidal wave of fear moved through Callie. "I don't want you to fight with me when I show affection for you."

"You make me sound like I'm closed-minded and closed-hearted."

"Callie," he said gently. "With me, you have been."

"Ouch," she said, and pure hurt pinched behind her heart.

"Tell me I'm wrong," he said.

Callie pressed her lips together, her emotions swirling and storming inside her. She couldn't argue with him on this, because she really didn't want to accept charity.

"Sometimes," Liam said. "I think you like *Miah* more than me."

"There's nothing between me and Miah except friendship," Callie said sharply. "I've told you that a thousand times. That's another stipulation." She decided on-the-spot. "You can't be jealous of Miah."

"I'm not jealous of Miah," he said.

"Liam."

"I like it when you say my name," he said, smiling at the ground.

Several things inside Callie released, and she gave a light laugh. "Liam, you're not wrong. I will try to be more open to what you say and how I feel about you."

"Thank you," he said. "I think those are all of my rules. Repeat them back to me."

"You don't want me to reject you, and you don't want me to tell you you can't buy stuff, and you want me to confide in you the way I do Miah."

"Oh, that last one is a great addition," he said. "One more." He tugged on her hand to get her to stop.

She looked up at him, and Callie thought if she did what he asked—opened herself up to a real relationship with him—she could easily fall in love with him. The very idea had her pulse in a tizzy. "What?" she asked through a dry throat.

"I don't want our first kiss to be when we get married."
Callie blinked. "So when...?"

"I don't know," he said. "I have to apply for a marriage license, and Rhett told me there's a mandatory seventy-two-hour waiting period. So we have a few days."

"When should we get married?"

"I was actually thinking right after the New Year," he said. "Oh, and I guess I have one more rule."

Weariness filled Callie, but her heart kept pumping, because he wanted to kiss her—soon. "All right," she said. "Better just say it."

"I don't want our marriage to be a secret."

"But it's kind of *not* real," Callie said. "Right? A sort of invented I-do."

"Sure," he said. "It can be invented...until it becomes real."

"Do you really think it will?" she asked.

Liam grinned at her and cocked his head to the side. "I do." He burst out laughing almost before he finished speaking, and Callie swatted his arm.

"You think you're so funny." But she felt like she was about to willingly step off a cliff and fall to her death.

"You're going to write up the rules, right?" he asked.
"Am I?"

"I know you, Callie Foster. You love rules."

She nudged him as they started walking again. "Fine, I'll write them up and text them to you."

"Perfect," he said, sweeping a kiss along her temple.

"Now, let's get back to the homestead before all the pecan pie is gone."

Callie went with him, the conversation on the way back to Seven Sons much easier, though her heart still felt caught in the icy grip of a hurricane.

Seventy-two-hours.

Married right after the New Year.

And he wanted a kiss before the wedding.

Callie hoped she wasn't about to make the biggest mistake of her life, and the moment she entered the homestead, she let go of Liam's hand and hurried over to Simone's side, so much to talk about.

4

Liam got up early the next day, and not because he was behind on his work for Pixelate, though he was. He'd looked up the hours for the county courthouse, and they were open today for three hours.

He wanted to apply for a marriage license before Callie changed her mind. Which was stupid, he knew. She could just as easily tell him she'd had a moment of weakness and didn't want to get married. Having the license didn't ensure anything.

He still pulled up to the courthouse in a tiny Texas town northeast of Three Rivers, which housed the office that issued the licenses, ten minutes before it was set to open. Walking around their ranches yesterday, holding hands...that had been pure bliss for Liam.

Of course Callie had rules for their marriage. Liam knew that in her mind, their marriage wasn't and wouldn't be real. That was fine with him, because he was sure that if she did what she said she would—if she'd open her heart and mind to him—that they could fall in love.

He felt like he was already halfway there, and he seriously needed to pull back on the reins. He couldn't pressure Callie. He just needed her to open the door and let him in.

And she'd said she'd try.

He waited an extra five minutes after the office was supposed to open, and then he went inside. "Morning," he said to the woman at the County Clerk's office. "I need to get a marriage license."

She seemed utterly bored as she passed over the paperwork. "Is your fiancée with you?"

"Uh, no," Liam said, his heartbeat throwing out an extra beat. "Does she need to be?"

"Well, most couples come in together," she said.

"I didn't see that requirement on the website," he said. He'd driven forty minutes north to the county building for this license. If he couldn't get it today, he wasn't sure when he could get back up to the courthouse.

"There's an FAQ on the website," the woman said, smacking her gum. "It's a PDF. It says it in there."

"So I can't apply without her." Liam looked at the woman from under the brim of his cowboy hat.

"No, sir," she said. "She has to show proof of her age, identity, all of that. She has to sign it in front of the county clerk. Unless she's in the military. Is she in the military?"

Liam really wanted to say yes, but his conscience wouldn't let him. "No, ma'am," he said, feeling deflated. "Okay, can I take these and fill them out and come back with her?"

"Sure thing, sugar."

"Thanks." Liam turned away from the window and headed back to his truck. Callie would be up, because she was an early-bird, but Liam didn't want to call her. They hadn't discussed when he'd get the marriage license, though it was completely implied that he would. The fee in Hutchinson County was seventy-six dollars, and he'd be surprised if Callie had that much in her bank account.

Twenty minutes later, he rolled into Three Rivers, and he said, "Call Callie Foster."

A blip sounded over his speakers, and then the cool, electronic voice said, "Calling Callie Foster." The phone rang, and Liam's anxiety grew.

"Hey," Callie said.

"Hey," he practically yelled, adjusting the volume on his radio so he could hear her better. "So I drove up to the county courthouse to get our marriage license, and it turns out, you have to come with me."

"Oh," she said. That was all. Nothing else.

"They're only open this morning for a few hours," he said. "And again on Monday or Tuesday before the New Year holidays." He looked left and right at a stop sign, deciding to turn right and head over to the bakery. "Which of those work best for you to go for a little drive?"

"It's up to you," she said. "You're the one with the busy work schedule."

Liam was busy, but not that busy. And he loved that it was work he could do any time, day or night. There was no clock to punch, and no one expected him to be anywhere at a specific time. He did have meetings from time to time, but they weren't very often.

"Let's go Monday morning," he said, the town of Three Rivers getting busier and busier the closer to downtown he got. "There was a cute little diner up there, and we could have breakfast afterward."

"Sure," Callie said, and Liam practically glowed. He had a date with her. A real date. He'd asked her out on three previous occasions, and she'd said no each time. His heart still throbbed painfully in his chest from all the humiliation he'd suffered.

"What about dinner tonight?" he asked.

"Okay," Callie said.

"Okay?"

"Liam, we're engaged," she said, her voice dropping to a whisper. Or a hiss; he wasn't sure which. "We should probably go out a few times before we get married."

"I know," he said. "I'm just a little surprised. I've asked you out before and been shot down."

"Well, consider this me trying to open myself up a little bit."

Liam chuckled and noticed the street in front of the bakery was packed. A mental groan pulled through him, but he knew why. Heidi Ackerman was seriously the best baker in three counties, and he really wanted a dozen of her cider doughnuts. "Hey, I'm at the bakery in town. You want anything?"

"If they still have that candy cane cookie, I want that," she said.

"That's just wrong," he said, getting out of his truck. "Candy canes should be outlawed for how disgusting they are."

"You bite your tongue, Mister," Callie teased, and Liam thought their engagement was off to a great start. No, he hadn't kissed her yet, but it was only a matter of time.

Liam tipped his head back and laughed, glad when Callie's giggles came through the phone too. "All right, I'll see what they have. Does Simone want anything?"

"She *loves* their double fudge brownies," Callie said.

"Okay, see you in a few." The call ended, and Liam joined the line waiting to be served at the bakery. The scent of maple syrup and chocolate hung in the air, along with the underlying hint of coffee. He was at least a head taller than the woman in front of him, so he could see the pastry cases that lined the back wall of the shop. Three people ran back and forth behind the case, filling orders and smiling like they were having the time of their lives.

Heidi Ackerman herself stood near the door, holding a tray of samples, and she smiled at Liam when he finally made it through the door. "Good morning," she said. "This is a new item I'd love your feedback on." She extended the tray toward him, and Liam didn't care what it was. He was sure it would be delicious.

"It's a macaroon base, with key lime cheesecake on top."

"Wow," he said, taking one of the delicate bites that she'd put in a pretty white paper lining.

"You just pop the whole thing in your mouth," Heidi said with a smile. "How's that ranch down south?"

"Doin' great, ma'am," he said, an idea forming in his mind. "I wonder if I could talk to your son about how he hires his ranch hands."

"I'm sure you could," Heidi said. "But it isn't that hard. Squire will just tell you to go by your gut."

Liam put the key lime cheesecake in his mouth, a moan of satisfaction coming immediately. The cookie base was chewy, with coconut and sugar exploding across his tongue. "This is so good," he said around the small bite. "I would eat a million of these."

Heidi smiled and nodded. "Thank you, Liam. How are your brothers?"

"Good, good." He took a step forward. "Go with your gut, huh?"

"That's right," she said, offering the tray to the person behind him in line. "But call Garth Ahlstrom. He's the one that will know who's available for hire. Squire doesn't deal with anything like that."

"Garth's the foreman?"

"That's right."

Liam was far enough from Heidi now that he couldn't keep yelling to her. She had other customers besides. He turned his attention back to the cases, searching for those cider doughnuts. A whole tray of them waited for him, and Liam decided he'd get a dozen.

When it was his turn, he did get his cider doughnuts, along with the double fudge brownie and two of the candy cane delights. There was nothing delightful about them to Liam, but whatever made Callie happy would make him happy.

The drive down the highway to the ranch went much faster now that he had sugar in the car with him. "Dough-nuts," he called to the house when he entered the kitchen. No one responded, so he could only assume his brothers had gone out onto the ranch. Jeremiah beat the sun up every day, and Wyatt might actually be out at Bowman's Breeds, where he now worked to train horses for the rodeo.

Footsteps sounded on the stairs, and Skyler came around the corner a moment later. "Did I hear the word doughnuts?"

"Cider doughnuts," Liam confirmed. "Where's Micah?" Their youngest brother was supposed to be here through the New Year, and then he'd be returning to tie up whatever loose ends he had. Liam understood loose ends, as he'd been the last Walker brother to move to Three Rivers when they'd bought the ranch almost three years ago.

Of course, his loose ends had involved a female, and he wondered if Micah's did too.

"Uh, he's on the phone."

"That doesn't sound good."

"It sounded intense," Skyler said. "I think he was telling Stephanie that he was moving here."

"I thought he'd broken up with her ages ago."

"I think he thought that too." Skyler shrugged and opened the pastry box. "Oh, you got tons." He took out two treats and turned to get out the milk. "Don't tell Jeremiah." With that, he took everything with him, and Liam shook his head.

"He'll kill you if he finds out."

"He's not gonna find out," Skyler said over his shoulder, his footsteps going back upstairs a moment later. Jeremiah was a bit anal about the kitchen and the food in it, and Skyler taking the whole gallon of milk upstairs? Jeremiah was definitely going to find out.

But Skyler had never been one to follow rules, and he sure did like making trouble. Most of the time, Liam enjoyed being at his brother's side while they did some mischievous thing, but now that he was forty, he supposed he'd rather focus on more important things than drinking straight from the milk carton or jumping off bridges into fast-moving rivers.

Like Callie Foster.

He turned back the way he'd come and once again bypassed his elaborate computer set-up in the office in favor of getting behind the wheel of his truck. He drove the quick half-mile to the Shining Star Ranch and grabbed the pastries he'd bought for his fiancée and her sister.

His fiancée.

Liam's smile was wide and instant, and he still wore it when Callie opened the door. "Hey, there," he said, handing her the bag with her cookies in it. "You look great."

She took the bag and actually looked down at herself. "These jeans are dirty."

"Yeah," he said, crowding into her personal space. "And sexy. I like them."

"Sexy?" Callie squeaked as Liam stepped past her and into the homestead.

"I like the shirt too," he said, though it was just a regular T-shirt.

"It literally has a cow on it." Callie closed the door behind him. "You're insane."

He chuckled as he went past what used to be Evelyn's office at the front of the house and into the living room. "Nah. Maybe I just like cows."

"Right." Callie joined him in the kitchen, where he put down Simone's brownie. Callie didn't wear any makeup that morning, and her dirty blonde hair looked like half of it was up and the other half was supposed to be.

"I can't think my fiancée is pretty?" Liam asked, grinning at her.

Callie stared at him, her eyes widening. "Your fiancée."

He glanced down at her left hand, but she wasn't wearing the ring he'd given her. "Are we not engaged?"

"We are," she said.

"So you'll wear the ring when I take you to dinner tonight." He wasn't really asking, and he didn't really like the level of shock in Callie's face. "Where's Simone?" he asked, to cover up the moment.

"Outside," Callie said, her voice on the hollow side of normal. She opened her bag of cookies and pulled out one red-and-white-striped catastrophe. "And yes, I'll wear the ring tonight when we go to dinner."

A smile spread through Liam's whole soul. "Great," he said, already thinking of how the date would end instead of how it would begin.

He couldn't help hoping and praying for a kiss that night. Did that make him delusional?

Probably, he thought. He just didn't care. He never thought Callie would agree to marry him either, but she had. Maybe she was full of more surprises too.

5

"Hey, so we need to talk about money." Callie didn't want to talk about money. She didn't want to talk about anything hard with Liam at all. She wished she was a regular fiancée about to marry a cowboy billionaire and be swept off her feet. Flown all over the world on an extravagant honeymoon while others tended to her chores here on the ranch.

"All right," Liam drawled. He sat down on a barstool, his eyes glued to her mouth as she lifted her cookie to take a bite. "I really don't understand what you like about those."

Callie smiled as she chewed. "They're sweet and minty," she said. "Delicious."

"Mint is so overpowering," he said.

"Well, if you want a kiss tonight, you better have minty fresh breath." Callie sucked in a breath as soon as the words left her mouth. She had no idea where they'd come from, and she felt wildly out of control.

Liam laughed though, and that only added fuel to the raging fire in her stomach. She wanted to make him laugh like that again. "Noted," he said. "What do we need to talk about with the money?"

Callie's nerves took over, finally subduing the hormones that had prompted her to flirt. "I haven't told anyone this. Not even Simone. But if I don't get caught up on the payments by January second, the ranch will go into foreclosure."

Alarm pulled across Liam's face. "Let's take care of that right now." He pulled out his phone, as if such things could be taken care of with an app. Maybe they could. He'd be the one to know, as he did everything with the latest and greatest technology. "How do I login to make a payment?"

"Let me get my laptop," she said.

"And then I want a tour of the house and ranch," he called after her as she started toward her bedroom.

She paused in the mouth of the hall. "You've seen the house and ranch."

"I've been over here," he said. "I haven't seen the ranch. I need to know what we're working with." He looked around the kitchen and living room, and foolishness rushed through Callie like a tsunami. Could he feel how outdated everything was? Would he insist on replacing everything?

Don't argue with him, she coached herself as she went to get her laptop. After all, she'd literally just asked him to get her caught up on her ranch payments, so if he wanted to get new curtains, she didn't know how to tell him no.

"All right," she said, re-entering the kitchen with her computer. "We can logon here." She sat next to him, surprised when he slipped his arm around her. So surprised, she flinched.

"Sorry," he murmured, immediately removing his hand.

"I just...it's fine," Callie said, but her voice was too high. She hadn't lied when she'd told Liam she hadn't dated in eleven years. Over a decade without a kiss, without holding a man's hand, without being in a place where a sexy cowboy like Liam could put his arms around her and she wouldn't jump.

"I'm kind of a touchy-feely guy," he said. "But I can see we're not there yet."

Callie cut a look at him out of the corner of her eye. "I like being touched."

His eyebrows went up, and his expression danced with amusement. "Is that so?"

"That came out wrong," she said, a laugh bursting from her mouth. "I mean, it's been a while since I dated, remember? I just maybe need some time to realize that you're my—" Her voice cut out, but she forced herself to keep going. "Fiancé, and it's okay for you to put your arm around my waist."

She tapped on the computer to wake it, and then she clicked to open the Internet. "It's a little slow."

Liam watched the computer struggle as it tried to bring up the web browser. "Is it the Internet service or your machine? Because this is not going to work for me, baby."

She looked at him, realizing he was dead serious. "I honestly don't know."

He pulled out his phone and tapped. "I'm putting Internet at the top of my list," he said.

"What list?"

"List of things that must work." He got up and went around the island. "Can I get a drink?"

"Yeah, of course. Cups in the cupboard by the sink."

He opened the right one and stepped over to the refrigerator.

"That doesn't work, remember?" She nodded to the sink. "But there's ice in the freezer in a real ice cube tray, and we just drink the water out of the tap."

He lifted one eyebrow, which made her smile, and set down his glass. "Refrigerator." His thumbs flew over the screen, and Callie's embarrassment grew. She wanted to argue that the fridge they had worked fine whether it produced its own ice cubes or not, but she remembered his rule.

Open mind, she told herself. *And Dear Lord, please help me to accept his help. Help me shelve my pride.*

The website finally loaded, and Callie said, "A-ha," as

she leaned forward to type in the address for her bank. With that pulled up, she logged in while Liam cracked ice out of the tray and filled his water glass. "You want anything?" he asked, and Callie really appreciated that he'd asked.

"I'd love another cup of coffee," she said, and Liam set about making that for her too.

"Cream or sugar?" He opened the fridge, but they still didn't have any cream. "No cream?"

"We're out right now," Callie said.

Liam said nothing, but the way his thumbs flew over his device spoke volumes.

"Okay, I'm in," she said, looking at the impossibly huge number indicating the amount she owed. She reached up and covered it, heat filling her whole body. "I'm so sorry, Liam. I feel like an idiot."

"That should've been a rule of mine," he said. "We don't apologize to each other, unless we've done something to hurt the other. I don't care how far in the hole you are. And you don't care that I ate four cider doughnuts before I even made it back to the ranch."

She smiled, glad when he returned the gesture. "But I still feel stupid. I feel stupid my fridge is broken and doesn't make ice. I feel stupid my computer is so old or the Internet doesn't work. Whatever it is. I feel so stupid that I let things get this bad." She looked at him, everything she'd kept secret about to be blown wide open.

Liam took both of her hands in his, gently guiding the

one away from the screen where she was trying to hide how much she owed. "Callie," he said, very seriously. "We all make mistakes. We all do things we're not proud of. We all feel stupid for something."

"Oh yeah?" she challenged. "Name one thing you've done that you're not proud of."

"How about me groveling at your feet for the past nine months?"

"You—didn't—you—" Callie didn't know what to say.

"I'm pathetic," he said with a gentle smile. "I feel stupid about that. I just keep thinking, she's not going to want me. I can't even control my emotions."

"I don't think that," Callie said quietly.

"And I don't think you should feel embarrassed because you got a little behind on your bills."

"Liam," she said slowly, really drawing out his name. "I'm not a little behind. Evelyn paid for a lot with her matchmaking income, and when she stopped doing that and married Rhett...I stopped paying the mortgage."

He blinked a few times. "Oh." He glanced at the computer, but Callie grabbed the lid and almost shut it.

"I'm so sorry," she whispered, feeling stupider and stupider by the moment.

Liam's eyes twinkled like black stars when he leaned closer. "It wouldn't matter if you'd never paid the mortgage once, sweetheart," he said. "I could buy this ranch with cash and have enough money leftover to buy another one. And another one. And another one. Now, please pass that computer over here and let's make sure our home doesn't go into foreclosure."

Our home.

Callie had fought so hard to hold onto this place. It was her home, and she didn't want to lose it. She reminded herself of that, and her desire to keep the Shining Star Ranch and the land it sat on in her family was more powerful than her humiliation.

So she did what Liam asked, and she cradled her head in her hands while he clicked and tapped and typed. Only three minutes later, he said, "Done. And will you email me everything I need to logon to this again and pay the mortgage moving forward?"

Callie could only nod, her gratitude so deep and so wide. She leaned into Liam, glad when he enveloped her in his strong arms. "Thank you, Liam." She'd never known such relief—nor such comfort. Being held by him, she could *feel* his strong feelings for her. Could he feel hers?

His lips touched her hairline, and Callie leaned into the kiss. "Anytime, sweetheart," he said. "Anytime."

"Hey," Simone said from behind her, and Callie straightened, causing Liam to release her.

"I brought you a brownie," he said. "I heard you loved the double fudge."

"Oh, wow," Simone said with a smile. "Thanks, Liam." Her eyes held dozens of questions as she joined them in the kitchen. "What's going on here?"

"You didn't tell her?" Liam asked.

"Simone is the best sister ever," Callie said, meeting her sister's eye. "But no, I thought we could tell her together."

"You didn't," Simone said, her voice hushing. She looked back and forth from Callie to Liam and back. "She said yes, didn't she?" Glee poured off of Simone in waves, and while Callie had known there was more at stake if they lost the ranch than just her life, she'd never felt it as keenly as she did in that moment.

"Yes," Liam said, grinning as widely as Simone. "She said yes."

Simone lifted her hand, and she and Liam gave each other high five. "Hey," Callie protested. "Were you two in on this together?"

"Of course not," Liam said. "I tried to contain my humiliation to my own ranch, thank you very much."

Simone unwrapped her brownie and took a bite. She chewed and swallowed while Callie thought about what Liam had said. He'd done a lot of things over the past several months that had annoyed her. She'd turned him down several times, from his offers to buy the ranch, to his offers to take her to dinner. She'd flat-out denied feelings for his brother and insinuations that she and Jeremiah had been having a secret relationship. After that, she and Liam hadn't spoken to each other for twenty-six days, and that had ended when he'd come over and apologized to her.

No, he wasn't perfect. But he was patient, and he was kind, and another blast of regret hit Callie that she hadn't been nicer to him. That she hadn't been better. And she wondered why he'd kept coming back....

"Let's take that tour now," Liam said. "Unless you've got another pressing chore."

Giving the tour would be a pressing chore—something that would press the life right out of her lungs. But the man had literally just paid over twenty-five thousand dollars to settle her account. If he wanted a tour, he was going to get one.

"Everyone's fed," Simone said, but Callie knew there was more to ranch work than just making sure the horses and cattle got enough to eat and drink. The reason they couldn't pay their bills was because they had to buy hay and other supplies from someone else. Most ranches produced their own hay, but Callie couldn't plant, cultivate, and harvest enough. Her equipment was old, and what she could do with just her two hands wasn't enough. Wasn't even close to enough.

"Let's take the tour," Callie said. "And you better bring that phone and a portable charger. I think you're going to be taking a lot of notes." Her stomach felt like she'd swallowed a brick instead of a delicious candy cane cookie, but she couldn't back out of their arrangement now.

In fact, she didn't even want to. As she left the house through the back door, all she could think about was where her first kiss with Liam Walker would be. And those weren't the thoughts of a woman who was being forced to do something against her will.

"Okay, so as you can see, we don't keep up great with the yardwork," she said, gesturing vaguely to the lawn.

"It's winter," he said. "We won't worry about that until spring." He glanced back to the house. "Does Simone do anything on the ranch?" He looked at Callie, and she couldn't find any judgment in his face. "Not that I care. I'm just trying to get an accurate picture of what I'm dealing with here."

"Not much," Callie said. "She spends most of her time in her antiques shop or looking for more items to refurbish. She'll help with feeding and stuff, if I need her to."

Liam nodded, his mouth drawing down. "Okay, got it."

Callie looked out over the Texas landscape she loved so much. "All right, let's get this over with."

Please let him still want to do this once he sees the disaster this ranch is, she prayed. She really needed God to hear and answer this one prayer more than any other she'd ever uttered. Because she desperately needed help, and not just financially.

6

L iam couldn't help feeling like he'd been duped, just a little. He knew the Foster sisters worked hard, but it honestly felt like neither one of them knew how to run a ranch. Callie and Simone didn't want to lose it either, but they sure didn't seem to even like ranching.

"Why do you want to keep this place?" he asked as they went through the back gate and onto the ranch. Everywhere he looked, something needed to be fixed or done. Jeremiah would go crazy over here, and Liam had been thinking about bringing his brother over for a consultation.

This ranch needed a foreman, and at least six cowboys working full-time to get it back in shape. Get everything cleaned up and cleared out. Go through inventory in the tool shed, the equipment shed, the hay barn. He had no idea when the last time the cattle had been checked by a vet, let alone the horses. Did she shoe them herself? Because farriers weren't cheap.

He wouldn't take notes, because honestly, he couldn't type that fast. Literally everything needed attention, and he could've typed that in and been good.

Everything.

"I grew up here," Callie said. "My momma died here. The ranch has been in the Foster family for four generations."

"Old ties," he muttered, halfway to himself. He understood those. He did. "Do you even like ranching?"

"Uh." Callie's hesitance answered the question.

"So you just want to keep the ranch," he said. "But you don't want to actually work it."

"I don't...know?"

"It's okay to want to keep it and not work it," he said gently. "I just need to know so I know who to hire and what to have them do."

"I grew up as the oldest," she said, her voice heavy. "Daddy didn't have any boys, so he taught me and my sisters to work the ranch. I never had the option to do anything else. Not like Evelyn or Simone did."

Liam heard a touch of bitterness in her voice. He wasn't the oldest, so he didn't understand those expectations. His life had always been up to him, and he'd chosen what he loved and was good at.

"Callie," he said. "I don't care if you stay in the homestead and watch TV all day, just so we're clear. But you want the homestead and the ranch, right?"

"Yes," she said.

"So you define what role you want to have, and I'll get people to do the rest."

"Well, I don't even watch TV, so that's not what I want."

"You don't watch TV?"

"Who has time for that?"

"Oh, I love a good British murder mystery."

Callie burst out laughing, and Liam was glad he could make her do that. "Shut up," she said. "You do not."

"I so do," he said. "I sometimes watch them while I'm working. They're awesome." He reached for her hand, glad she didn't flinch away from him this time. "Do you know what you'd like to do?"

"I haven't thought about it," she said. "I've always just done what I could."

"What you thought you were *supposed* to," he said, his heart bleeding a little bit for her. "But if you could do anything, anything at all, what would that be?"

"I like to cross-stitch," she said.

"That's a hobby, sweetheart," he said. "Not a career. Like a job. what do you want to do for a job?"

"Nothing?" she guessed. "I don't know, Liam. That's a hard question."

"It shouldn't be," he said, looking over at her. Callie

was a strong, beautiful woman. He'd always liked her generous spirit and quick, kind smile. She'd taken all of the brothers under her wing and taught them about small-town Texas without a single complaint. She put up with their loud parties next door, and all the new construction at Seven Sons that had taken about a year to complete.

She loved her family fiercely, and she loved this ranch. But he couldn't understand how she had no idea what she wanted her life to be.

"When you look around this land, and think about the house," he said. "What do you see yourself doing?"

"Taking care of the cowboys," she said.

"So you want to be the ranch matron." That role fit her to a T, and he smiled at her. "That's the perfect job for you. Feeding them lunch and making sure everyone feels important and cared about." He squeezed her hand, a slip of peace entering his soul. "You're really good at that."

"Am I?"

"Yes," he said simply. "And we get a foreman to run the ranch. You have cowboy cabins, I assume?"

"Yes," she said. "They're over there, tucked against those trees." She pointed west, but Liam couldn't see them from this far away.

"How many?"

"Five or six," she said. "No one's lived in them in years."

So they'd need a lot of work, and Liam hoped Micah would move to Seven Sons sooner rather than later. Then

Liam could employ his carpenter brother's hands to help him get everything back in good repair.

"Horses here," Callie said, and Liam saw five or six horses in the pasture in front of him. It did look like someone took care of it, and bit of relief moved through him.

"I'll admit I don't know the first thing about ranching," he said, putting his foot on the bottom rung of the fence separating him from the horses.

"You don't? You work at Seven Sons, don't you?"

"Uh, a little." Liam shrugged and held his hand out to one of the pretty bays that came toward him. "The cowboy hat and boots are more for show, sweetheart."

Callie laughed, and Liam liked that. "I don't believe that. I know Miah's told me you've been out on the ranch before."

Liam turned toward her and slung his arm over the top rung of the fence. "Oh? You been askin' about me?" He grinned at her, but part of him wanted to know.

Callie tucked her hair and ducked her head. "I mean, there was a time when we weren't speaking, you know? I had to know where you were so I wouldn't run into you."

All of the air got punched out of Liam's lungs. He wanted to say so much, but it took him a moment to draw in a breath. "I hated those times," he whispered.

"Me too." Callie lifted her eyes to his, and Liam didn't have any gum with him. No breath freshener. The last minty thing that had touched his mouth was his tooth-paste, hours ago.

He leaned down and kissed Callie anyway, instant heat filling his body. He pulled in a breath without removing his lips from hers, thrilled when her fingers slid up the back of his neck and into his hair.

She was kissing him back.

Liam had imagined this moment for a long time—too long. He'd planned the most romantic places, and fanta-sized about the perfect conversation they'd have before he'd lean down and make sure she knew how he felt about her.

This kiss was so much better than any of that, though he'd never thought he'd kiss her next to the horse pasture on her own ranch.

He broke the kiss, every fiber of his being vibrating like he'd been hooked up to a powerful energy source. He didn't know what to say, and that was a first for him. Callie wrapped her arms around him and leaned into his chest, giving him the opportunity to hold her, breathe in the soft floral scent of her hair, and bask in the glory of this moment.

Liam closed his eyes, wanting to memorize everything about this situation, right down to the smell of dust and horses in the air, the mid-morning sun on his back, and the shape of Callie in his arms.

"Do you want to keep going?" she eventually asked, and Liam nodded. He held her hand as they moseyed around the ranch. Callie pointed out the things she did, and those seemed to be in good repair, from the hay troughs for the cattle, to the stables where the horses were sheltered. The fields closest to the epicenter of the ranch had been cleared for the winter, but Callie didn't actually know how big the Shining Star was.

"I feel way out of my league," Liam said as they started down the road that would lead in front of the abandoned cowboy cabins.

"Tell me about it," Callie said miserably.

"At least you know more than how to fill a water trough," he said. "That's what I do at Seven Sons, and only if Jeremiah says he needs me."

Callie stepped in front of him, and Liam met her eye. "So we help each other," she said. "That's what, uh... people do, right?"

"People?" he asked, because he wanted to hear her say the words.

"Husbands and wives," she said, lifting her chin a little. "You can't be good at everything, Liam."

"I know that."

"Do you?" she teased. "I think you sometimes forget because you're so good at everything."

"I am not," he said.

"Name one thing you can't do."

"I'm a terrible golfer," he said. "I can't throw a ball to save my life. I mean, I can, but it doesn't go where I'm aiming."

Callie giggled and snuggled into his embrace again. "Keep going. I like this game."

Liam rolled his eyes though she couldn't see him. "I'm good at making desserts. I like trying different ice creams the best. And flavored popcorns."

"I can't wait for that," she said. "But I've already gained a ton of weight this year, so I might have to pass on the ice cream."

"You're perfect the way you are," he said.

She backed up, a dangerous glint in her eyes now.

"What?" he asked, but he should've just taken her hand and asked her to tell him about the cabins on his right.

"Nothing," she said.

"I think you're beautiful," he said. "I've told you that before."

She said nothing, and Liam decided to let the subject drop. He didn't need to grab a shovel and start digging himself into another hole. Maybe then she wouldn't marry him. Maybe they'd go another month or two without speaking.

They arrived back at the homestead, and Callie took him upstairs to the bedrooms there. Honestly, he'd gut the whole thing and start fresh. New paint. New flooring. All new appliances and furniture.

An idea started forming in his head, but he knew Callie would never agree to it.

"And that's it," she said once they made it back to the

kitchen. She picked up her bag with the candy cane cookie in it and looked inside.

"Cal, what about a honeymoon?" If he could get her out of the homestead for a bit, he could hire a whole team of people to come in and spruce things up. She'd lived here her whole life—and so had that carpet in the family room.

"A honeymoon?" Her eyes rounded, and Liam had his answer. "I don't...do we need to do that?"

"Do we need to do any of this?" Liam asked. "I just settled your account. We don't need to get married at all." And there the words were. He'd offered to buy her ranch and give her the deed.

She'd said no.

He'd asked her out on dates.

She'd said no.

Rhett had suggested applying for historical status.

That hadn't worked.

She simply wouldn't take charity from the Walker brothers, and so Liam had gone to his last resort.

But they didn't really need to get married.

Callie stared at him, searching his face. He didn't need to buy a bride. In fact, the idea of her marrying him as a sort of repayment for him paying her bills really left a bad taste in his mouth. His stomach squirmed, and he fell back a couple of steps.

"I'm going to go," he said, because he wasn't comforted by her silent stare-fest either. He'd spoken true. They did not need to get married for him to help her with the ranch. He could fund everything silently and effectively from half a mile down the road, in the safety of his own office.

He pulled open the front door and nearly plowed into a man standing there. "Oh," he said, trying to stall his forward momentum. He did, and he also noticed the freshly pressed suit the man wore.

One quick glance over his shoulder revealed the shiny, black SUV parked in the driveway. So he was a land shark, and he smelled blood here at the Shining Star.

"Do you own this property?" the man asked, his voice as greasy as his hair.

"I sure don't," Liam said, turning as Callie came up behind him. "She does."

"Ma'am, are you aware this property is going to auction next week?" He actually extended his hand for Callie to shake.

She stood beside Liam, her displeasure rolling off of her. Liam detected anger too, but the suited man on the porch just smiled like he'd invited them to a picnic. "I'm here to offer you top dollar for this ranch."

"The ranch isn't for sale," Callie said.

"Everything is for sale," the man said, his smile stuck in place. "You can't pay for this place, and the worst thing that can happen is someone buys it out from under you in an auction." He clicked his tongue as he shook his head. "Bad business, those auctions. Places go for very low. Very low indeed."

Liam thought this guy was a very low human, and he took a half-step in front of Callie. "It's not going to go to auction," he said. "She just paid up on her mortgage this morning."

Surprise moved across the man's face. "Oh, well. Hopefully that posts before the auction is announced." He saluted them and spun around. Liam stood there and watched him stride back to his car, and then Callie sagged into him.

"What does that mean?" she asked.

"It doesn't matter," he said. "We paid the bill."

"*You* paid it," she said.

"It doesn't matter who paid it," he said. "The bank doesn't care where the money comes from." He glanced down at her, and she wore a terrified look on her face. She blinked, and it disappeared.

"I'm going to go call the bank," she said. "Make sure the payments are there."

"All right." He watched her bustle into the kitchen too, picking up her phone and opening that Jurassic computer. He'd replace that too. Rewire the house with lightning fast Internet. Install security cameras. The works.

He turned away from Callie and left the house, bringing the door closed behind him. Would she even marry him now?

Why did he want her to so badly, especially if he knew she didn't love him and had only agreed to it so he'd pay her bills?

Hopeless fool, he told himself as he went down the steps and got behind the wheel of his own truck.

"Guide me, Lord," he said, but no promptings came. So he went back to his own ranch and sat down in front of his command center. After all, he had work to do, and no one at Pixelate cared if his personal life was in complete turmoil.

7

C allie couldn't believe what she was hearing. "But I paid this morning," she said. "Like, an hour ago."

"I realize that, Miss Foster," the man on the other end of the line said. He'd said his name when she'd been transferred to him, but Callie couldn't remember it. Right now, she was having a hard time remembering her own name.

"The bank is still concerned about your future ability to pay your bill," he said. "So while your account will be marked current by the end of business today, there's still a chance of foreclosure."

"How big of a chance?" she asked, feeling lightheaded. She collapsed onto the couch and glanced over when Simone walked in the back door.

"That's up to the loan officer," the man said. "Her name is Lois, and she won't be in until the fifth."

"The ranch was supposed to go into foreclosure on the second," Callie said, her throat so, so tight.

"Oh...yes...I see that."

And? Callie wanted to scream. She ran her hand down her face and bent over, a full-blown panic attack starting. She couldn't breathe. Couldn't think. She rocked back and forth, trying to find a way through this dark maze her life had become.

Simone's touch on her back brought her back to the present, and she looked up at her sister.

"What's going on?" she whispered, but Callie just shook her head.

"Can't someone else look at the account?" Callie asked. "I mean, I *paid* this morning."

"Ma'am," the man said again, and he sounded like he was working really hard to be patient with her. "You've had a notice of foreclosure for sixty days."

"I just got the money today," she said. "And I paid before the sixty days were up." She hadn't even told her sister about the foreclosure, and absolute guilt hit her squarely in the chest.

"The loan officer will have to review the situation," he said.

"Will there be an auction?" Callie asked, thinking of that slimy man on the front porch. She also thought about how Liam had stepped right in front of her to defend her. When he'd said they didn't need to get married at all, Callie's brain had stalled. Of course they didn't need to get married for him to logon to her bank and pay her mortgage. He'd done that a couple of hours ago, no marriage license needed. No diamond ring. No dress. No rules for how they could live their lives.

"Possibly," the man said. "That's generally what happens when a property goes into foreclosure. We try to get whatever we can for it, to recoup some or all of the loan."

"But I've paid," Callie said, pushing her confusing situation with Liam from her mind.

"Ma'am," the man said. "I really don't know how else to tell you this."

"Tell me like I'm five years old," she said. Simone threaded her fingers through Callie's and squeezed. Her eyes were so earnest and afraid, and Callie couldn't believe she'd brought them to this point.

"You were ten months behind on your mortgage," the man said. "So yes, I can see a pending payment here that will bring your account current. But the fact remains that we have no guarantee of future payments, and your account has been flagged as high-risk for us." Tapping sounded on his end of the line. "Over the past five years, you've only made one payment on time. Honestly, ma'am, I don't see us hanging onto this loan."

Callie closed her eyes, her mind going dark. The man continued to talk, something about how he couldn't really say, he wasn't a loan officer, her account could be sold to another bank, blah, blah, blah.

What she needed to know was how to get the loan officer to keep her account and stop the auction from happening.

"What do I need to do?" she asked when he finally stopped talking. "What's the solution?"

"I see you have a savings and a checking account with us."

"That's right."

"Your checking account is in the hole right now, ma'am. And you have seventy-three dollars in savings. If those accounts had more money in them, or if there was another account you had linked to yours, where we could see that you had the means to continue to pay the loan...." He let the words hang there, and Callie thought of Liam's bank account.

She hated herself keenly in that moment.

"Can I ask how you paid your bill this morning, ma'am?"

"I got a gift," she whispered. Liam *was* a gift to her, and so was his money. He'd said they didn't have to get married, but Callie wasn't sure how to accept charity from him if they weren't. Could he really just write the checks while she...did what, exactly? Ran the ranch further into debt?

"The loan officer will want an LOE for that."

Callie pinched the bridge of her nose. "A what?"

"A letter of explanation. And will you be getting more gifts? We generally frown upon that type of income, as it's not reliable enough to pay something that comes due every month."

Callie just wanted this call to end. Just when she'd thought she'd hit rock bottom. "Thank you," she said, hanging up even as the man started to say something else.

"Callie," Simone said. "What is going on?"

She leaned back against the couch and closed her eyes. "We're going to lose the ranch. There could be an auction, and it's been in foreclosure for months, and even though Liam paid this morning, it might be too late." Tears streamed down her face. She opened her eyes and looked at Simone. "I'm so sorry. I can't do this. I've ruined everything."

Simone gathered her into a hug and held her tight. She didn't say it was okay, because it wasn't okay. They had no money. And in eight days, they might not have a place to live.

She couldn't stand to be comforted right now, and she broke the embrace with her sister. "I can't fix this. I thought I could, but I can't."

"I thought you were going to marry Liam," Simone said.

"I said yes." She studied her hands. "But it doesn't matter. He paid the mortgage this morning, and it still doesn't matter." She looked up at Simone. "And we don't need to get married for him to pay our bills. It's not necessary."

"You like Liam," Simone said, as if that mattered at all.

"I do," she said. Callie liked Liam a whole lot. "But what kind of marriage is it if he's just around to pay the bills?" She shook her head. "He'll end up resenting me, and I already feel so guilty. I mean, what does he get out of doing this?"

"He gets you," Simone said.

"So what? He's *bought* me?" Callie's fury came roaring back. "And I have to do what he says?"

"He's not like that."

No, he wasn't. But it was a very slippery slope, and Callie knew she could slide right into his bed to show him her gratitude after he'd hired the cowboys they needed to get the ranch running well again. Or after he bought a new refrigerator that actually made ice. Or when he paid for anything at all. And she'd never been with a man, and she was absolutely terrified of being intimate with anyone, most of all Liam, who she wanted to think so highly of her.

But how could he?

He'd pay for things, and she'd have sex with him? Liam wouldn't respect her then.

She bolted to her feet. "I'm *not* a prostitute."

"Callie," Simone called, but she couldn't stay in the house for another second. She burst out the back door, great wracking sobs shaking her shoulders. She ran as far as she could before her lungs felt like they'd burst.

She bent over and braced her elbows against her knees, sucking at the air. "Help me," she begged. "Please help me."

God knew what she wanted. She'd been praying for a way to save the ranch for years now. And those Walker brothers had moved in right next door.

When I learned to accept help from who God put into my life, everything got better.

Callie straightened, a sense of calmness coming over her. "So Liam's in my life," she said to the still air around her. "I'll accept his help. But I'm not sleeping with him so he'll pay my bills."

He doesn't expect you to. She wasn't sure if the voice was hers or someone else's, but she managed to wipe her tears.

She pulled her phone from her pocket and called the bank again. After another transfer, she got the same man she'd been talking to. "Yes," she said. "Callie Foster again. What if I linked my husband's account to mine? Would that be enough?"

"That depends, ma'am," he said. "But a balance big enough to cover things for a while would definitely help."

Callie nodded, her solution becoming crystal clear. "How do I do that?"

"Does he have an account here?"

"I don't know," she said.

"You don't know where your husband's bank account is?"

Callie didn't appreciate the condescending tone, but she ignored the river of fury-frustration moving through her. "We're not married quite yet," she said. "I'll find out."

"If he had an account here, that would be best."

"Thank you." Callie hung up and faced east. She couldn't see the homestead at Seven Sons from here, but she knew it was there. Everything to the east was far superior to the buildings and accommodations here at the Shining Star, and Callie started another walk.

She'd once asked Evelyn if she was doing something illegal or something to be ashamed of when she'd married Rhett the first time. She hadn't been—and Callie wasn't either.

She went in through the back door of the homestead at Seven Sons, like she'd done countless times before. Jeremiah stood in the kitchen, his back to her as he looked at his phone, something whirring in the microwave.

He turned when he heard her footsteps, and Callie burst into tears.

"Hey, whoa," he said kindly, abandoning his phone and his food to hurry over to her. "What's wrong? Are you hurt?"

Oh, she was hurt all right, and she had no idea how to make the pain go away. He gathered her into his arms, but there were no sparks. No heat building in her. No desire to kiss this Walker brother. Miah was her best friend, though, besides her sisters and Liam, and it was nice to have his support.

"I've really messed up, Miah," she said, pulling away and remembering her promise to Liam. "Where's Liam?"

"In his office, I think." He stepped back, the concern

still plain in his eyes. "You're going to marry him, aren't you?"

"Yes," Callie said, a vision of how Miah had gone nuts when he'd found out about Rhett and Evelyn's marriage running through her mind.

Miah's jaw jumped, but he just nodded. "He's in the office." He went back over to the microwave, his shoulders definitely more tense than before. Callie left him in the kitchen, because while she'd confided in him a lot over the past few years, ultimately, he wasn't the one she wanted to be with.

Liam sat in a huge desk chair, a pair of head-phones on as he clicked and worked. He had four screens in front of him, and she didn't understand a single thing on any of them. He muttered something to himself, reached over with his left hand and tapped on the furthermost left screen, and said, "I said, light him up." He moved both of his hands, one of which held a drawing stylus, as if completing a complicated magic spell as he made a loud whooshing noise.

He wasn't wearing his cowboy hat, and Callie remembered the feel of his hair between her fingers. She wept, which was an improvement over the debilitating sobs from earlier, and entered the office.

She put a delicate touch on Liam's shoulder, but he still startled and almost stabbed her with that stylus. He hurried to pull the headphones off his ears as he said, "Oh.

Callie." He rose from his chair, that same concern that had filled Miah's face entering his. "What's wrong?"

"I have another huge favor," she said, wondering if she'd loathe herself forever.

"Okay," he said, not agreeing to it immediately. She knew this man liked her and had for a long time. So the fact that he wasn't willing to just agree to anything before he heard it testified that he had an operational brain and he was using it. He could say no. He wasn't letting her use him for his bank account.

Or maybe he was.

Callie was so, so tired of thinking about it. But she could be brave for thirty more seconds. She could.

"The ranch will likely still go into foreclosure," she said. "And yes, there will most likely still be an auction. I could still lose the ranch, because the bank has labeled my loan as high-risk."

He reached for her hand and squeezed it, his nonverbal way of asking her what the favor was.

"I'm wondering if you can open an account at my bank and put enough money into it to show them that we can pay the loan payments." She drew in a shuddering breath but held back her tears. Thankfully. She was so tired of feeling weak and crying over this situation. "I need that account linked to mine."

Ten more seconds.

"And I have two accounts that are basically over-drawn, and I need money in both of those too."

There. Done.

She kept her eyes on Liam's, because she didn't want to be ashamed in front of him. She simply needed help, and God had brought him into her life. It seemed wholly unfair that He couldn't have spread the wealth out a little bit, but Callie was willing to bury her pride to save her ranch.

"Oh, one more thing," she said. "I know you would never do this, and that you don't think this, but it's something that's been tormenting me, and I just have to say it."

"Say it," he said quietly.

"I am *not* a prostitute. You don't *own* me because you paid my bills."

There. Now she was done. The ball was in his court, and whether he could throw it or bounce it or punt it, she didn't care.

Well, she did. She really hoped he'd take it, hold it, and then say, *Let's go to the bank right now.*

She waited, watching the perfect storm brew into something dark and dangerous in his eyes.

8

Liam had so many thoughts and feelings moving through him at the same time, he didn't know which one to isolate and grab onto.

He'd heard everything Callie had said, and he was willing to open a bank account at her institution. That was easy. Transferring money could be done with an app, in less than five seconds. So moving money into her two accounts—also easy.

Dealing with a prostitution comment? Not so easy.

No, he didn't think of their arrangement like that, and he hated that she'd been tormented with such thoughts.

"You're angry," Callie finally said.

"Kind of?" He shook his head and pulled his hand away from her, unsure of how to label the emotions inside him. "I don't think I own you."

"I know that," she said quickly, before he'd even

finished his sentence. "I said that. I know you don't think that or feel that way. I just...*I* feel that way, because I feel so stupid, and so guilty, and so, just—I hate myself." Her chin quivered, but she didn't let the tears out. "I want you to respect me. I want you to think highly of me. Out of anyone, I don't want to disappoint you. I don't want you to resent me. I—" She cut off and turned away from him.

In that moment, Liam fell a little harder for Callie Foster. "I'm falling in love with you," he said simply, and love was complicated, and confusing, and Liam hadn't been in this position for a very long time.

Callie spun back to him, those beautiful brown eyes wide. "That's what you say?"

"What do you want me to say?" When she said nothing, Liam attempted a smile. It didn't quite sit right, but then again, nothing between him and Callie was exactly right at the moment.

Except that kiss.

Oh, that kiss. He couldn't stop thinking about it, and while the woman had plagued his thoughts for at least a couple of years now, having tasted her lips was a new form of exquisite torture he wanted to repeat as often as possible.

"I think highly of you," he said. "I know you've been doing the best you can, with the limited resources you have. I respect you and your sisters. I've already told you to stop apologizing and stop feeling guilty." He threw up his hands in a quick display of *I don't know what else to say.* "So let's go to the bank."

Callie stepped into his personal space, those eyes so hopeful as she searched his. "I believe you."

"Good," he said. "I wouldn't lie to you, Cal."

She cupped his face in her hands and kissed him, a sweet, chaste union of their mouths that was as erotic as the deeper kiss they'd shared by her horse pasture earlier. "Thank you, Liam," she whispered against his lips. "I'm falling in love with you too."

She settled back onto her feet, removing her hands from his face. He kept his eyes closed for a moment, because her words were just too much for him to handle while he looked at her. "You wouldn't lie to me either, would you?" he asked, finally opening his eyes.

She looked right at him, right into his soul. "Of course not."

That was good enough for him. He took her hand and said, "My keys are in the kitchen. Do you want to wait here while I get them?"

"Yes," she murmured, and Liam left her in the doorway of his office so he could go down the hall to the kitchen. He knew Jeremiah had come in from the ranch, because the scent of sugary ham and rich gravy had filled the house a few minutes ago.

"I'm running into town with Callie," he said to his brother, who looked up from his phone.

"Yeah? Is she okay?"

"I think she will be," Liam said, opening the drawer where the brothers kept their car keys. "Do we need anything for the weekend? What are you making for Sunday dinner?"

"As a matter of fact," Jeremiah said. "I have a grocery list, and I'd love it if you'd go. I have those rascally goats to deal with this afternoon. They broke their hay basket *again*. I'll text you?"

"Sure," Liam said, reaching up to tip his hat only to realize he wasn't wearing his cowboy hat. He looked at Jeremiah for an extra moment, trying to see in him what Callie did. They'd been instant friends since the moment Jeremiah had arrived on the ranch, and Liam didn't begrudge them that. "What did Callie say to you when she got here?"

Jeremiah looked at him again, alarm in his eyes now. "Nothing. She burst into tears and asked where you were."

Liam hated that he needed this reassurance from his older brother. But Tripp wasn't here, and Callie and Jeremiah had always been so close.... "Okay," he said. "See you in a bit."

"Yeah."

Liam left Jeremiah in the kitchen and went to retrieve his hat. He may not be a born and bred cowboy like his brother, but he sure did like dressing the part. "Callie?" he asked when he arrived in the office and she wasn't there. He turned as if she'd be hiding in the corner, but she wasn't.

He grabbed his hat and stuffed it on his head before walking out the front door. But she wasn't waiting for him on the porch either. Confused, he turned back to the house just as she came out of the bathroom across the hall from the office. "Hey," he said. "Everything okay?"

She drew in a long breath that didn't shake. "Yeah." She smiled at him. "Yes, I'm going to be okay." She slipped one arm around his waist and looked up at him. She'd washed all the evidence of tears from her face and slicked her hair back into a ponytail. She looked put together and refreshed, but Liam could see the turmoil just below the surface. He wanted to ease as much of it as he could, and he honestly didn't expect anything physical from her in return.

He did want her to talk to him. Confide in him. Trust him. He wanted her to let him spoil her and to share her life with him. He was falling in love with her, and he really wanted to keep doing things that contributed to that.

"Ready?" she asked, and Liam led her out onto the front porch.

"Yeah," he said. "I think I'm ready."

———

Two hours later, she said, "I need to call Simone."

"Get 'er done," Liam said as he clicked the button to unlock his truck. She didn't get in right away, but wandered a few feet down the sidewalk as she made the call.

He'd been surprised at how long it took to open an account and move money around. But there had been so many questions, from "How much is the balance on her loan?" to "Are you related to or affiliated with anyone having ties to the Middle East?"

He was moving a very large amount of money, and the woman at the bank had said it could take three days to clear. He didn't mind. Moving a couple hundred thousand dollars from one place to another left him plenty of money to do other things—like buy groceries, their next stop.

As he waited for Callie to talk to her sister, he wondered how often she checked her loan. He could pay it off tomorrow and save a ton in interest—but he didn't know how she'd react. He told himself to *go slow*, so she wouldn't get scared away.

She finally climbed in the truck, and Liam asked, "All set?"

"Yep." She flashed him a grateful smile. "What are we having for Sunday lunch?"

Liam had gotten a text from Jeremiah only a few minutes after they'd left the ranch. "I honestly don't know what all of the things he sent make," he said. "It might be sausage and tortellini soup."

"Ooh, I love that stuff," she said.

"I'm going to make chocolate covered caramel pretzels."

"You know a way into a woman's heart," she said with a giggle, and Liam was just glad he had the real Callie Foster back.

"Oh, is that one of your favorites?" he asked innocently.

"You know it is." She gave him a playful look that made him think of kissing her again and faced the front again.

"Tell me some of your other favorites," he said.

"Men in cowboy hats."

"Check."

"Men who can sing."

"Oh, that's a strike for me. Tripp is a great singer though."

"I've heard you sing."

"You have? When?" He glanced at her, enjoying this new game between them. Everything had been made of tension and corded steel in the bank, and Liam didn't like it.

"At church," she said.

"Again, that's Tripp," he said. "We just sound the same."

"I don't think you sound all that similar."

"We're identical twins," Liam said.

"But you're different."

Of course, Liam knew he was different than Tripp, but everyone outside of the family still had trouble telling them apart. "Anyway," he said. "What else?"

"Sunsets."

"Nice."

"Horses. Dogs. Cream in my coffee."

"Love all of those," he said, making a turn that would take them to the organic market that Jeremiah liked. He knew she was out of cream for her coffee, and he hoped he could buy her some groceries too. "I'm going to call about the Internet at your place on Monday." He glanced at her. "Okay? I have to have screaming fast Internet to work." He looked back at the road. Back to her. "They might have to come rewire."

"Okay," she said with a smile.

Liam wanted to reach over and take her hand in his, but the bulky console between them didn't allow him to. She hadn't argued with him over what he wanted to pay for, and he really liked she was keeping one of the rules they'd set for their marriage. "Thanks," he said. "And you'll be getting some groceries at the store too, right?"

"I...think we have what we need."

"Callie," he said, plenty of warning in his voice. "I opened your fridge this morning. You didn't have cream, and you literally just said one of your favorite things was cream in your coffee."

She looked at him, but he couldn't hold her gaze for long and keep them in the right lane. "This is one of those things you don't want me to argue about, isn't it?"

"Yes," he said simply.

"Fine." She folded her arms. "Then I guess I'm going grocery shopping too."

"Great," he said in a falsely cheery voice. "Oh, and do you want to sit by me at church on Sunday? I mean, then you'll know what a terrible singer I am, but you seem to like knowing about the things I'm bad at."

"Sit by you?"

"Yeah," he said. "And if you wear the diamond, we'll really be able to stir up the rumor mill in town." He kicked a devilish grin in her direction, thrilled when her laughter filled the cab of his truck. He wanted to bottle the sound and listen to it whenever he worried if he was doing the right thing or not. Let her listen to it when she felt like crying, so she'd know she was happy once. *They* were happy once.

He'd already been through plenty of hard things with Callie, and he sent up a prayer that perhaps God could try to make their path a little easier from now on. *Just a little,* he thought as he pulled into the organic market.

"Okay," Callie said. "I'll sit by you *and* wear the diamond."

"Now we're talkin'."

————

Liam left for church before the other brothers, hoping to make a clean getaway. They usually all rode in together, but since Micah was still here, as well as their parents, they'd have to take two vehicles anyway.

"You're leaving already?" his mom asked, startling Liam as he headed for the front steps. He skidded sideways, seeing a fall in his future. He grabbed for the porch railing and managed to keep from toppling down the steps. "Momma," he said, his heart pounding in his chest. "You scared me."

"Mm hm," she said, rising from the rocking chair on the porch. She was already dressed for church, her hair perfectly curled and poofed. "Looks like you were sneaking out."

"I wasn't," Liam said, wondering how his mother could make him feel like he was twelve years old again—when he had actually snuck out to see a girl he liked. "Plus, I'm forty years old, so I can kinda do what I want." He smiled down at her.

She grinned at him and reached up to cup his face in her hand. "Going to see Callie?"

"We're going to church together," he said. "You want to sit by us?" He really hoped she'd say no. He loved his mother, but sitting by his fiancée and his mother in one day felt like a lot.

"If there's room," his mom said. "But we're not leaving for a few more minutes."

"So I'll see you over there," he said, starting down the steps. The homestead had an attached three-car garage, but Liam never parked in it. Jeremiah did, and the rest of the space was filled with tools and boxes and anything else the brothers didn't know what to do with. Skyler had brought a fridge and a microwave with him, for crying out loud. As if the enormous kitchen wasn't big enough and didn't have the proper appliances.

Liam drove the half-mile to Callie's, only to find her waiting at the gate. "Hey," he said, rolling down the window. "You lost, ma'am?"

"Very funny," she said, trying the door. "Unlock it for me."

Chuckling, he did, and Callie climbed into his truck. "You look pretty," he said, drinking in the sight of all those curves in the little black dress she wore.

"Thanks." She smiled at him, and all traces of the weepy, worried woman he'd spent yesterday with seemed to have disappeared. They didn't talk much on the way to church, which had Liam's nerves a bit on-edge for a reason he couldn't name. He'd spent a lot of time with Callie where they didn't talk.

He hadn't checked for the diamond ring, and he didn't want to be obvious about it. They finally reached the church, and Liam practically shot out of his seat so he could round the truck and help Callie down. They hadn't arrived too early or too late, and there were several people walking into the little white building with the cross on top.

Liam found the glinting gem on his fiancée's finger, and he couldn't help the grin that covered his whole face.

"Yes," Callie whispered. "I'm wearing the ring." She

glanced around as if the police would jump out from behind the nearest car and arrest her for doing so.

"Looks nice on your finger," he said, his voice a bit on the throaty side.

"All right," she said. "Let's go. I already feel like everyone is staring at us."

Liam glanced around, but he didn't notice that anyone was looking at them for longer than usual. Inside the building, he led her through the foyer and into the chapel, immediately scanning for someone he knew. He realized he didn't need someone he knew—he was with someone he knew.

The only person he wanted to sit by.

"There's Tripp," Callie said. "Should we sit by them?"

"Sure," Liam said, though his pulse rippled now. He hadn't said anything to Tripp about his proposal to Callie, as his brother had been dealing with a lot of his own personal things the past week or so. He'd bought a house, moved into it, and celebrated Christmas with his wife and stepson.

Liam missed Tripp, that was for sure. So when he appeared at the end of the row where his brother sat, his arm around Ivory, he sure was glad to see Tripp's face.

"Liam," he said, rising. "You want to sit by us?"

"Yeah. There's room for two, right?"

Tripp's gaze moved to Callie, and that same grin that had exploded onto Liam's face now appeared on Tripp's.

"There sure is." He waited for Oliver and Ivory to move down, making room for Liam and Callie.

"Can I sit by you?" Ollie asked, climbing right onto Liam's lap before he even answered.

"'Course you can, bud." He held the boy easily on his lap, ignored his brother's interested stare, and glanced at Callie. "Everyone's staring, aren't they?"

"Bet your life on it," she whispered, and Liam chuckled quietly though he felt like he was sitting on nails. He wasn't used to being the center of attention, and he didn't want people talking about him over their Sunday lunches.

People continued to come in, and Liam finally settled enough to feel the peace that always came from attending church. He closed his eyes and listened, feeling like everything he'd done in the past couple of days was the right thing.

So he reached over and took Callie's hand in his, squeezing to let her know how much he liked sitting on this bench with her, ready to worship. At least that was the message he hoped she got, and he sure liked it when she squeezed his hand back.

Now, if they could survive the meet-and-greet after the sermon, *that* would be a miracle.

9

Callie adored the way Liam held Oliver on his lap. He whispered things to him throughout the meeting, and once, he reached over to Tripp and took a graham cracker and held it for the boy until he was ready to eat it.

He was kind, and gentle, and he'd make a great father. Her nerves rioted, because she couldn't give him that opportunity. Callie had thought she'd dealt with her feelings of loss, but she struggled against the rising feelings of inferiority. She hated them, and she didn't like that Liam was marrying her when he could find someone he could really love, who could give him more than a broken-down ranch and a broken-down body.

His hand landed on her knee, and she glanced over at him. He leaned closer to her, and she definitely enjoyed the scent of his cologne and the minty freshness of his breath. Her desire for him skyrocketed, and she tipped her head toward his mouth as he whispered, "Do you think he's right?"

"Who?" she whispered back.

He grinned at her and tipped his cowboy hat toward the front, where Pastor Daniels stood at the microphone. She honestly hadn't heard a word he'd said, and her pulse bounced in her chest. Up and down. Up and down.

"You weren't listening." Liam shifted on the bench beside her, moving closer to her as he brought his arm around her shoulders.

"I'm distracted," she whispered back to him, really enjoying the extra warmth from his body.

"I can see that, sweetheart."

"It's your fault." Callie hadn't flirted with a man in a long time—and never in church. Maybe she and Liam had come to be sitting together on this bench in an unconventional way, but the fact was, they were still here.

"My fault?" His deep, throaty cowboy chuckle set all of her cells to vibrating, and she laughed quietly with him.

His brother nudged him on his left side, and Liam straightened up. Good thing too, because Callie was pretty sure old Jean Hillstone behind them was about to shush them, and Callie didn't need to be reprimanded at age forty-three.

Callie tuned into the pastor's words after that, and she learned that he was talking about second and third and fourth chances when it came to the Lord. "In fact," Scott Daniels said. "There will always be another chance with God."

Callie really wished God worked at the bank where her loan was still being considered for foreclosure. Or that she could see Lois in the congregation—not that she knew who her loan officer was.

But the pastor's words did stir her faith, and she leaned over and whispered in Liam's ear, "Yeah, I think he's right." After all, she was going to get a second chance to make the Shining Star back into what it should've been all these years.

———

Later that afternoon, Callie woke when someone opened her bedroom door. She expected it to be Simone, so when her sister crawled into bed with her and hugged her from behind, Callie smiled.

"I slept too long, didn't I?"

"Almost," Simone said. "Evelyn just called to see if we were coming, and she said Jeremiah says lunch is at least twenty minutes out."

Callie stayed still, enjoying the comfort in her sister's embrace. She was going to miss simple Sunday afternoons with Simone, as they'd both mourned the loss of Evelyn over the past year. Callie was happy for Evelyn, of course.

She didn't want her to be stuck here, at a ranch that was falling apart, her business failing and her heart broken.

But she sure did miss her. She kept a cute little house on Quail Creek Road, and Callie wanted to go over and help her sister get the nursery ready for her new baby that was coming this summer.

"Knock, knock," Evelyn called, but neither Simone nor Callie moved.

"We don't have to go to lunch if it's too much," Simone said.

"I don't know if it's too much or not," Callie said just before Evelyn came into the room.

"Oh, I see what's happening here."

Callie rolled over and pushed herself up, leaning back against the headboard. Evelyn came around to her side of the bed and peered down at her. She reached out and tucked her hair behind her ear. "You okay?"

"I'm good," Callie said.

"You and Liam are engaged?"

"Yes," Callie said, looking into Evelyn's eyes. "It's not...we're calling it an invented I-do." She glanced over at Simone. "Did you tell her?"

"No." Simone shook her head and smiled. Callie hadn't explained much more to Simone after running out of the house on Friday. She and Liam had gone to the bank. They'd gone grocery shopping and to dinner, and she'd gotten home late.

She'd worked around the ranch as much as she could on Saturday while Liam spent the day with his parents, who were flying back to Grand Cayman just after the New Year. They hadn't talked about asking his parents to stay for the wedding, as they didn't have a date for the nuptials. He'd said he'd handle his parents, and Callie didn't argue. She didn't want anyone at the wedding, and they hadn't talked about it much. They'd mostly been setting ground rules and going out together.

"Callie?" Evelyn asked, and she pulled herself back to the moment.

"I do like Liam a whole lot," Callie said. "We get along for the most part, and he's going to help us keep and fix up the ranch." She smiled, but it wobbled on her face. "I was so far behind on the mortgage, the property went into foreclosure. We would've lost everything this upcoming Friday."

Evelyn sat down on the bed, a shocked look on her face.

"I love this place so much," Callie said. "But I can't keep it up myself. I know it's almost in ruins, and walking around with Liam on Friday, showing him the ranch and talking about everything that needed to be done...it was torture." She looked at both of her sisters. "But he has a lot of money, and he's going to help me get it all fixed up." She ducked her head, shame moving through her. "I'm sorry, guys. I really am." Helplessness filled her. "Maybe I should've sold this place years ago. I just...couldn't let it go."

"I wouldn't have been able to either," Simone said. "I'm sorry I haven't helped out as much."

"You didn't know," Callie said. "I made sure of that. It's my fault, and well, I'm going to try to fix it." She'd been thinking a lot about what role she wanted to have on the ranch, and it wasn't the CEO. Nor the one who got up and did all the chores. The fence-fixer, or the horse trainer, or the agriculture specialist. She couldn't be a veterinarian, and she couldn't wrangle all the cattle.

She wanted to take care of the paperwork and oversee the cowboys. She wanted to feed them and make sure they had someone who cared about them. She wanted to find a place to keep bees and collect honey, which she could bottle and take to her friends in this town where she'd grown up and which she still loved.

And with Liam, she could do all of that. The ranch would be as beautiful as Seven Sons next door, and she'd opened her heart and her mind to the cowboy who could make it all possible.

"Can you guys forgive me?" Callie asked.

"Nothing to forgive," Simone said. "And you're not the only one who's been responsible for the ranch." She looked at Evelyn and back to Callie. "I could've done more. It was just easier to go out to my shed and put my head down."

"Rhett's offered to help," Evelyn said gently, and Callie's eyes darted over to her.

"He has helped," Callie said. "He's been working out here without pay for over a year."

"*We* would've done more," Evelyn said. "I...somehow, I thought you were doing okay. I didn't know."

"And that's because I didn't tell you." Callie reached for her sisters and drew them into a three-way hug. "Now, if we're eating with those boys, we better get going. You know how Miah gets if someone's late to dinner." She wiped at her eyes, realizing she was a little teary. "I love you guys. You know that, right?"

"Of course. We love you too," Evelyn said, leaning away. "I wanted to ask you guys one more thing." She looked at her hands and then her sisters again, and Callie felt a nervous tremor move through her.

"Go ahead," Simone said when Evelyn remained quiet.

"If the baby is a girl," she said. "Rhett and I have already talked about naming her after Momma."

Callie's emotion reared up in her throat, and she nodded. "That's perfect," she squeaked, because it was.

"Do you know if it's a boy or girl?" Simone asked.

"Not yet." Evelyn smiled down at her stomach. "We don't have any boy names yet."

"Well, you're not due until June," Callie said. "So I think you have time." She smiled at her sister and nudged her so she'd get off the bed. "Look out. I have to get up and get dressed. Do something with my hair." They were definitely going to be late for lunch.

Evelyn got up and drew Callie into a hug when she got out of bed too. "Are you okay? I mean, I don't have to talk about the baby."

"I'm...it's okay." Callie held onto her sister tight, tight. "I struggle sometimes, but I'm so happy for you. You know that right?" She drew back and held her sister at arm's length. "And I'm going to spoil that baby like crazy, so I hope you're ready for that." She gave a light laugh, her phone buzzing as her alarm went off.

Evelyn giggled and nodded. "I actually can't wait for that." Her phone rang, and her husband's name sat on the screen. "Oh, boy. I'll handle this. You get ready."

Simone slid off the bed too, saying, "I'll head over now and let them know you're coming." She and Evelyn left the room as Evelyn answered the phone with a falsely bright voice.

Callie went into the bathroom and looked into her eyes. She'd never liked them all that much, as they weren't a deep, rich brown and they weren't light either. They were just like her hair—an in-between color that had no name.

She sighed and reached for a washcloth, turning the water on hot. She brushed her teeth and washed the sleep and weariness from her face. She wet her hands and smoothed her hair back, noticing how thin it was. She'd curled it in anticipation of sitting beside Liam at church, and she thought her high, curly ponytail was actually pretty cute.

She changed out of her yoga pants and random T-shirt, and by the time she stepped back into her bedroom to get her phone, it was flashing with three different colored lights. Texts, social media messages, and a missed call.

"Liam," she whispered when she saw that last one.

She read his texts first, his last one saying, *I'm out front. Come out when you're ready.*

She quickly turned and headed for the front door, more excited to see him than she wanted to admit. He sat at the bottom of her front steps, turning when he heard her come outside. "Your Internet is *really* bad. I can't even check my email here."

"You're going to call on that tomorrow, right?" she asked.

"First thing," he said. "What time did you want to head up to get the marriage license?"

Callie thought through her morning routine. "I can get all the animals fed by about ten," she said. "Shower, and we can go?"

"So ten-thirty?"

"You think it only takes me thirty minutes to get ready?" She reached for his hand and acted like she could help him stand. She stepped into his arms while he chuckled.

Liam

"We're late already," he murmured. "And Jeremiah's in a snit as it is."

"He can start lunch without us," Callie said. "He won't die." She liked holding onto Liam, and she liked finding him on her steps, and she wanted to spend the day with him tomorrow. "I sure do like you, Liam." She looked right into his eyes. "You know that, right?"

"Yeah, Cal," he said. "I know that." He touched his lips to hers then, and Callie got the kiss she wanted.

10

Liam woke way earlier than he needed to, his mind moving through the dozens of tasks he needed to accomplish that day. The Internet company wasn't open, and he couldn't go get a marriage license at five in the morning. Pretty much the only thing he could do was hit the gym, so he did that, unsurprised to see Tripp there.

"Hey, brother," he said, joining his twin near the free weights.

"What are you doin' here?" Tripp asked, setting the handheld weight back in the rack. He grabbed Liam and hugged him, clapping him on the back.

"I should be asking you that," Liam said. "You only come to the gym when you're avoiding something else."

Tripp laughed, and he was happier than Liam had seen him in a long time. Only a handful of weeks ago, he'd been at the lowest point Liam had ever seen him. But now that he had Ivory and Oliver back, everything in Tripp had changed.

To Liam, that was a testimony that love could heal even the hardest of hearts, and shine light into the darkest of places. He thought of Jeremiah, who'd been suffering for years after his fiancée had left him standing at the altar.

Liam could still remember keenly how he and Tripp had jumped up and stood shoulder to shoulder while Rhett had helped Jeremiah down the few steps where the altar had been and away from all the eyes of their friends, family, coworkers, and neighbors.

Jeremiah had never been the same, and Liam hoped he'd get another chance for happiness in his life. He thought about what Pastor Daniels had said at church yesterday, and he believed that there were unlimited chances with God too.

"So you and Callie," Tripp said, glancing at him. "I need all the dirt. I hate not being at the ranch."

"You do not," Liam said. "You love your new house and your wife and your stepson."

"Yeah." Tripp grinned. "Yeah, okay. I love those things too." He nodded to the bench press. "Spot me?"

"Best kind of workout," Liam said, because he could stand there and not do much.

"Yeah, you get to talk," Tripp said, putting the weights on the bar and then situating himself on the bench beneath it.

"Yeah, so Callie and I have had a rough year," Liam

said, though Tripp knew this. "She warmed a little after you barked at her about how much I liked her."

"Hey, I asked if I should apologize for that." Tripp adjusted his grip on the bar and lifted it off the support.

"I'm not complaining," Liam said. "She started talking to me a lot more, and she told me some things about the ranch." He shrugged, but Tripp was focused on his workout. "And when she finally told me the ranch was in foreclosure, I drove to the jewelers, and I bought her a ring, and I asked her to marry me."

"When did that all happen?" Tripp asked, grunting as he pushed the weight up again.

"A week before Christmas," he said. "She said she needed time to think about it. She said yes on Christmas Day, after dinner."

"So you're marrying her."

"Yes," Liam said.

Tripp settled the bar back in the supports and sat up. He stood and looked at Liam, his eyes sharp and already gleaming. "It's real?"

"It will be," Liam said, not wanting to admit outright that they had rules and he wouldn't be sharing a bed with his wife.

"Hey, it's worked for two of us," Tripp said with a grin. "And I totally think it'll work for you too." He bent and picked up his water bottle. "Now you better get some sweat going, bro. Otherwise you drove all the way here for nothing."

Liam chuckled, but Tripp was right. "I think it's leg day," he said, moving over to the bench that would work out that part of his body.

By ten-thirty, he'd showered, worked for a few hours on his CGI project, and spent twenty minutes on the phone with Garth Ahlstrom. He hadn't told Callie yet, but they'd be stopping at Three Rivers Ranch after they got their marriage license. Garth had told him a few things about hiring cowboys, and Liam wanted to get some more information about the cowboy cabins, the daily chores on a functioning ranch, and how much to pay good cowboys.

Before he could get out of his truck to go get Callie, she came out the front door. The sight of her made his throat dry, and he got out of his truck to greet her. "Morning," he said, grinning like a fool and not even caring. His conversation with his brother from that morning rang through his head like a gong.

I totally think it'll work for you too.

Liam maybe was a little too optimistic, but Callie stepped into his arms and kissed him, so maybe not. "You ready for this?" he asked, walking her over to the passenger-side door.

"Yes." She wore a cute pair of jeans with a festive red sweater, and a light brown leather jacket over all of that. She'd done her hair and put on makeup, and Liam was sure an angel had just climbed into his truck.

"Are you going to stand there and stare at me all morning?" Callie laughed, and Liam backed out of the doorway where he had been standing and staring.

He got behind the wheel, and Callie asked, "Are you ready for this, Liam?"

He knew she was asking about more than just a drive and a marriage license. "Yes," he said with as much confidence as he could muster. He liked her. She liked him. They had great chemistry together, and while maybe most people waited until the *I love you*'s were said to tie the knot, Liam thought they had a chance. A real chance.

"Okay," he said as he backed out. "Today, I want a childhood story."

"Oh," she said with a laugh. "You do, huh?"

"Yes," he said. "And I have six brothers, so I have a lot of them." He glanced at her. "But you start first. Tell me something about the ranch that made you want to keep it for the rest of your life."

"Oh, I don't know." Callie looked out her window. "I think the stories binding me to this ranch aren't very happy."

"No?"

"I mean, not really." She exhaled, and it sounded heavy to Liam.

"Okay, well, I'll tell one first." He looked at her, and she nodded. "So my dad started building apps when I was a teenager. For a while there, we didn't have anything. Like, I wore Jeremiah's shoes and my mom actually sewed patches on Rhett's jeans." He shook his head, the child-hood memories right there in his mind. "We had this family down the street that had fruit trees in their front yard. Apricots and peaches, and the lady that lived there was like, totally in love with her trees."

"And you stole her fruit," Callie said, her face lit up with happiness. "And you know there are peach trees and apricot trees on my ranch, right?"

"I didn't know that," he said, because there was so much about the ranch he didn't know. He had to compart-mentalize it, or he felt like shutting down. Putting his headphones on and disappearing into the CGI. He'd done that a lot when he'd first moved to Three Rivers, and he didn't want to do it again.

"And we didn't steal her fruit," he said. "Tripp and I wanted money for the movies, so we went to her house and asked her if we could pick her fruit for a few bucks."

"Oh, wow, I wasn't expecting that."

"Yeah, well, we got in plenty of trouble too. This just wasn't one of those times, and if you want some real stories, you should ask Jeremiah."

"He's told me some," Callie said. "There was this one about him and Skyler and something about pumpkins?" She laughed, and Liam did like the sound of that. He didn't like that she'd shared this same experience with his brother.

Jeremiah had assured him several times that he wasn't

interested in Callie, and Callie didn't have feelings for him. Liam knew that intellectually, but his heart throbbed all the same. "Yeah," he said, wishing he hadn't brought anything up.

"And that's it?" Callie asked. "You went down the street and picked the lady's fruit? She paid you and you went to the movies?"

"No, she paid us, and we paid for Skyler, Micah, and Wyatt to go to the movies," he said. "See, they were kids, and their tickets were cheaper. We, uh, we snuck in the back."

"You scoundrel," she said, laughing again.

"I still feel bad about it," he said, smiling with her.

"Well, you have a ton of money now. Why don't you just send them the five bucks and an anonymous note?"

He looked at her and found those eyes he loved so much sparkling with amusement. "I could totally do that. Maybe my conscience would be eased."

"Is that all you have on your conscience?"

Liam looked out of the corner of his eye. "Uh, not even close."

"Keep going," she said, and she sounded playful, but there was a more serious glint there too.

"I didn't realize this was a confessional drive," he said, uneasy now, because so many of his regrets centered around her. "But I think another thing I'd like off my mind is the last woman I dated."

"Oh." Callie blinked, and Liam hurried to add, "I

mean, it's not like I think about her all the time or anything. Jeremiah's told you why we moved here, right?"

"I know he had a fiancée that broke his heart. He hasn't said much about it. But Evelyn told me you Walkers don't date."

"Well, that's obviously not true," he said. "I mean, two of us are married now, and me and you are engaged."

"After three years," she said. "So why did you come to Three Rivers? You came last, I think."

"Yeah," he said. "Yep. I was trying to decide if I really wanted to leave this woman I'd been seeing. I mean, kind of seeing."

"Kind of seeing? How do you do that?"

"We were on-again, off-again for about two years," he said. "When I wasn't with her, I was miserable. When I was, I was angry. Tripp kept telling me our relationship wasn't healthy, but I don't know." He shrugged. "I couldn't see it. I was in love with her."

"What was her name?"

"Okay, don't laugh," he said, looking at her as they made it out of town and started on the highway north of Three Rivers. "Portia Petlova."

"Oh, a Russian girl." Callie's voice was way too high.

"She wasn't Russian," Liam said.

"Petlova?"

"She was born in Texas," he said, laughing.

"All the good ones are," Callie said, joining him. The rest of the drive became easy, and Liam was glad for that.

They went into the courthouse, and the same woman sat at the County Clerk's desk.

"Oh, you're back," she said, smiling up at Liam.

"Sure am."

"You know, sometimes people come in like they need a marriage license when they don't," she said. "I'm glad to know you weren't one of those."

Liam had no idea what to say, so he just kept smiling. Callie was the one who stepped forward and said, "Here's our application. My driver's license."

Liam dug in his back pocket for his wallet, producing his ID as well. Everything checked out, and before he knew it, Liam was signing the application.

"Did you two take the marriage education class?" the woman asked.

"The what?" Liam asked.

"It's a class that helps premarital couples, and you get a sixty-dollar discount on the marriage license fee if you take it. You also don't have to wait seventy-two hours to get married if you take the class."

Liam looked at Callie, who stepped a little closer to him. "We're not going to get married today or tomorrow," she said. "We can wait the seventy-two hours."

"And I have the money." He looked back at the clerk. "We didn't take the class."

"You still can," she said, stamping something on their application. She started giving instructions on how long it would last, and when it needed to be back to the office

Liam

after the wedding, and when they'd get it back. It all seemed to happen in a blink of an eye, and then Liam was walking out the door, Callie's arm in his, and the paperwork they needed to say I-do—even if it was an invented one.

11

C allie couldn't explain the giddiness inside her as she and Liam left the courthouse. "I guess we're really doing this."

"Yeah, I think so," Liam said. "And I hope you have your thumbs ready and your best listening ears on, because we've got a stop to make before we get lunch."

"A stop?"

"Yeah, I forgot to tell you I talked to Garth Ahlstrom this morning, and he's expecting us at Three Rivers Ranch."

Dread filled Callie's stomach. "Oh."

"What?" he asked. "What does that mean?"

"It means that Three Rivers is the premier ranch in the entire Texas Panhandle," she said. "You'll see it, and I'll be even more embarrassed."

"The premier ranch in the entire Texas Panhandle?" Liam scoffed, and that made Callie smile.

"Besides Seven Sons, of course," she said.

"Of course." He made the turn onto the dirt road that led out to the ranch. "Besides, Three Rivers is just the biggest. The way Jeremiah tells it, it's Shiloh Ridge that's the premier ranch."

"Well, that's true." Callie hadn't stepped foot onto Shiloh Ridge Ranch in years. She'd probably die from embarrassment if Bear Glover or any of his brothers and cousins even looked twice at the Shining Star.

"And, Cal, I've been out here before. I've already seen it."

Her nerves wouldn't be quieted, and she swallowed as Liam rounded the bend and the ranch spread before them. Every building looked brand-new and well taken care of. The grass was green, and this ranch possessed an energy the Shining Star hadn't had for a very long time.

"Look, don't be worried," he said. "We're here to get the help we need. You have nothing to be embarrassed about." He pulled past the big glass building that had a huge sign above it. Courage Reins.

He turned onto another lane that led in front of more buildings and parked next to a couple of other trucks.

"Well, your truck is the nicest one," she said just as a cowboy came in between two buildings.

"There he is," Liam said, reaching into the center console for something. "Are you ready?"

She watched the cowboy stop and wait, and then he looked at Liam with that notebook. "Yes," she said, gathering her courage as close as she could.

Liam smiled at her, and they got out of the truck together. "Hey, Garth," he said brightly, striding over to the other cowboy and shaking his hand. "We talked on the phone earlier."

"Hullo, Liam. I'm Garth."

Liam stepped back and tugged Callie to his side. "This is Callie Foster. She owns the Shining Star Ranch, south of town."

"Right next door to you," Garth said with a smile. He shook Callie's hand too, and he possessed a quiet spirit that calmed Callie. "I understand you two have some questions about hiring cowboys, their room and board, all of that."

"Right," Liam said.

"You wanna come take a look?" Garth hooked his thumb over his shoulder, already turning back the way he'd come.

"Yeah, of course." Liam secured Callie's hand in his, and she had no choice but to go with him.

"So we have two cowboys in a cabin," Garth said. "That's fairly normal, depending on the size. Their room and board is part of their pay." He kept talking about the vehicles they drove, the allowances they got, their work schedules. Liam took notes on all of it, and then they followed Garth up the steps of one of the cabins.

"So Bennett and Beau live here. They're fairly clean."
He knocked, and then opened the door and went inside. "I
told them you were coming, so don't be alarmed. We don't
have cabin checks here, and we don't invade their space
without talking to them first." He turned and looked at
Callie. "How many cabins do you have?"

"Um, five," she said at the same time Liam said, "Six."

She jerked her attention to him. "Six?"

"I'm pretty sure there's six, sweetheart." Liam gave an
awkward chuckle and looked at Garth. He did not seem
like the type who wouldn't know exactly how many
feathers each chicken had on his ranch, and Callie found
him intimidating.

At the same time, she wanted a foreman just like him.
"How much do you pay your cowboys who live and work
here full-time?" she asked.

"Thirty thousand, plus the room and board," Garth
said.

"And what about you?" she asked. "I mean, you don't
have to tell me." She shot a glance at Liam. "But I need
someone like you at the Shining Star. How much does
someone like you cost?"

Garth smiled at her and stepped back onto the porch.
"I live three cabins down," he said. "It's bigger than the
other cabins, and my family lives there with me. On top of
that, I get fifty thousand."

Callie looked at Liam. "I don't have a bigger cabin
than the others."

"My brother is a carpenter," he said, almost under his breath.

Garth looked back and forth between them. "Are you two going into business together?"

Business. The word reverberated through her head, and Liam said it out loud, his voice incredulous.

"Yeah." Garth looked back and forth between them. "I've been out to Seven Sons, Liam. Your brother Jeremiah is a good cowboy, and he runs a tight ship." He glanced at Callie. "I haven't seen your ranch ma'am, so I can't speak to it. But it seems like you two need some help with it."

Understatement of the year.

"We do," Liam said. "Can I go back inside?" He stepped back into the cabin, leaving Callie on the porch with Garth. She didn't like the way he studied her, but thankfully, his phone rang, and he pulled it out of his back pocket.

"It's my wife. Excuse me." He stepped over to the corner of the porch, and said, "Hey, baby." That softened him considerably, as did the two kids who came running down the gravel path in front of the cabins a moment later.

They ran right up the steps, yelling about something, and Garth scooped them both up into his arms, laughing. Ah, there was the Texas cowboy that Callie knew, and she blinked, having a vision of Liam doing the same thing with their kids.

Shocked, she turned away from Garth and his boys and went back inside the cabin too.

"This is nice," Liam said. "Two bedrooms. One bathroom. Living room big enough for two sofas. Kitchen. Table. Back door, with a little patch of lawn."

"Liam," Callie said. "I want to adopt."

"What?" He looked at her, clearly confused about the two different conversations they were having.

"Did you want to see the barns?" Garth asked from behind them. "My boys are dying to give you a tour."

"We want to see it all," Liam said, and he was obviously more excited about being here than Callie was. She told herself this was a good opportunity for her, to tour this very functional ranch.

So she put her heart into the tour, and she asked questions about the bull pens, the amount of acreage they had at Three Rivers, and how many men it took to keep the ranch running how it did.

"We have seventeen full-time cowboys," Garth said. "Seasonal workers during harvest and branding time."

"Do they rotate?" Liam asked. "And how big is this place?"

"They don't rotate," Garth said. "I have people over animals and people over crops. Men over fences and groundskeeping. We've got three distinct entities out here, and sometimes we share cowboys."

"Yeah, my brother works for Bowman's Breeds," Liam said. "Wyatt Walker?"

"Yep, I know Wyatt," Garth said. "Hard worker, that one. Knows his way with horses, too."

"That he does," Liam said with a smile, clearly enjoying himself. Callie's stomach growled, and she nodded toward the huge building at the end of the row. They'd been in the barns, seen the chickens, visited the stables. Garth had answered nearly every question under the sun, and she appreciated his time.

"What's that building?" she asked.

"That's where my daddy works," one of the little boys said. He was probably seven or eight years old.

"That's the admin building," Garth said. "We have our meetings in there. Squire Ackerman has an office. So does his wife, who runs all of our financial affairs here at the ranch. She's an accountant. My office is in there, and we have a general controller who runs the front desk. That way, we all know who's supposed to be doing what, we all get paid, and all of our sales are recorded properly."

Callie's head swam. No wonder the Shining Star was in ruins. This place—though three times as big as her family ranch—had seventeen full-time cowboys, a general controller, a foreman, offices, schedules, accountants.

"Thank you so much," Liam said, shaking Garth's hand.

"You want to meet some of my best boys?" Garth asked, and Callie wanted to say no. But before either of them could say anything, he added, "Here's Bennett and Beau now. How were things out in pasture seven?"

"Just peachy," one of the cowboys said. He extended

his hand to Callie. "I'm Bennett Peterson." He indicated the cowboy in the white hat next to him. "Beau Rogers."

"Nice to meet you," she said.

"Yeah?" Bennett took a step closer. "I'm not sure I've seen you around."

"Bennett," Garth barked, but the cowboy in the dark hat didn't back down.

"I own a crumbling ranch fifteen minutes south of town," she said. "And me and my fiancé sure are hoping to get it all fixed up." She smiled broadly at the cowboy, watching his eyes glaze over the moment she said *fiancé*.

"Lucky guy," Bennett said, stepping back.

Liam said, "Thanks."

"Oh." Bennett looked back and forth between them, obviously surprised. Callie really didn't like that, especially because it was the second person who hadn't been able to tell she and Liam were together. Was it possible she was the only one who could feel the crackling electricity between her and Liam?

And why did that bother her?

"Thanks for your time," she said to Garth before crouching down in front of his boys. "And you two are amazing tour guides."

They grinned at her, and Callie sure did like the sight of children on a ranch. In that moment, a girl came tearing around the corner. "Mac—oh. There you are. Come on. My baby brother can walk."

"Can we go, Daddy?" Mac asked, looking up at Garth.

"Yes," he said. "But you come back as soon as Trina says to, y'all hear?"

"Yes, sir," the boys chorused, and then the two boys ran off.

"There's more kids here?" Callie asked, unable to help herself.

"Oh, yeah," Garth said. "Squire has four children. Pete and Chelsea have three. I've got my two boys, and that girl, Sabrina, is Cal's. His wife was a professional tennis player, and they just had a baby a year or so ago. Ethan and Brynn don't live on the ranch, but they bring their kids out from time to time. Three Rivers Ranch is a family-friendly place." He tipped his hat as his phone rang again. He answered it with, "Yeah, boss?"

Bennett and Beau were talking to Liam, and he was frantically scribbling in his notebook. Callie hung back, because while she'd actually enjoyed getting hit on, she was ready to leave.

She wanted a family-friendly ranch. She wanted kids. She wanted white gravel paths and rustic cowboy cabins full of light and charm. She wanted a foreman, and she wanted all of her fields planted and harvested each year.

"You ready?" Liam asked, and Callie nodded. And through all of that, she wanted Liam Walker too.

They got back in the truck, and she looked at him. "Did you think it odd no one could tell we were together?"

"Yes," he said. "Thank you. Like, what was that about?"

Callie burst out laughing. "I don't know, but this much I do know. That was completely overwhelming. I feel so... inadequate."

"Tell me about it," Liam said.

"You?" she asked. "Why would you feel inadequate?"

"Because." He navigated them down the road, leaving the perfection of Three Rivers Ranch in their rear-view mirror. "I feel like I've made you promises I might not be able to keep." He looked at her, a nervous edge in those perfect eyes. "And what were you saying about adopting?"

Callie's brain hurt, and she closed her eyes. "I just... can we talk about all of this later?"

"Sure thing," Liam said, his voice a bit wounded. Maybe. Callie couldn't tell. She closed her eyes and leaned her head back, everything Garth had told them about cowboys and schedules and jobs blending into one giant ball of noise.

"And I know you don't want to talk right now," he said. "But I want to put the topic of our honeymoon back on the agenda."

"We have an agenda now?" she asked without opening her eyes.

"Yes," Liam said.

Callie smiled and reached for his hand. He gave it to her, and she squeezed his fingers. "I don't care what other people can't see," she said. "I know we're together."

"I thought you said you didn't want to talk."

"I don't," she said. "Now get us back to town quick, or I might start gnawing on your arm."

Liam burst out laughing, and all the tension and all the unsaid words between them didn't matter. Callie laughed too, knowing there'd be plenty of time to talk everything to death—and wholly dreading it.

12

"Family meeting," Liam said that night.

"Oh, boy," Jeremiah said, still wiping the kitchen counter.

Liam ignored his brother and walked into the living room. Wyatt already sat there, a pair of reading glasses perched on his nose as he looked at something on his phone. He looked up, surprise in those green eyes Liam knew so well. Then he put his phone down and waited.

Liam sat next to him and waited for Skyler, Micah, and Jeremiah to come over.

"You guys still do the family meeting?" Micah asked.

"It's saved us a few times," Jeremiah said. "We live here together, and it's not all roses and sunshine."

"Yeah, because of you," Wyatt said, a broad smile on his face.

"Okay, okay," Liam said. "This isn't a bash-Jeremiah session."

"Thank you," Jeremiah said. "Though I can admit I'm a little grouchy sometimes." He looked around at the other brothers. "Sorry about that." He nodded, keeping his head down for an extra beat.

"We all have flaws," Micah said, looking back at Liam. "So you called the meeting. Are you in charge? That same rule applies."

"Yes," Liam said. He took a deep breath and thought about his fantastic morning with Callie. They hadn't talked about the honeymoon, or adopting kids, or anything to do with the wedding.

No, their conversation at lunch had centered around the ranch. Hiring cowboys. She'd started making a list on her phone, and she'd already texted it to him. He'd noted that she'd never sent him the rules for their marriage, and they didn't have a date yet anyway.

But Liam would like to be married in four days.

"Okay, so I got the marriage license today," he said, watching Jeremiah. Surprisingly, his brother didn't look like he wanted to commit murder. "Callie and I don't have a date yet, but I'm going to try to get something set in the next couple of days."

"When are you thinking?" Micah asked. "I'd like to be here, and I do have to go back to Temple for a bit."

"I'm thinking this weekend," Liam said.

Skyler whistled like this weekend was a tall order.

And it was. As far as Liam knew, Callie hadn't planned a single thing.

"We'll just have the wedding at the Shining Star," he said. "We just need someone qualified to marry us and the family."

"And food," Jeremiah said, as if lunch was the most important part of any wedding.

Liam looked at him. "You don't have to, Jeremiah. We can cater something."

"By this weekend?" Jeremiah shook his head. "I'll do it. I know what you guys like, and if it's just family, it's really just a Sunday lunch after church."

Gratitude filled Liam, and he cleared his throat. He knew how hard weddings were for Jeremiah. "Thank you," he managed to say, and Jeremiah clapped him on the knee.

"Now, what's this meeting really about?"

"The Shining Star," Liam said. "I'm taking Callie to Hawaii for a honeymoon, and we'll be gone for fifteen days."

Skyler whistled again, this time like *woooow, cowboy. Hawaii for fifteen days? Dang.*

Liam grinned at Skyler, and asked, "Right?" They chuckled together, and Liam sobered again. "I'm going to ask a huge favor. This week, as Callie gets a wedding put together and Jeremiah makes a menu, I'm going to be hiring anyone I can to come work on the ranch. Some permanently. Some inside, as I want to do an entire remodel on the house. I want everything cleaned up and hauled away. I want men ready to work. I want Callie to come home to absolute perfection at the Shining Star."

He took a deep breath and surveyed his brothers. "I know we have a ranch to run too, but I'm asking all of you to help me get the Shining Star, well, as shiny as a new penny while I'm gone. I'll pay everyone."

Wyatt scoffed, his first contribution to the conversation. "Yeah, because we need your money." A beat of silence filled the room, and then all five of them started laughing. Liam missed Tripp and Rhett in that moment, and he wished all seven brothers were at Seven Sons tonight.

When they'd quieted, Liam said, "I'll talk to Rhett and Tripp."

"I'm sure they can come help," Micah said. "And I'm sure we'll all do what we can." He looked around at everyone. "Right, guys?"

"Yes," and "yeah," and "yep," came from the brothers.

The enormity of what Liam was asking them to do hit him, and he sagged back into the couch. "I don't know if it can be done. Have any of you seen that place?"

Jeremiah raised his hand halfway, as did Wyatt. "It's not in great shape," Wyatt said. "And that's just the outside. I haven't been in the house."

"I have," Jeremiah said. "And it's not pretty in there either." He met Liam's eye, but Liam couldn't sit up. "It needs a complete renovation. Fifteen days?"

"I called the three-day bathroom guys," Liam said. "They can come. If you guys can do the demo, I can get carpet and flooring guys in. I've already ordered the new appliances. Maybe Micah can work on the back deck, and I'm going to ask Evelyn to pick out new furniture and curtains and stuff like that. I'll ask Tripp to move my computer setup into the office over there." He had so many things to do. So many people to ask. So many phone calls to make.

But he wasn't working this week due to the holidays, and he literally had nothing but time and money.

"I'll get as much help as I can for the outside," he said. "Maybe we could spare Orion, Dicky, Wallace, and Simon."

"We can," Jeremiah said. "And I just had a guy call me the week before Christmas, looking for work. Seemed like a good man. I can get you his name."

"Great," Liam said. "Callie has six cabins over there. I don't think she needs twelve people to run the ranch, but she'll need at least that many to get everything cleaned up."

Liam had ten men already. And Simone and Evelyn to help with the more feminine details the homestead needed. A dozen people to help, and he wanted it to be the best present Callie had ever received.

"And I want it to be a surprise," Liam said. "So not a word to Callie."

"Deal," Skyler said. "Now, are you going to make that peanut butter banana ice cream, or what?"

Liam burst out laughing, but he did get up and head into the kitchen. Jeremiah was a genius with savory foods, but it was always Liam who made the desserts at Seven Sons. He hoped after he and Callie were married that he'd still be welcome here to spin up a delicious sweet treat to share with his brothers.

———

THE NEXT DAY, Liam had made nine phone calls before lunch. He hadn't seen Callie, but he had both of her sisters on-board for the remodel plan, and Evelyn was so excited, she'd shrieked and said she and Simone would go to the furniture store that afternoon. Simone had offered to put some of her custom pieces in the house, and Liam had said, "Tell me how much they are, Simone, and I'll buy them."

For once, one of the Foster sisters hadn't argued with him and said his money wasn't welcome. She'd just said, "All right, Liam," and hung up.

He'd talked to the Internet company, and they'd actually be there that afternoon between three and six. He'd called a lawn care company and scheduled them to come get the front and back yard cleaned up. He'd ordered all the flooring—carpet and a waterproof vinyl that looked like hardwood.

He wasn't sure there was time to paint, and while the cabinets were old, if Micah could stain them, they'd probably look brand-new.

He looked down at his desk, his head pounding. Floors. Appliances. Internet. Yard. Furniture. Bathrooms.

"Cowboys," he said to himself, getting up and stretching his back. Jeremiah hadn't come in for lunch yet, but Liam went down the hall to find something to eat. His brother hadn't given him the name of the cowboy who'd come looking for work either, and Liam wasn't sure how to find people who were available.

After pulling out the cheesy spaghetti casserole they'd eaten last night and sticking the whole container in the microwave, he started tapping and searching on his phone. There had to be a job board for cowboys in the Texas Panhandle.

Before he could find what he needed, the back door got flung open, and the perfect storm that was Jeremiah entered. "You have got to be kidding me," he practically roared. His dark eyes shot fire at Liam, who wanted to vacate the kitchen immediately. But he held his ground, because he needed information Jeremiah had.

The microwave beeped, and Liam almost didn't want to turn his back on his brother. He pulled the food out and put it on the counter as Jeremiah said, "Well, can't you move us?"

Whoever he was talking to was obviously trying to placate him, but they weren't saying what Jeremiah wanted to hear. "Fine," he barked. "Thank you for trying." He ripped his phone away from his ear, and Liam actually thought he'd throw it through the nearest window.

"What's goin' on?" Liam asked.

"Nothing." Jeremiah glared at him and sat down at the bar. "Is some of that for me?"

"Yes, of course," he said, turning to get two plates out. "Listen, I need help with hiring. Is there a job board or something?"

"Oh, sure," Jeremiah said, his temper cooling quickly. And the fact that he wouldn't say what that phone call was about had Liam's radar on high alert. "Let me text you."

Liam served some pasta to himself and Jeremiah and rounded the island. "Are you really not going to tell me what that phone call was about?"

Jeremiah gave him the side-eye, and Liam's phone chimed. "Is that you?"

"Yes," Jeremiah said. "That's a great job board. Make a post there, and you'll get a ton of cowboys and cowgirls calling you. Oh." He went back to his phone, and Liam wondered if he should just let the call drop. "That's Cayden Murphy's number. Hopefully he'll still be looking for work. I liked him."

Liam nodded, glancing at his phone as it chimed again. He swiped and opened Jeremiah's texts to get rid of the notification. "And you didn't like whoever you were talking to on the phone." He lifted his eyebrows, and Jeremiah's shoulders deflated.

He got up to get himself a fork, and while he was facing Liam, he said, "This is a secret. I find out you've told anyone—*any*one, even Tripp or Callie—and I will rip you apart."

"Wow." Liam couldn't even eat. "I don't know if I want to know." Callie was going to be his wife, and Tripp was his twin. "And I don't know if I can't tell Tripp."

"Twin thing," Jeremiah said, returning to his spot next to Liam.

"Yeah."

"And you're marrying Callie."

Liam's heart skipped a beat. "Yeah." He twirled some noodles around his fork. "I'd still like to know, because you seemed pretty mad, and maybe I can help."

Jeremiah went silent, and Liam continued eating. He finally said, "It's about a woman."

Liam choked unintentionally, but wow. "You should've warned me." His food forgotten know, he twisted fully toward Jeremiah. "And keep talking."

13

Jeremiah couldn't believe he'd mentioned a woman to Liam. His brother's entire being had lit up, and Jeremiah couldn't back out now.

He knew Liam would tell both Tripp and Callie. He couldn't ask him to keep secrets from the two of them, but he knew the gossip would end there. Callie had kept plenty of secrets for him, and Tripp had a new life with a new wife and stepson to deal with.

"We have a really nice reserved spot for the New Year's Eve parade," Jeremiah said. "And Brenda called me to find out if we wanted to bring something to share with the other people in the reserved area." He lifted one hand in a strange, wavy gesture. "I guess it's a tradition among the people who get the reserved spots." He blew out his breath.

"What could we possibly take?"

"She'd actually heard you were a genius with desserts. She suggested that." Jeremiah cocked his eyebrows at Liam, who said nothing. "I said we could take some of our home-smoked jerky, and she got really excited about that."

"That's a better idea," Liam said. "I'm swamped right now."

Jeremiah knew, and he worked hard not to roll his eyes. He couldn't blame Liam for his vision; the twins had always had extraordinary expectations for themselves and everyone else. They dreamt big, and achieved big, if Liam's contract with the entire Marvel universe was any indication.

"Anyway," Jeremiah said, his heartbeat speeding again, because he knew the next part of the story. "Brenda started telling me who else was in the reserved section, and she said we were *lucky*—" He rolled his eyes. "Because we were located right next to Wilde & Organic, and they always brought amazing hummus, and home-made pita chips, and fruited honeys."

Jeremiah was actually excited about the honey, as he loved his beehives and the honey that came from them. A day he pulled frames out of hives, spun them, and strained honey into bottles was a very good day.

Pathetic, he told himself. He was almost as excited about the honey as he was sitting by Whitney at the parade. *Absolutely pathetic.*

"Sounds good," Liam said, clearly not getting what Jeremiah was saying.

"Yeah, except Whitney Wilde's family owns Wilde & Organic, and she's going to badger me *to death* about shooting out here, and I'm not even going to be able to enjoy the parade."

Or maybe he'd enjoy it too much. Sitting next to the beautiful Whitney Wilde...oh, yeah, his heart was excited about that. It was almost like it had forgotten completely how shattered it had been by the last female Jeremiah had let into his life.

Liam started laughing, but Jeremiah didn't see what was so funny. He stabbed at his food, barely tasting the cheesy pasta, and that was a real shame, because he'd worked hard on this, and it had been delicious last night.

"You know what I think?" Liam asked.

"No," Jeremiah said. "And I don't care." Liam would say it anyway, and he'd probably be right.

"I think you like this Whitney Wilde, and you're worried you'll want to hold her hand at the parade."

"No," Jeremiah said. It was Whitney's bright red lips that kept him awake at night, though he was thinking about holding her hand now.

"And you're hoping she'll sit right beside you and talk to you in that pretty, Texas voice she has." He practically sang the words at the end of the sentence, and annoyance ran through Jeremiah.

"You don't even know if she has a pretty, Texas voice," Jeremiah said, scoffing. But she did.

Liam laughed again. "You said it was about a woman," he said, still chuckling. "So just admit you like her."

"I *don't* like her," he said. Jeremiah warred with himself. He kept his eyes on the counter a few inches in front of him. "But I think I could, and she torments me with that voice, and I may have thought about kissing her."

Pure panic streamed through him, and he expected Liam to laugh again.

He didn't.

Jeremiah took another moment, and then he looked at his brother. "I don't—I can't go through what I did with Laura Ann."

Liam simply looked at him, his eyes searching for something. "Your life didn't end in Austin with Laura Ann."

"I know that." But Jeremiah really wasn't sure if he did.

"I think if you like this woman, you should maybe... how do I say this nicely?" He exhaled, and Jeremiah almost didn't want him to say it.

"Go on," he said anyway.

"Get out of your own way," Liam said. "Get out of your head. Hold her hand if you want to. Kiss her if you want to."

"I don't know what I want."

"You were *livid* about sitting beside her and her family," Liam said.

"That's my default," Jeremiah said. "That way, everyone stays away."

"Including Whitney."

Jeremiah nodded. "But she doesn't seem to care how many times I hang up on her or tell her to stop calling."

Liam grinned like the Cheshire Cat, and that didn't settle Jeremiah's stomach. "Maybe she's the one who can handle being with the Many Moods of Jeremiah."

"Oh, come on."

Liam laughed then, and Jeremiah couldn't deny the fact that yes, he went from zero to sixty pretty quickly sometimes.

Maybe she's the one. The thought terrified Jeremiah to his very core. He managed to finish eating, and Liam said, "I won't tell anyone. But maybe you should just give yourself a chance." He knocked a couple of times on the counter and got up. "Now I have to go hire some cowboys."

———

TWO DAYS LATER, Jeremiah left the evening feeding in the capable hands of his cowboys. Orion would make sure every living creature got fed for the night, and then they'd join the Walker family in town. Jeremiah wanted to check-in early with Brenda for the New Year's Eve parade, and fine. Maybe he wanted to talk to Whitney before the crazy started. With all of his brothers coming, the Seven Sons section of the parade route was going to be loud and obnoxious.

The parade didn't start until six-thirty, and by then it would be dark. The grandstand, where they got to sit, would be lit until the parade started, and a general excitement ran through Jeremiah as he pulled into the reserved lot where he should be able to park.

"Name?" a man asked, holding a clipboard and pen, his cowboy hat covering his eyes.

"Jeremiah Walker," he said.

"With Seven Sons?"

"Yes, sir."

"How many vehicles will you have?"

"Probably five," he said. "Is that okay?"

"Yep." The man made a note on his clipboard and handed Jeremiah a blue tag. "Put that in your window. Park anywhere." He grinned at him. "Good to see you again, Jeremiah."

"Oh, Brit, I didn't even recognize you." He stared at the man he'd seen at plenty of community ranch meetings. "What's different?"

He laughed and shook his head. "My wife is going to win this bet. I shaved my beard."

"Oh, right." He laughed too, the sound breaking up some of the tension in his chest. "Good luck with whatever bet you've got." He eased past Brit Bellamore and found a parking spot. He hauled as many camp chairs as he could carry over to the spot marked with a little sign that had hand-lettering on it. *Seven Sons Ranch.*

He wasn't blind, and he could see the Wilde & Organic sign too. Whitney's parents were there, spreading blankets and setting up a table. Panic blipped through Jeremiah. What did they need a table for?

"Evening, Jeremiah," her father said, and Jeremiah nodded at him.

"Evening, Larry. Ma'am."

"We brought chips and salsa," she said. "Homegrown tomatoes from our farm."

No wonder they needed a table. "Thank you, ma'am," he said, but he didn't cross the line and go sample any. He started setting up the chairs he'd brought over, returning to his truck for the rest. He'd told his brothers he'd take care of everything, because it made him feel useful. Important. Worthy.

So much in his life had died when Laura Ann had fled the state, and Jeremiah needed something to make him feel alive. Cooking for his family and taking care of the ranch did that, and so far, it had been a good mask for what really troubled him.

The fact that he could feel very little. He didn't have a relationship with the Lord anymore, though he still went to church. He barely prayed, because God wasn't going to answer him anyway. He'd relied on his own strength and his own wit and his own talent around the homestead and ranch, and it was working so far.

Is it, though? he asked himself, wishing the doubts weren't there. A couple of Whitney's brothers and sisters had arrived, and they were passing out sandwiches and opening bags of chips. Micah and Skyler had said they'd stop and get food for the parade, so Jeremiah went back to his truck one last time to retrieve the home-smoked beef jerky he'd brought to share with the other grandstanders.

"Do you want to put that over here?" Molly asked, and Jeremiah looked over to their patch of grass. It was filled with life and people and a pulse. He was still waiting for his brothers to show up—and Whitney.

"Sure," he said. "There's room?" He stepped over the rope that had been set up to separate the spaces and piled the jerky on the table.

"There's always room for more food," Molly said with a smile.

"We can take this rope down," Jeremiah said. "It's just my brothers. Well, and the Foster sisters." And Ivory. But they had plenty of room, and he removed the rope between their two spots. The rope stuck on a spike in the ground, and he bent to untangle it.

In that moment, he knew Whitney had arrived. He hadn't seen her. But she had a presence that called to him, and sure enough, when he straightened and started coiling the rope, she stood at the table with all the food on it.

She wore dark jeans that disappeared into a pair of brown cowgirl boots with red stitching. Her red and white flannel top seemed tailored for her curves, and all that beautiful, dark hair had been curled and clipped just so, spilling down her back where it begged Jeremiah to fist his fingers in it as he kissed her.

Stupid Liam, he thought, as if he were fourteen years old again. As if it were Liam's fault this woman had been tormenting him for six months.

Oh, no, that was Tripp's fault, and Jeremiah was going to give him a piece of his mind the moment he showed up.

Whitney turned as if she could feel the weight of Jeremiah's stare on her. Their eyes met, and something formed between them. He couldn't be the only one who felt that, could he?

A smile danced across those bright red lips, and Whitney lifted a piece of his beef jerky to her mouth. She came toward him, and everything in the world was suddenly too hot.

"You alone tonight, cowboy?" she asked.

"Nope," he said, glad his voice didn't sound strangled. "My brothers are coming."

"I assume this is yours." She held out her beef jerky.

"Yeah," he said. "Do you like it?" For some reason, he *really* wanted her to like it.

"Yeah," she said. "It's great." She took another bite and looked at all the empty chairs. "Where are you sitting?"

"Uh—"

"Whitney," a woman said, and she turned to her sister. "Can Dalton sit by you? He won't get out of the car unless he can sit by you."

"Of course," Whitney said, turning back to Jeremiah. "My fifteen-year-old nephew. He and my sister don't get along that well."

"Being fifteen is hard," Jeremiah said.

Whitney looked at him, searching his face for something. She took so much from him, and he didn't even realize what he was willing to give her. "I have two sides," she said. "I'd love to sit by you during the parade." She tucked her hair behind her ear and took another bite of that beef jerky, tormenting him.

"Jeremiah, where do you want us?" Rhett asked, and Jeremiah looked at his brother. He'd arrived with Evelyn and Simone, and Jeremiah waved in a general direction of the chairs.

"Anywhere," he said.

"We can talk about the ranch," Whitney said. "And how you made this." She popped the last bite of jerky in her mouth and turned around. Twisting back to him, she said, "If you want."

Oh, he wanted to sit beside her. He'd tell her anything she wanted to know. An idea popped into his mind, and he let it marinate while he dealt with chairs and blankets as more people arrived.

Micah and Skyler showed up with pizza and sodas, and Jeremiah made sure his chair was situated right next to Whitney's, at the back of the crowd, out of the way. He liked that she'd set up there, though she'd probably done it for her nephew.

"I had a thought," he said once he had a plate of pizza balanced on his lap and a cold can of diet cola in his arm rest.

"Oh, boy," Whitney said. "Sounds dangerous." She sat beside a surly teenager who wore sunglasses though twilight had already fallen.

Jeremiah chuckled, because he couldn't help himself. Liam was sitting way on the other side of the square, with Callie practically on his lap. He didn't need to know what Jeremiah was doing over here. No one needed to know.

"My brother is getting married and leaving the ranch," he said. "I was thinking...maybe for a wedding present, I'd give him a picture of it."

Whitney's head swung toward him so fast, Jeremiah thought for sure she'd get whiplash. Her eyes soaked him in, hope filling them so quickly that Jeremiah felt bad for denying her the opportunity to shoot at Seven Sons for all of these months.

"What are you saying?" she asked.

"I'm asking you to come out to the ranch and take some pictures," he said. "Landscapes. Of the best features of the ranch. Not brides. Not families. And it's *not* an open invitation to shoot at the ranch."

A smile curved those lips, and Jeremiah couldn't help staring at them. He cleared his throat and yanked his gaze away. "And then, I don't know. We can pick one of the best ones to print for him. They can hang it in their house." He lifted his pizza to his lips and took a bite. He said nothing while he ate, and when he finished the first slice, he finally dared to look at her again.

"What?" he asked, because she was still staring at him, wonder etched in her expression. "Do you not take land-scapes? How much would it cost?"

Whitney cleared her throat too, and Jeremiah knew then that the attraction sparking through him was defi-nitely not one-sided. "I can take landscapes," she said. "And you'll only have to pay for the print. I can get it at wholesale, though."

"I can pay you for your time."

Whitney put a coy smile on her face then, and she leaned closer to Jeremiah. He instinctually bent his head toward hers too. "I'd rather you paid for dinner."

"Dinner?"

She giggled, and the sound was going to drive him straight to madness. "That's right, cowboy. You can pay for dinner after the shoot. We'll go together."

"Jeremiah," Wyatt said, and Jeremiah wanted to rip off his brother's face. "We have a problem."

We'll go together.

To dinner.

With Whitney Wilde.

And he'd pay, which made it a date.

Light and joy filled him as he turned toward Wyatt. "Yeah?"

"Orion says he has a flat. Needs us to go get him and the others. Can we take your truck?"

"Sure," Jeremiah said. "Take it." He turned back to Whitney to confirm their date.

"I need the keys, bro," Wyatt said, stepping in front of him.

"Oh, right." Jeremiah dug in his pocket and produced the keys, hearing the slightest wisp of laughter from Whitney. Wyatt glanced at her, took the keys, and left. Thankfully. "Sorry, where were we?"

"You were just going to ask me to dinner," Whitney said. "Or maybe I asked you." She grinned again and looked at her nephew. "How did you hear it, Dalton?"

"You asked him, Aunt Whitney," the boy said in a near monotone, staring straight ahead. "And old people flirting is weird."

Whitney laughed and swatted his arm. "Watch your mouth. I'm not that old."

Dalton's mouth twitched, but he wouldn't let a full smile show. Jeremiah knew exactly how the kid felt, because he was smothering his own smile too.

"So?" Whitney asked, the playfulness still loud in her voice. "Are you going to take me to dinner after the shoot or not?"

"Depends," Jeremiah said, facing the street again.

"On what?"

He cut a look out of the corner of his eye. "I haven't decided yet."

14

C allie couldn't believe the beauty of the light parade. She'd been before, as a little girl, but it almost took an act of God to get her off the Shining Star lately. And by lately, she meant the last decade or so.

Simone did the grocery shopping. Evelyn was the public face of the family. Callie went to church and she worked the ranch. She went to town to visit her father and grandmother. That was all she'd ever needed to do.

"You okay, Gran?" she asked, looking over at her grandmother now. "It's a little chilly." She was glad she'd bundled up in the thickest coat she had. Liam had brought a blanket too, and she already sat under that.

"Just fine, dear," her grandmother said. "I haven't been to this parade in a while."

"Me either," Callie said, her excitement growing as the holiday music continued to play. Three Rivers had a lot of town traditions, and this New Year's Eve celebration had really picked up in the past several years.

The scent of roasting meat and fried food filled the air, and a whole food truck extravaganza was going on in the downtown park behind them.

"You guys are set for Sunday?" she asked, looking past her grandma to her father. "Do I need to come and take a suit to the cleaners?"

"I can do it," her father said with a smile. "And yes, I'm ready."

Callie couldn't believe she was getting married on Sunday. *Married.* She glanced at Liam, who was turned toward Tripp. They were talking in low voices about something, and Callie looked back at her family. Rhett and Evelyn sat in front of them, with Simone as well. Wyatt and Micah had chairs there too, but they'd left to get the other cowboys.

Her two sisters, her father, and her grandmother were everything she'd had for so long, but now.... Now she had the whole Walker family too.

"Okay," she said. "It's not going to be a big wedding. Just family."

"That's the perfect kind," her grandma said, reaching over to cover Callie's hand with one of her weathered ones. "We're very excited for you and Liam."

"Thank you, Gran." Callie squeezed her hand and turned when the lights flashed. A cry went up, and people who had been out on the street started moving back to their seats.

"Five minutes," a man said over the loudspeaker. "Please clear the road and be ready for the lights to go out in five minutes."

She squeezed Liam's hand, and he turned toward her. "I'm so excited," she said.

He grinned at her and pressed a kiss to her forehead. "Yeah? What are you excited about?"

"I haven't been to this for ages," she said. "I heard it's gotten really good." The diamond on her ring finger felt amazing too. She looked up into Liam's eyes. "I haven't been...happy about anything for so long. I haven't had a single thing to look forward to."

Compassion filled his gaze, and he leaned down and touched his lips to hers in a sweet, meaningful kiss. "I'm glad, sweetheart."

"I'm willing to talk about the honeymoon," she said. He'd tried to bring it up on Tuesday morning too, when he'd suggested a wedding date of Sunday. He'd already gotten the Internet up to speed, and he claimed the only thing they needed to do now was tie the knot. Say that invented I-do.

But she'd been adamant that she didn't need to go on a honeymoon. She had a ranch to run, didn't he know?

"You are?" he asked.

She nodded, thinking about the rules they'd set for themselves. None of those had changed, though her relationship with Liam was definitely something different than it had been even a week ago.

"Well, good thing I already bought those tickets to Hawaii, then," Liam said, his grin as big as the whole state of Texas.

Callie gaped at him, shocked for a moment. Then she realized she should've known he'd already have a plan—with tickets bought—for their honeymoon. No matter what she said, Liam did what he wanted.

"You deserve it," he said, as if he could sense her growing irritation with him. "And you need a break from that ranch, and we need some time to ourselves."

"Liam," she said, a new type of knot forming inside her. She leaned closer to him, glad the music was still playing loudly. "You know what people do on their honeymoon, right?"

"Our rules stand," he whispered. "But tell me you don't want to go to Hawaii."

"I've never left the state," she said, the fear right there.

"I know, sweetheart. And I can tell you're a little worried about it. But you don't need to be. It's just a few hours on an airplane."

"I've never been on an airplane."

"What?" Liam searched her face then, but the lights went out completely, arousing another cry of surprise from the crowd. His lips brushed the side of her face and touched her earlobe. "Then this is going to be a grand adventure for you. I can't wait." He straightened as the first float came toward them. It was lit with blue and white light, creating a heavenly atmosphere as it advanced down the street slowly.

It was the Three Rivers town float, with a cowboy standing on it, along with a pretty woman in a pioneer dress. A statue of this woman sat in the square too, and she'd been a jilted bride, left by her cowboy boyfriend in the middle of the Texas Panhandle.

Now, she seemed like an angel, and Callie clapped as the float went by. She stood when the American flag marched by, one hand over her heart. She sang the national anthem with the hay wagon singers, and she clapped along when the high school marching band went by, lights sewn into the seams of their uniforms and laced around their big bass drums.

Liam didn't bring up their rules, their honeymoon, or their wedding during the parade. They just watched, and laughed, and ate too much red licorice, which Wyatt had brought as his contribution to the family snack pile.

Callie enjoyed every minute, and she had no idea people lived like this. Without fear that the envelope they'd been dreading would be waiting for them in the mailbox when they got home. Without the weight of so much debt piled on their shoulders. Without the debilitating panic that had been following her for years.

The parade, concert, and fireworks ended before midnight, and Callie helped clean up the area where she and all the Walkers had been sitting. A woman laughed, and she looked over to find Jeremiah talking to Whitney Wilde.

Not just talking. *Flirting.* The man was flirting with her, a wide smile on his face as he ducked his head. She said something else, and Jeremiah nodded before she left with a teenage boy.

Callie's first instinct was to go find out what in the world that was all about. But she held back, because she didn't need to be involved in Miah's life quite so much anymore. A pang of sadness ran through her, because she loved Miah like a brother.

"I've got it, sweetheart," Liam said, and Callie blinked. Turning back to him, she picked up the blanket he'd brought and smiled. "You ready?"

"Yes," she said. "Did my father get everything?"

"Yeah," Simone said. "They're off already."

Callie stepped off the curb with Liam and headed through the parking lot to his truck. "That was so much fun."

"I think so too," he said, loading everything into the truck bed. He took her into his arms, and Callie gazed up at him. A measure of love moved through her, and she tensed. She'd liked Liam for a long time. He'd always made her heart beat wildly in her chest. He'd replaced Jeremiah as her best friend, despite the setbacks they'd had over the last several months.

He was going to help her keep the ranch, and so much gratitude filled her.

"Cal," he whispered, taking off his cowboy hat. He ran his nose down the side of her face, and she closed her eyes. "I'm falling in love with you. All the way. For real." He kissed her before she could respond, and she poured her emotions into her touch, hoping he could feel that she was falling for him too.

When he finally pulled away, Callie was breathless, and the parking lot was almost empty. "I'm not ready for the night to end," she said.

"No?" Liam swayed with her. "I bet we could find somewhere that's open. We could watch the ball drop."

Callie really wanted to kiss him at midnight. She wanted to start a new chapter of her life with this man. Get the new year off to the right start.

"We can do that at the ranch," she said, because then she wouldn't have to kiss him in public.

You literally just did, she thought.

Liam nodded and walked her over to the passenger door. "All right. Let's head back to the ranch."

At the Shining Star, Simone was nowhere to be found. Callie wondered if she'd decided to sleep at Evelyn's that night. She sent her a quick text so she'd know, and then she snuggled into Liam's side.

He fell asleep during the concerts and chatter on the New Year's Eve show on TV, but Callie woke him up with five minutes to spare. "It's almost time," she whispered.

"Time for what?" he asked, still groggy.

"Time for us to celebrate a new year together." She looked at him, watching him become more alert.

"This is important to you."

"The last few years have been terrible for me," she admitted. "And here I am, with you, and all this possibility in front of me." Callie wasn't quite sure how to articulate what it all meant to her. "It's just...amazing. *You're* amazing, and I want you to know how much I appreciate you, and what you're doing, and just...everything."

Liam cradled her face in his hand. "I think you're amazing too."

"I want to start this year right," she said. "And I want to be with you." She kissed him, even though it wasn't quite midnight yet. Even though no one had counted down. Even though the ball hadn't dropped.

And she was still kissing him when all of those things happened, hopeful that the coming year could be the one where she finally found true happiness.

———

THE NEXT DAY, she opened her closet and took out a dress she hadn't looked at or thought about in a very long time.

Her mother's wedding dress.

The bag crinkled as she pulled it from the back of the closet, behind so many other things Callie never looked at, thought about, or wore.

"Mama," she said, though her mother had been gone

for a long time now. She lovingly laid the dress on her bed and unzipped the garment bag. The dress was old and frail, yellowed along the collar and the cuffs. But it held so much of who Callie was that she hadn't been able to let it go. Just like the ranch.

She wasn't going to wear the dress to marry Liam. No, she and her sisters would go to town tomorrow to find something that would work in a pinch. She didn't have time for tailoring, and she honestly didn't even care if the dress was white.

But she needed something of her mother's for the wedding, and while she hadn't sat behind a sewing machine for a while, she could still make a straight line. She'd made a handkerchief for Evelyn's wedding out of part of the train of their mother's dress, but Callie was thinking this time, she could make something out of the lace.

A necklace. A coin purse. A pillow. Maybe she wouldn't have to sew at all. She carefully clipped a section of lace from the back of the dress, preserving the front, and rezipped the dress into the bag.

After carefully replacing the dress in the back of the closet, she held the lace in her hand and closed her eyes. "I wish you were here, Mama," she said. "Did you love Daddy so much when you married him?"

Of course, Callie believed her mother and father had been desperately in love. She wanted that kind of love with her husband too.

"And maybe you'll have it," she whispered to herself. Callie had been abiding by all of Liam's rules. She'd been very open minded and hearted toward him. So much so that she could feel herself falling for him after only a week. She hadn't told him he couldn't buy things, and in fact, he was financing a frivolous honeymoon to Hawaii. She'd stepped back from Miah, and she'd been confiding in her husband-to-be.

So maybe, just maybe, her happily-ever-after was on the horizon after all.

15

L iam looked down at the sheets of paper in front of him. Unlike Wyatt, he didn't need glasses to see them, and he could plainly tell that he had enough good men and women ready and willing to show up to the ranch on Monday morning.

Problem was, he didn't have anywhere to put them until the cabins were cleaned out.

"They can do it," he said. "Day one: clean up your own cabin. Go buy what you need to live there." He could leave a credit card here while he and Callie flew to paradise. He'd spent three days interviewing cowboys and cowgirls, and now he just needed to make some offers and get people out here.

He was getting married in two days, and there was so much to do. Not for the wedding itself. No, Liam had a perfectly pressed suit ready to be worn. A really nice dress hat. His best boots polished and ready.

Jeremiah was going through the menu with him that night, and he'd shop for everything tomorrow. Callie had gone to town with her sisters that morning to find a dress. Everyone in the family had been invited and confirmed they'd be there. Not only that, but Skyler was a licensed minister, and he'd agreed to marry Liam and Callie.

So even if the I-do wasn't very real, at least no one else needed to know about it. Liam wouldn't have to look at Pastor Daniels and feel guilty for taking him from his family to perform a fake marriage.

"It's not fake to you," he muttered to himself. In fact, he'd been dreaming of the day he could marry Callie Foster, long before he'd found out about the financial troubles at her ranch. In the week since he'd logged on to her bank and paid her mortgage, she'd completely transformed.

He realized he'd only seen glimpses of the woman she could be without the threat of financial ruin and eviction, and he'd still fallen in love with her.

Judging from the way she'd kissed him on New Year's Eve, Liam didn't think Callie was faking much with him. She liked him a whole lot. He wasn't so far removed from the female species that he couldn't tell when a woman liked him. But he didn't think she *loved* him, and he'd never imagined himself marrying a woman who didn't love him.

Wasn't that why he'd ended things with Portia permanently, left Austin, and came to Three Rivers in the first place?

Yes, his brain said. *Doesn't matter*, his heart said, pounding loudly as if to get its point across. And he sided with his heart. It didn't matter that he'd left Portia because she couldn't commit to him. Because she didn't love him.

Callie wasn't Portia, and she *could* fall in love with Liam. They just needed more time. He once again had the thought that he should postpone the wedding. Surely Callie wouldn't lose the ranch now that he'd caught up her balance and put money in her accounts at the bank.

He felt uneasy for some reason, and he couldn't quite put his finger on why. He wanted to get the Shining Star up to its full operational capacity, and he'd do that whether Callie married him or not. But she wouldn't let him unless they were married.

So they had to get married.

He couldn't believe he was still going back and forth with himself about this.

All at once, the sky opened, and a beam of heaven's light shone into his mind. He knew why he didn't want to marry Callie this way. He felt like he was forcing her to do something she didn't want to do. He'd given her a big enough incentive to say I-do, and she was going to.

But she didn't want to.

And he didn't want to be someone she didn't want.

He sighed, his head aching from all the circular

thoughts. Why couldn't the stars just align, and he could meet a woman who fell madly in love with him from the start?

Someone came in the back door, and the house creaked as boots hit the floor. Liam shook his head to clear it and picked up his phone. He didn't know what to do about the wedding, but he knew he could make phone calls and hire the people he needed to work the ranch.

No, not him. The people *Callie* needed to work the ranch.

He frowned as he dialed the first number, making his voice falsely bright when Cayden Murphy picked up. "Heya, Cayden," he said. "It's Liam Walker, out at the Shining Star. I'd love to have you on full-time. Are you still available?"

"Absolutely," Cayden said.

"And you need a cabin?"

"Yep."

They'd already talked about all of this. Liam went on to explain a bit about when the job started—bright and early Monday morning—and that Jeremiah would be there to give out assignments. "He'll be in charge while I'm on my honeymoon," Liam said. "And it's going to be an intense two weeks. I already know that. I'm going to be asking you to work fourteen or fifteen hour days, seven days a week. I'm willing to pay double-time for every hour during those first fifteen days."

He took a breath, realizing what he was asking people to do. "Do you think you can do that?"

"I can try," Cayden said. "Does the ranch really need that much work?"

"It really does," Liam said. "If you'd like, I'm going to be doing a tour of it tomorrow morning." The idea came into his mind as it came out his mouth. "Then you'll be able to see. We can take care of paperwork then too, if you can make it."

"Name the time," Cayden said.

"Let's say nine," Liam said, scratching out a new note on the pad on his desk. *Figure out paperwork for hiring.* His to-do list never seemed to get any smaller, and he held onto the thoughts of a serene, sandy beach in Hawaii, Callie beside him, as they dozed in the sun. He wouldn't have to worry about his to-do list then.

"See you at nine," Cayden said, and Liam put a check mark next to his name on the list as the call ended.

Before he could make another call, someone stepped around the corner. "Fifteen or sixteen hour days?"

He looked up at the feminine voice, thinking his careful plans to surprise Callie with a complete overhaul of the ranch and homestead had just been blown wide open. His adrenaline surged at the woman standing there.

"Simone," he said, breathing out. "You scared me. I thought I'd just spoiled everything for Callie." He was anticipating her being angry about the renovation already, but that would happen after it was already done. If she found out before...Liam might not get a chance to make her his wife and give her the time she needed to fall all the way in love with him.

Simone smiled and entered the office. "Can I talk to you for a second?"

"Of course." If Simone was back, so was Callie, and he'd need to close the door on his office before he made the rest of his phone calls.

The youngest sister, Simone was definitely the quietest of the three Foster women. She was smart and resourceful, though. And very artistic and talented. "It's about a cabin," she said, looking him straight in the eyes. "I want to live in one of them."

Whatever Liam had been expecting her to say, it wasn't that. "Oh."

"I know that only leaves you with five for cowboys and whatnot," she said. "But I don't want to live at the homestead with you and Callie." She dropped her chin to her chest and studied her hands. "You two need your privacy, and I've been toying with the idea of moving out anyway."

"You have?" Liam didn't dare think too much about why he and Callie would need their privacy, and it was easier to focus on Simone leaving the Shining Star.

"I mean, a little," she said. "I work there, obviously. But I'm not as tied to the house as Callie is." She looked up at him. "I can fix up my own cabin."

"Yeah, okay," Liam said, because he didn't know how to deny her. It was her ranch, not his. "I'm sure we can build more cabins too. Micah's really good with that kind of stuff."

"Not in fifteen days," Simone said.

"Well, we'll see how many of these people need housing," he said. "Maybe we can put some of them here for the time being." In fact, most of the bedrooms upstairs here at Seven Sons were empty. "I'm sure it won't be a problem."

Simone nodded and stood up. "Thanks, Liam." She took a few steps toward the door and then turned back. "I'm glad you and Callie are doing this, you know." She smiled, and Liam felt her good spirit beaming right out at him.

"Me too," he said. "Thanks, Simone."

She left, and Liam got up and closed his office door, actually surprised he knew how to do that. He never closed the door, because people were always welcome here. But he didn't want Callie walking in while he was explaining the situation to her new ranch hands. He turned back to the desk, many more phone calls to make—and they weren't going to dial themselves.

———

LATER THAT NIGHT, he stood on the opposite side of the bar while Jeremiah bent to take a huge Dutch oven out of the oven. "Wow," he said. "Smells good."

"I hope so," Jeremiah said. "It feels like stew weather,

doesn't it?" His brother had been in an unusually good mood the last few days, and Liam wondered what had happened on New Year's Eve.

"Sure," Liam said. "Is this what you're serving at the wedding?"

"I think so," he said. "It's full of heart, and it's easy. Put it together in the morning, serve it that afternoon." He looked at Liam for approval, and all Liam had to give him was utter gratitude.

He cleared his throat, because there was so much emotion there. "Thank you, Jeremiah," he said, and everything was laid out between them.

Jeremiah tossed the oven mitts on the counter and came around the island to take Liam into a tight, brotherly hug. "I'm so happy for you. I know you've liked this woman for a long time."

"Too long," Liam whispered. He backed up quickly and blinked back the moisture in his eyes. "What if I'm doing the wrong thing?"

"Impossible," Jeremiah said. "You're the only one who can help her, and who knows? Maybe you two will get your real wedding like Tripp and Rhett." He went back around the island and opened a drawer. He put spoons on the counter and lifted the lid on the Dutch oven. "Now, let's taste this."

Liam didn't need to say more than had already been said, so he picked up the spoon and dipped it in the broth. It looked thick and delicious, and the scent of beef and tomatoes and spices had his mouth watering while he blew on the piping hot stew. "You're going to tell me about Whitney, right?"

Jeremiah put his spoonful of stew in his mouth, and Liam did too. A groan came out of his throat, and he nodded. Smiling, he said, "Yes, this is perfect. Wedding stew."

"I'll get those sourdough rolls from Wilde & Organic too," he said. "Butter, jam, honey...." He let his voice hang there. "And punch. We'll be set, right?"

"Right." Liam sat down at the counter. "Now dish me up a whole bowl of that and start talking about Whitney."

"You're a bit of a bully, you know that?" Jeremiah glared at him. "What if I don't want to talk about Whitney?"

Liam chuckled, because out of the twins, he knew he was the bossiest. "Oh, you do."

Jeremiah grumbled something under his breath as he ladled stew into bowls. When he was seated next to Liam, he said, "We're going out."

Liam flinched and coughed, his stew bowl skidding a few inches across the counter. "Again, no warning. Come on, man."

Jeremiah started laughing, and it might have been the first time that Liam had heard any happiness in his brother's tone. "Sorry. She actually asked me out, and I confirmed."

"Wow. On New Year's Eve?"

Jeremiah nodded and stirred his stew. "And I—oh, this part is a secret."

"Really?"

"Really, really," he said, filling his mouth with stew after that. Liam did the same, because Jeremiah had already told him a lot already.

He swallowed and asked, "So...do you think you're ready to be dating again?"

"I guess we'll see," Jeremiah said. He kept his head down, but Liam still saw the flush as it crawled up his neck. "I held her hand on New Year's Eve too. It felt... good. Nice."

"Good," Liam mimicked, teasing his brother. "Nice."

"Yeah," Jeremiah said, smiling. "Like, I just need a human connection." He shrugged. "I hope I don't screw everything up."

"Why would you do that?"

"Because," he said, and nothing more. Liam thought he knew what he meant, because he'd been praying he wouldn't mess everything up between him and Callie by becoming her husband.

Help us both, he thought as he took another bite of stew. Surely the Lord could do that, couldn't he?

Liam sure hoped so, because he was getting married in less than forty-eight hours, and he didn't know how to back out now.

16

"Andy said it would lay like that," Evelyn said, swatting Callie's hand away from her waist. "Leave it alone."

"I don't like it," Callie said. She'd enjoyed shopping with her sisters, and they'd found a long, lacy dress at Andy's boutique. She liked the woman, and her cowboy husband had been there too. Watching her and Lawrence interact had been cleansing for Callie, and she'd recommitted herself to going through with this wedding.

And now the day was here.

But she didn't like the dress now. It felt more yellow than off-white, and that stupid pleat on her waist had added another ten pounds where Callie certainly didn't need it.

Friday's shopping with her sisters had been fun, but

exhausting. Not only did she buy her wedding dress, but a swimming suit. And every woman needed a dark room and utter silence to recover from bathing suit shopping.

Or maybe that was just Callie. No matter what, the spandex now sat in her suitcase, which she'd also had to buy. But, thanks to Liam's transfers, Callie had money in her account for all of it. Guilt had eaten at her for most of the afternoon on Friday, and thankfully, Liam had been busy with hiring the cowboys for the ranch.

Which only added to her guilt.

But she said nothing, because she'd promised Liam she wouldn't argue about what he chose to spend his money on. And she did need help around the ranch. With the holidays and then their honeymoon, Liam was sure to be behind on his work, and she knew he'd landed the largest contract in movie-making history.

She turned away from the mirror, tired of looking at the dress. Desperation filled her, and tears pricked her eyes.

"Why are you crying?" Evelyn asked, running a brush through a section of Callie's hair and wrapping it around the curling rod.

"This isn't...I'm getting *married* today."

"And it's not what you imagined it to be," Evelyn said. "Is that it?" She wore a sharp look in her eye Callie didn't like.

"Yes," Callie said.

"Remember how I got dressed in a locker room?"

Evelyn asked, not looking at her. Instead, she stared somewhere over Callie's head. "And then got married without Daddy and Gran there, without even Simone. Remember that?"

Foolishness hit Callie, but she nodded miserably anyway. "I'm sorry, Evelyn."

"This might not be the wedding you want," Evelyn said. "But it's the one you're getting, and at least your whole family and his whole family are here." She released the curl and she seemed satisfied with it, because she moved on to another section of hair. "And Callie, that man is in love with you."

"Stop it," Callie said, though Liam's own words from New Year's Eve rang through her mind, her heart, her soul.

"Whether he's said it or not, I don't know," Evelyn said like she was suddenly the oldest sister. "But I can see it."

"She has freaky pregnant-lady vision," Simone said, turning from the counter where she'd been wrapping Callie's bouquet. "So just listen to her."

"She's not wrong," Evelyn said, releasing another curl. "And if she plays her cards right, she could have the last name of Walker too."

"What?" Callie asked, practically kinking her neck to look at Evelyn. Simone was a much easier target, so she looked there. "What's she talking about?"

"Oh, Evelyn has some crazy idea that Micah Walker

likes me." Simone rolled her eyes and shook her head. "I've said maybe five words to the man."

"He does," Evelyn insisted. "And if you listen to me, you could have yourself a cowboy billionaire brother too."

"Fine," Simone said. "Let's say I believe you—which I don't. Not really. What would Evelyn-the-matchmaker do to set us up?"

"Oh, now you just want to use my keen eye."

Simone giggled and shrugged, pressing another piece of green floral tape around the stems. "If I can't, who can?"

"She has a point," Callie said.

"I just want the record to show that I could see things like this before I got pregnant," Evelyn said.

Callie rolled her eyes. "What record, Evvy?"

"Just say it." Her sister laughed as she wrapped another piece of hair. She'd moved behind Callie, and she couldn't see her.

"Fine," Callie said. "Let the record show that Evelyn has always known who to set us up with, even before she got pregnant." Of course, her sister's business had failed, though she had had several good years.

"Thank you," Evelyn said, an air of importance about her words. "And I can't really tell you what to do right now. I need some time to think about it."

Callie burst out laughing, but she caught sight of Simone's face. She and Evelyn were clearly having a silent conversation without her. She silenced her laughter and asked, "What's going on?"

"What? Nothing." Evelyn pulled on her hair a bit harder. "Stop moving so much. I'm going to have to re-do this whole thing."

Callie held still, because she didn't want that. If it were up to her, she'd pile her hair on top of her head and call it good. But Evelyn had said it was her wedding day, and she might not get another one.

The words had stung Callie, because she was sure her sister was right. She wasn't exactly young, and she didn't have a whole lot to offer a man. Especially one like Liam, and his interest in her was as baffling as it was flattering.

She decided she didn't care what her sisters were plotting. She and Liam would be married very soon, and then Callie was leaving the ranch. Leaving town. Leaving the state. She'd never fantasized about traveling much, but since Liam had mentioned Hawaii, her enthusiasm for the trip had grown and grown and grown.

She did need a break from the Shining Star, and she couldn't wait to live a day without the pressures of animal feedings and financial obligations hanging over her head. On the ranch, there was never enough time, energy, or money for what needed to be done. In Hawaii, she imagined it would be the complete opposite.

Liam had not given her any details about the trip, other than to "pack for the beach, sweetheart," and "don't forget to bring your ID. You can't fly without it."

Good tips, as Callie had never flown before. Her stomach bubbled just thinking about it, and she almost felt like a small child anticipating Christmas Day. Knowing Liam, everything would be high-end, catered, or plated in gold.

And Callie didn't completely hate that. He knew how to pamper a woman, and she could admit that it had been far too long since someone had taken care of her. No, she was the one who took care of everyone else, starting at age nine, when her mother had died. She'd learned to do laundry under her grandmother's hand, and she'd learned to feed horses from her grandfather. She started making dinner for the family when she was eleven, and she felt like the glue that had kept everyone together though she was suffering too.

She never let it show, and the emotion she felt over her mother's death felt suffocating. Out of the three girls, she remembered their mother the best, and it felt like a very great tragedy that Mama wasn't here today to see Callie get married.

Even if it wasn't entirely real.

"Okay," Evelyn said a few minutes later. "You're ready. Stand up and let's see."

Callie did what her sister wanted, and she faced Evelyn and Simone. Evelyn's chin wobbled as she started to weep. "It's just the hormones," she said in a teary voice. She gathered Callie into a hug and held her tight. "I love you so much."

Callie's first instinct was to apologize for putting them in this situation in the first place. If she'd have been honest with her sisters—she curbed the thoughts before they could derail her. Again.

She couldn't go back and change the past. All she could do was move forward. *One step at a time,* she thought.

Simone made their hug a three-way affair, and Callie thought her heart would burst. "I love you guys," she said, holding back the tears. She'd already spent too long on her makeup, and she didn't want to redo it. "Are you sure—?"

"Yes," Simone said before Callie could even finish the question. "You've already been through this. You've prayed about it and gotten your answer. Don't doubt it now."

Simone had always been the steady one in terms of her faith. Callie felt whipped all over, from one side of a rushing river to another. She'd tried holding onto the anchor of what she believed, but it was slippery, and she constantly felt like she was about to be thrown off. Cast aside, with the wrath of God about to be rained down upon her.

She nodded anyway, deciding that for this one day, she could use some of Simone's faith that this marriage was the right thing to do.

Drawing in a deep breath, she accepted the bouquet from her sister. "All right," she said. "What's next?"

"You stay here and relax," Evelyn said. "We'll go see how setup is coming. Do *not* let Liam in. I've already overheard him and Rhett talking about how he wants to see you before the wedding."

Callie wanted to see him too. She needed his reassurance that he wanted to marry her. That he wasn't just doing this out of pity. But she just nodded and watched her sisters leave the room. Callie had often retreated to her bedroom when things around the ranch had seemed dire. The walls of this room, though large, had often felt like fences she couldn't get past. They were no different now, and Callie paced out of the bathroom and into her bedroom.

The next person who knocked on the door definitely wasn't Liam, nor was it Evelyn or Simone. Callie moved toward it, asking, "Who is it?"

"It's Daddy, baby. Open up."

Callie fumbled with the lock but managed to get the door open. "Daddy." She practically fell into her father's arms, already trembling.

"It's time, honey-bug," he said, reverting to her child-hood nickname. It was actually one Mama had given her, and Callie pulled in a tight breath.

"Help me with my necklace," Callie said, moving over to her dresser and picking up the piece she'd made. "It's lace from Mama's dress." She showed it to her father, who took the necklace as if it were made of smoke and might disappear under his touch.

"Would you look at that," her dad said, a smile on his

face. "That's beautiful. Your mother would've been so proud of you."

Callie wished she could tell her father the truth. That since the moment Grandpa had died and her dad had retired, Callie had failed. And without this marriage and without Liam, the bank would've taken the ranch already.

So she wouldn't blurt out the horrible truth and crush her father's spirit, Callie turned around so he could put the necklace on for her. He looped it around her neck and his hands shook as he worked the clasp.

"Got it," he said a few seconds later, and Callie turned into his arms.

"Love you, Daddy."

"I love you too, sugar," he said. "Now, Evelyn's probably going to lecture me about taking too long." He gave Callie a knowing smile that said he didn't mind if Evelyn lectured him. He cocked his arm toward her. "Ready?"

Callie was absolutely not ready, but she laced her hand through her father's arm and said, "Yes," anyway.

For the ranch, she told herself as she left the safety and security of her bedroom. But with every step she took, her thoughts started to center on Liam.

She liked Liam. She liked him a whole lot. He liked her. They got along great—when they weren't arguing about money. Since she'd quit doing that, every moment with him had been fun and memorable.

Maybe she really did just need to open her mind and heart to him in order to be happy with him.

Her father opened the back door, and they stepped onto the deck. The wood got scraped as cowboy boots found their footing and chairs got moved slightly as people stood. Callie scanned everyone, and sure enough, it was just her family and Liam's. No other friends from town.

She focused on the handsome, kind, hardworking, wonderful man waiting for her at the altar, and suddenly Callie's fears vanished.

17

L iam couldn't believe the woman walking toward him was his. Or about to be, at least legally.

She was in many other ways too, and Liam needed to tell her how he really felt. He'd been back and forth about it for the past couple of days, but he didn't want to say or do anything that would scare her away.

And getting married was scary enough for Callie. And then leaving her ranch. The state of Texas. Getting on an airplane. Maybe he'd save the "I love you's" for Hawaii.

Her father stepped next to him and said, "You're a lucky man, Mister Walker," a smile plastered all over his face.

"Thank you, sir," he said, taking Callie's hand as her dad passed her to him. "I sure am." He pressed a kiss to Callie's forehead, feeling calmer than he had all day.

They faced Skyler, who beamed back at Liam with so much joy coming from him. "Well, you two," he drawled in a fake Texas accent. "You finally made it here."

"Oh, boy," Liam muttered under his breath at the same time a brother behind him scoffed. Laughed. Sucked in a breath. Liam knew it was Tripp, and sure enough, his twin appeared at the altar too, right between him and Callie.

"Sky," he said in a stage whisper. "No theatrics. This is serious, man."

"Sit down," Rhett said, joining them and tugging on Tripp's arm.

"You guys can't go anywhere without adult supervision," Jeremiah said, and Liam looked helplessly at nearly his entire family standing at the altar with him.

"Would you guys stop?" he hissed. "You're ruining this."

Callie giggled, quickly covering her mouth. Her eyes widened, and they flew to Liam's. "Sorry, I—" She laughed, her nose crinkling up so cute and the happiness he wanted for her pouring from her.

"I'm uninviting all y'all," Liam said, sounding a lot more upset than he actually was. "Everyone better dang well sit down right now." He let the threat hang there, and thankfully, all of his brothers sat down. Except for Skyler, who gave Liam an apologetic smile.

"We're gathered here today for the union of Liam Ronald Walker and Callie Hart Foster."

Liam's middle name wasn't Ronald, but he wasn't going to stop his brother. Let Skyler have his fun. Whatever. He just wanted to get to the I-do's.

"Love is a beautiful thing," Skyler said, and someone behind Liam made another noise. Liam ignored whoever it was and glared at Skyler, who finally got the message. "Do you, Callie Foster, take Liam Walker to be your lawfully wedded husband, to have and to cherish forever?"

Liam looked at Callie, every muscle in his body so dang tight. What if she said no? What a disaster that would be. He saw everything he'd done over the course of the last ten days flash before his eyes. He couldn't even imagine the number of phone calls it would take to undo the work he had arranged to be done at the homestead.

"I do," Callie said, the words ringing in Liam's ears. He grinned, the relief inside him strong.

"And do you, Liam Walker, take Callie Foster to be your lawfully wedded wife?"

"I do," he said.

"By the power vested in me by the *mighty* state of Texas—" Another chuckle from behind Liam, and he was pretty sure that was Wyatt—"I now pronounce you husband and wife. You can kiss 'er now, Liam."

That last bit was a bit untraditional, but Liam supposed everything they were doing didn't really fit in a mold, from the snickering to the bickering at the altar.

He looked at Callie, and everyone else just fell away. "I love you," he murmured, the feeling burning through him so strongly he couldn't deny it. He pressed his lips to hers before she could say anything, but he caught the flash of surprise in her eyes.

Everyone cheered, and wow, he knew his brothers were loud, but this was bring-the-sky-down loud. Callie laughed, breaking the kiss, and Liam took her by the hand and faced everyone.

Finally.

It was done.

He grinned and hugged his brothers, as well as everyone in her family.

"All right," Jeremiah said a few minutes later, clapping his hands together. "Lunch will be served in exactly ten minutes next door. Everyone has a place card, so if you'll kindly make your way over to Seven Sons, we can get these two out the door on time for their flight."

Liam gave Jeremiah a grateful smile, and he stood back while everyone chatted and laughed and started to go down the steps to the yard. The noise went with them, but Callie stayed.

"Sorry about Skyler," he said. "Is your middle name even Hart?"

Callie burst out laughing, a snort coming out as she shook her head no. Liam laughed too, and he slung his arm around her waist. "And you just went with it." No wonder he loved her.

"Well, I knew your middle name wasn't Ronald, and

you didn't say anything." She gazed up at him, and Liam just had to tell her again.

"What I said is true," he said. "I'm in love with you."

Callie's fear blipped across her face for a single heartbeat. There. Disappeared. "I know you are," she said. "Thank you, Liam. For everything." She tipped up and kissed him, and Liam distinctly noted that she hadn't said she loved him too. But he didn't need her to right now. What he had at the moment was enough.

"We better go," she murmured against his lips. "Jeremiah will be livid if we're late to our own luncheon."

"He can wait." Liam wrapped his arms fully around his wife and kissed her again. She may not have articulated to him in words how she felt about him, but Liam could feel her passion and desire for him in her touch. In the way she slid her fingernails up the back of his neck. In the way she clung to him like she needed him to stand.

And he was willing to be her support, her anchor, her bank account, until she fell for him all the way.

———

Hours later, Liam kept a tight hold on Callie's hand as they navigated the Amarillo airport together. The luncheon had been beautiful, and both Liam and Callie had hugged Jeremiah and thanked him profusely. He had enough stew to feed the new cowboys at the Shining Star for a few days, and Liam had put Callie in his truck and then said he'd forgotten something.

Back inside, he'd handed Jeremiah the folder with all the notes. The names. The phone numbers. The dates and timelines for installers and appliance deliveries and yard care.

"Go," Jeremiah had said. "I can handle this."

So Liam had gone. They arrived at their gate without incident, and Liam groaned as he sat down. "I ate way too much stew."

She smiled at him and took his hand in hers. "I'm scared."

He loved that she would tell him things like that, and he lifted her hand to his lips. "Me too."

"You? What are you scared of?"

He shrugged, because he didn't want to admit he was scared she could never love him. "I don't know. That you'll hate flying. Hate this honeymoon. Hate the beach."

"I'm going to *love* the beach," she said. "I've always wanted to go."

"Why haven't you then?" As soon as he asked, he wished he hadn't. "Never mind. I know why you never went."

Callie gave him a soft look, those gorgeous eyes broadcasting her forgiveness of his stupid question. The Texas Panhandle wasn't exactly close to any white, sandy beaches. Not like the ones they'd be able to lie on in Hawaii, at least.

"If you did have the money," he said. "And all the time in the world. Where would you go?"

"Hawaii," she said.

"Really? That's your first choice?"

"Well, I've always wanted to see the sheep farms in the highlands of Scotland too," she said, her face taking on longing expression. "They have castles there too. I love sheep and castles."

Liam chuckled and tucked her into his side. "Sheep and castles. That actually sounds better than Hawaii."

"Oh, no, you go to Scotland in the summer," she said. "Not January. It'll be freezing there right now."

"Where should we go next Christmas?" he asked.

"I don't want to travel at Christmastime," she said. "I love being home, on the ranch, with all the traditions you guys have at Seven Sons."

"Yeah." Liam sighed. "I like those too." Just the fact that she hadn't said they wouldn't be together next Christmas made him happy, and he leaned his head back and closed his eyes. He couldn't believe that this morning he was single, and now he was married.

Pure happiness filled him, and he felt content for maybe the first time in his life. Liam had always been wanting for something. The education. The next big job. The huge contract that said he was the best in the country at what he did. The woman.

And right now, he had it all.

"That's us," Callie said, standing up. "I think they just called us."

"Did they?" Liam glanced around, and sure enough, their flight had started to board. "Yep." He reached for her bag and gestured for her to go in front of him. She walked with purpose, never missing a step. Anyone looking at her would never know she'd never been on an airplane before.

She found their seats and gazed at them. "This is amazing," she said while Liam put her bag in the overhead bin.

She had a childlike look of joy on her face, and he asked, "Do you want the window or the aisle?" already knowing which she'd pick.

"Window." She slid into the seat, and Liam sat beside her. He knew the novelty would wear off, but he sure did like it when she squealed and gripped his hand as they took off, and the nervous vibe that hit him when they landed in Los Angeles.

"One more flight," he said. "And then we can hit the beach."

"Are we really going to do that?" she asked. "I'm exhausted."

"Me too," he admitted. "So maybe we save the beach for tomorrow."

They boarded. Took off. Flew across the ocean, which was new for Liam too. Landed on the island of Oahu. Everything was a shade brighter than in Texas. The blues were bluer, the greens greener, the white sand almost blinding.

He collected all of their baggage, got their rental car, and loaded everything up. By the time they arrived at the luxury resort he'd booked on the North Shore, the sun was starting to go down on the island. Which meant in Texas, it was way past his bedtime.

His heart started pounding after he checked in. They only had one room. *Remember the rules,* he told himself. *Remember the rules.*

He was not going to pressure Callie. He'd made sure this room had two beds so he could have his own. He was too tall and too broad for a sofa bed, but he'd called—twice—to make sure the room had two beds.

Callie had fallen silent, and Liam wondered if she was reminding herself of the rules too. Maybe she was just tired. She was still beautiful and vibrant as they got off the elevator on the highest floor in the resort.

"Oh, Liam," she said. "Look at that." She gazed out the window at the glorious sunset, the sky an array of gold, orange, yellow, red, and pink.

"It's gorgeous," he said, taking a moment to experience God's hand on Earth. Gratitude moved through him that he'd been brought to this point safely. "Come on, sweetheart," he said. "We'll have this same view in our room."

"How do you know?"

"Because I paid for an ocean-view room." He nodded her down the hall, and she keyed them into the room. Sure enough, the sunset shone right into the room too, and Callie dropped everything she was carrying to go stand at the glass.

"I just love it," she said.

Liam dropped everything in his hands too and let the door slam closed behind him. Because there was only one bed.

"This isn't right," he said, causing Callie to turn from the window.

"What's not?"

"Our room," he said. "It should have two beds."

Callie looked around as if she was just seeing the rest of the room now. Everything inside Liam ached. How was he supposed to explain to the front desk clerk that he needed a room with two beds for him and his wife?

"I'll call them." He swiped off his cowboy hat and set it on the TV cabinet. He started for the phone on the side of the bed closest to the window, but Callie stepped in front of him.

"It's fine, Liam."

He paused, even the most glorious sunset in the world unable to distract him. "It's fine?"

She looked up at him, those eyes so wide and so full of fear. She slid her arms around his waist and pressed into him. "I'm in love with you too."

Liam couldn't believe what she'd just said. His brain felt like it was smoking it was moving so fast. He wanted to ask her to repeat it. He wanted her to lay out her evidence.

Liam

A dozen different thoughts screamed through his mind, the loudest one saying, *Kiss her, you idiot! Kiss her now!*

So he did that. She kissed him back too, and Liam had never felt anything as wonderful as being loved by a good woman. "I love you," he whispered, running his hands through her hair.

"I love you, too."

And suddenly, Liam didn't need a room with two beds. This one would do just fine.

18

J eremiah woke before the sun on Monday morning, his back already aching. But he could deal with the pain, because he was going to see Whitney today. Not until the late afternoon, but still.

Today.

He whistled his way through breakfast, ignoring Wyatt's questions about why he was in such a good mood when they literally had to work themselves to the bone for the next fifteen days.

He arrived at the Shining Star at seven-fifteen for a seven-thirty roll-call meeting. Several cowboys were already there, and Jeremiah started introducing himself around. Liam had given them a tour of the ranch, and he'd made a preliminary assignment sheet as well. Not surprisingly, the Walker brothers were the last cowboys to arrive, and Jeremiah held up his hand to begin.

"Okay, ladies and gents," he said. "We have a ton to do over the course of the next two weeks. The three-day bathroom guys will be here at ten to start on one of the bathrooms, and we need the floors out by then. So." He glanced down at his sheet. "I'm putting eight of you on the homestead today. It's demo day, and we're literally taking out everything. All the furniture, except the beds. The kitchen cabinets and counters stay. The walls and windows, obvious, but curtains are coming down. Pictures off the walls. Everything. Callie's sisters will be here in half an hour to make sure we keep what needs to be kept, and our Dumpster should be here in ten minutes."

He glanced over his shoulder as if the trash receptacle was there now. It wasn't. "Okay, listen for your name." He started reading names, glad when they stepped forward so he could give them further directions.

"Cayden, you and Jarrod start with furniture. Blaine, you and Shawn do the same." He turned to the next person. "Wilson, I want you to start getting everything off the walls. Then I want you on the floor removal crew. Mike, Tanner, and Trey, you're all on floor demo. I think the front office is already empty. I'd start there while the others get the furniture out of the rest of the rooms. The upstairs bedrooms haven't been touched in years, so you could also get the furniture down from up there and then start pulling up the old carpet."

"You got it, boss," Trey said, and the eight of them moved off.

Jeremiah turned to his cowboys and his brothers. "Liam hired a lawn care service for the front and back yards. They're going to come in and weed, mow, fertilize, and landscape. But we need cabin demo and then people to start going through barns, stables, coops, all of it. They need to be cleaned out and cleaned up. Outside, inside."

Jeremiah wanted to cry. He knew what it was like to show up on a ranch that hadn't been properly cared for, and Seven Sons hadn't been bad at all. Some broken-down equipment that had been left behind, and a general feel of disuse around the place.

"We'll take the cabins," Orion said. "And when we finish there, we'll come help on the ranch."

"I guess that leaves ranch clean-up to us," Rhett said. "Come on, boys. We know how to do this."

"Anyone else, go with Rhett." Jeremiah nodded to his older brother, who was striding toward the corner of the house. "He'll put you to work."

With everyone on their assignments, Jeremiah waited out front until the Dumpster crew arrived. Liam had ordered two, and Jeremiah signed the paperwork. "We're going to need you to come get these tonight and bring them back tomorrow." He looked a the guy. "Can you do that?"

"Yep," he said. "There's a hundred-dollar dump fee per unit. And a twenty-five dollar transportation fee."

"No problem," Jeremiah said. "It's demo day."

The man chuckled and looked toward the house. "Good luck."

"Thanks." Jeremiah was going to need it. As the Dumpster delivery man rumbled away, Evelyn pulled up with Simone.

"Ladies," Jeremiah said, giving them both a quick hug. "I've got people bringing things out already." He indicated a pile accumulating on the lawn. "Liam said he ordered all new furniture, so I'm assuming we can junk everything."

"Yep," Simone said, glancing around. "Did Liam tell you I was doing one of the cabins myself?"

"Oh, right." Jeremiah spun toward the west fence line. "I sent Orion and my crew out there. I forgot to tell them."

"I'll go," Simone said. "I really want to do it myself."

"It's just demo," Evelyn said. "Let them do it for you. Then you can put it all back together."

"Yeah?"

"Liam has a whole flooring crew coming on Wednesday to do everything," Jeremiah said. "It'll take them a few days, but yeah. Let my guys tear everything out and put new stuff in. Then you can decorate it how you want."

"I'll just go help them," Simone said. "How about that?"

"Sure," Jeremiah said.

"And I'll stay here and make sure they don't throw out something that Callie will freak out about."

"They're just bringing out furniture and stuff," Jeremiah said.

"Well, she has boxes in every closet in the place," Evelyn said, one hand resting on her nearly flat stomach. "I'll just make sure."

A couch came out the front door, and Jeremiah directed them to one of the Dumpsters. "All furniture, guys. Evelyn will be going through boxes and pictures and stuff. That goes on the lawn right over here."

He was tired already, and it wasn't even eight o'clock in the morning. But demo day was off to a great start, with enthusiasm high for the massive project in front of them all.

———

"Jeremiah. Jeremiah?"

Jeremiah sat up, realizing that he'd fallen asleep. A groan came out of his mouth as Wyatt called for him again. "Coming," he said peering over the edge of the loft in the stable. He'd snuck away from the chaos and activity next door just to check on his horses. Fine, and to make sure that Seven Sons was fit for a pretty woman to show up with her camera.

"Jeremiah?" Wyatt asked, entering the barn. He looked straight up at Jeremiah as if he expected to find him snoozing in the loft, among hay bales and old horse blankets.

"Sorry," he said. "I'm up. What time is it?"

"Four," Wyatt said. "And Whitney Wilde is here. She has her camera." He looked like he'd run her out of town himself.

"Yeah, I know." Jeremiah swung his leg over the side of the loft and scampered down the ladder. "I invited her to come shoot a picture for Liam to hang in his new house."

"Wow." Wyatt looked as surprised as he sounded. "That's an awesome idea."

"Thanks," Jeremiah said. "She's at the house?"

"Yeah, I left her on the front porch when I called you and you wouldn't answer."

Foolishness rushed through him, because he should've set an alarm so he didn't have to be tracked down by his brother.

Thankfully, Wyatt didn't seem to have any questions about Jeremiah and Whitney's relationship. Jeremiah did, though.

"I'm meeting with Martin Payne tomorrow morning, remember?" Wyatt asked as they walked back to the homestead.

"Yep," Jeremiah said though he had forgotten. "Sign us on for a year, Wyatt. I like what they've been doing." He glanced at Wyatt, who just nodded.

"I think we get a discount if we sign a year-long contract," he said.

"Great," Jeremiah said, wondering if Liam had thought about pest control for the Shining Star. He didn't want to text his brother on the first day of his honeymoon. "Ask them if Shining Star has a contract with them," he said. "And if they don't, sign them up for a year too, with their fertilization and field-prep formulas."

"Yeah?"

"Yeah," Jeremiah said. "The photo can be my gift to Liam for the wedding, and the crop-dusting can be for Callie." Callie had been the first woman Jeremiah had started to trust again after everything with Laura Ann. He loved her like a sister, and he wanted everything at the Shining Star to work out for her too. Probably not as much as Liam—*obviously not as much as Liam*, he thought—but he could provide pest control for the next year.

"You're good with the gifts," Wyatt said. "You always have been."

"Have I?"

"Always," Wyatt said. "Remember when I joined the pro rodeo circuit?"

"Yeah, of course." Jeremiah passed the barn with the huge Texas flag he and his brothers had painted the first month they'd arrived in Three Rivers.

"You bought me a kit with sore muscle gel, painkillers, and a rice bag." Wyatt chuckled. "I don't know where you got the idea—probably the Internet or something—and at first, I was like, what is this? But that was the very best gift I'd ever gotten. I still buy and use that arnica gel for my back." He clapped Jeremiah on the shoulder. "I didn't even get Liam or Callie a present."

"Sure you did," Jeremiah said, his heart starting to pound and not from the brisk walk in from the stables. "You're working for free on their ranch for the next fifteen days." He grinned at his brother. "How are things going over there?"

"Good," Wyatt said. "With a lot of hands, the work goes fast. The Dumpsters are full, and the yard is too. Half of it is stuff we'll reload into the house, and the other half is trash."

"So more Dumpsters."

"We could probably use two more," Wyatt agreed. "And fill them tomorrow and then go back to just two."

"Okay," Jeremiah said. "The folder with the company info is on Liam's desk. Will you go call them while I deal with Whitney?" He made "dealing with her" sound difficult, and Wyatt chuckled again.

"Sure thing." Wyatt detoured up the steps to the back deck while Jeremiah continued around the corner of the house to the front porch.

Whitney was not sitting there, as Wyatt had said she would be. Instead, Jeremiah found her down the front driveway, crouched down with her camera up at her eye as she took pictures of the stars on the open front gate.

Jeremiah moved under the huge oak tree in the front yard to watch her. He leaned against the giant tree trunk and swallowed. Her dark hair fell in absolutely straight lines over her shoulders, and the last time he'd seen her, that had been curled. He could practically smell her perfume from his position fifty yards away, and he had a love-hate relationship with the way his heart was pulsing in the back of his throat.

No doubt about it, this woman had gotten right under his skin.

She straightened as if she'd heard his thoughts and turned back toward him. A smile filled her face, those red, red lips making desire swim through Jeremiah.

He lifted his hand in a wave to her but made no effort to step away from the tree trunk. She came toward him, and he just watched her take one slow step after another.

19

Whitney Wilde couldn't look away from the smirking cowboy leaning against the oak tree like the ancient trunk needed him to hold it up. She needed him to hold her up, what with the way her legs were shaking with every step she took.

He was so dark, and so dreamy, and so delicious—and he didn't even know it. At least he acted like he didn't know it. Whitney could still feel his fingers in hers from the New Year's Eve parade, and her pulse practically jumped through her skin. She'd flirted with him shamelessly—right in front of Dalton too—and he'd rewarded her with an agreement to take her to dinner after this shoot and the hand-holding.

And wow. She hadn't been able to stop thinking about him since.

"Howdy, cowboy," she said when she was only a few

paces away. She paused, because she wasn't sure they were to the point where she could just continue right into his personal space. She wanted to. Oh, she wanted to.

But Jeremiah had all of his walls up, and just because they'd had a few conversations where he hadn't hung up on her didn't mean they were to the point where she could sweep a kiss across his cheek.

"Hey," he said. "You started without me."

"You made it clear I'd get one hour here," she said. "And you were late."

He smiled and ducked his head, toeing the ground with those heavy-soled work boots. She liked them as much as the cowboy boots she'd seen him wear before. "Did you decide where you wanted to go to dinner?" he asked.

"I think you're a beef man," she said. "And there's a new place in the north part of town, where all those posh houses are."

"A new place?"

"I've been," she said. "All grass-raised beef. They have fancy stuff like steak tartar and regular stuff like a ribeye."

Jeremiah grinned at her, the left side of his smile lifting a little higher than the right. Adorable. Whitney would never tell him that, as such a word would probably offend the rough, tough cowboy.

"You think I'd order a ribeye?" he asked.

Feeling flirty and brave, Whitney stepped right up to him and tiptoed her fingers up the front of his shirt, where all the buttons were. "Yep." She popped the P. "You're not fussy enough for a filet mignon, and you'd have to be in the right mood for a T-bone." She cocked her head and shrugged one shoulder in a move she hoped said *fun, flirty, maybe you can kiss me after dinner.* "So it's a ribeye."

"Maybe I'm in the right mood," he said.

Whitney backed up, her intentions for their dinner very clear. "Maybe," she said. "And we do still have an hour of shooting to get through. You might be ready to commit murder by then."

"Oh, boy," he said with a laugh. "Shooting a few land-scapes is that bad?"

"No," she said. "I think it's great fun. But you...you might not think so." She turned and took a few steps away. "Now, come on. You said you'd show me a few things you wanted me to see. You wanted my 'artistic eye' if I remember right."

"I did say that," Jeremiah said, finally pushing off the tree trunk. "Let's start out at the barn."

Whitney had a feeling she'd start and then go wher-ever he said, and she fell into step beside him. "So," she said. "Where were you living before you came to Seven Sons?" They hadn't had much of a chance to really talk and get to know one another at the parade. And before that, he either didn't answer her calls or told her no before he'd said hello.

"Austin," he said. "You? Let me guess: you've lived here forever?"

"Something like that," she said, hardly able to take in the beauty of the ranch. The landscape would be something spectacular in the spring, after the rains came and made everything grow again.

"Your family has a farm, right?" he asked.

Surely he knew that already, but Whitney said, "Yep," anyway.

"Do you work there?" he asked. "Or just do the photography?"

Whitney thought of her other half. Lake Winters. What would Jeremiah do with the knowledge that she liked posing newborns with pumpkins, turnips, and cornucopias?

Only during Thanksgiving, she told herself. The baby photography she was doing now usually included more rustic winter vegetables, with plenty of greens, beets, and gourds. In fact, she'd just switched out the photo at the front of Wilde & Organic and counted her business cards. Three had been taken in December, but she hadn't booked any new baby shoots.

Since she wasn't married or in the young, married couple scene, she didn't know how else to find customers. She had the display board at the store and word of mouth.

"Whitney?" Jeremiah said, and she blinked her way out of Lake's mind and focused on the handsome man at her side.

"Sorry," she said. "I do the photography full-time, but I

stock the produce section at the store in the morning. No farm work."

Jeremiah nodded and pointed up ahead. "There's the barn."

Sure enough, a huge, beautiful barn stood in front of them. It looked like it might fall down at any moment, but also appeared to be made of the finest wood Texas had to offer. "Wow," she said, drinking in the American flag. "Patriotic."

"We've got Texas on the other side," he said. "But this view, if you stand over here." He started to his left, crossing through the corner of the backyard, which seemed trimmed and perfect, despite it being January. "The view of the land beyond is all Seven Sons Ranch."

"And over there?" She indicated the land to the west.

"That's the Shining Star," he said. "See that fence there? That's where Callie's ranch starts."

She heard something fond in Jeremiah's voice when he spoke of Callie. "Callie?"

"Callie Foster?" he asked, looking toward her ranch. "I mean, she married my brother yesterday. I guess she's Callie Walker now."

Whitney couldn't actually tell how Jeremiah felt about that, so she said nothing. The best thing about being a photographer was the fact that she could hide behind the lens during moments where she needed a bit more time to gather her thoughts.

"The barn is beautiful," she said, adjusting her focus

to get the barn in the foreground and the background. *Click, click, click.* "Let's see that Texas flag." She flashed him a smile, glad to find Jeremiah watching her.

Around the other side of the barn, the huge Texas flag filled her vision, and she couldn't help laughing. "Well, you Walkers are Texas cowboys to the bone," she said, still giggling between the words.

"I'm going to take that as a compliment."

As Whitney had always pictured herself with a through-and-through Texas cowboy, her comment was definitely a compliment. She positioned her camera, not finding a shot here. "I don't like the close-up," she said. "You're right; the view beyond isn't the same from this side." She twisted to look behind her. "Could we go farther out, and get the barn in the background?"

"Sure," he said. "Whatever you think will work." He led her down perfectly manicured paths, past a pen of goats. Whitney stopped to take some close-up shots of the animals, pure joy moving through her.

"I love goats," she said. "We have some of those on the farm."

"Oh?"

"Yeah," she said. "My brother works with the animals on our farm, and we do some local sourcing of goat and lamb."

"I love your store," he said.

"It's my parents' store," she said. "But I love it too. You're a real chef, aren't you?"

"Oh, I don't know about that."

But Whitney did. She knew Jeremiah cooked for his brothers here at the ranch, if only because she'd overheard her sister and her mother talking about how much he shopped at the store. Usually the person who shopped did the cooking.

"We often have vegetables we can't sell," she said. "I could bring them to you."

"What kind of vegetables?"

"Everything," she said. "My brother Johnny is the chef in the Wilde family. He'll take things that are a bit soft or look a bit neglected and turn them into something great." She looked at Jeremiah out of the corner of her eye. "I bet you could do the same."

"What kind of something great?" he asked, not denying his skills in the kitchen this time.

"He made a vegetable ratatouille last week that was amazing."

"Ratatouille," Jeremiah said. "Wow. I'm a bit more... rustic in my cooking style."

"So, what?" Whitney asked. "Stews? Chicken and vegetable bakes?"

"Both of those, yeah."

"You'll have to make dinner for me sometime," she said, adding a smile to her statement.

Jeremiah didn't confirm or deny making dinner for her. Whitney looked up and paused, the shot before her filling her view. "Hold for a moment." She lifted her camera and took a few shots to test the light looking into the west. The sun was on its way down, spreading its rays wide across the sky in front of her. And with the path, the fields, the fences, it felt like the only way a ranch should look.

Jeremiah stopped walking, and Whitney crouched down, getting the pretty dirt path in complete focus close up, with the horizon line beyond. She switched her focus so the path was blurry close up, with the near sunset in sharp focus.

"Okay." She straightened and continued for a few more paces before turning back. "Oh, wow."

The light cascading over the land now, the barn in the distance, was absolutely the vision she'd hoped to find at this ranch. She took a dozen pictures and looked at Jeremiah. "Where else?"

He indicated she should go down the path to her immediate left. "I think the best view of the ranch is just past the cattle yard." He looked over at her. "It's a bit of a walk."

"I wore my cowgirl boots," she said, lifting one up as if he hadn't seen them yet. But she had a feeling Jeremiah Walker didn't miss a single thing.

He smiled at her, their steps in tandem. His hand brushed hers, and the next thing she knew, he'd taken her hand in his. "Okay?" he asked, not looking at her.

"Okay," she managed to push through a very narrow throat. Holding hands with this man was much more than okay. Sparks raced up and down her arm, making her feel like she'd never been touched by a man before. And maybe she hadn't, now that Jeremiah had touched her. No matter what, his touch had sparked something inside her she'd thought long dead.

"Besides photography, what do you like to do?" he asked.

"I'm an outdoor person," she said. "I spend a lot of time in front of my computer editing, so when I don't have to do that, I like to get out and enjoy Texas."

"Hiking? Biking? Sitting by a lake?"

"All of the above," she said. "What about you?"

"Oh, the ranch and the kitchen consume me," he said, no shame in his voice. "Though I suppose I let them."

Wow, honesty. Whitney sure did like that. She caught sight of a horse, and she slipped her hand away from Jeremiah's to hold her camera to get a shot.

"That's actually Liam's horse," Jeremiah said. "Pretzel. Let's move him over to the other pasture, and maybe you could get him in the view I'm thinking of."

Before she could respond, he nickered as if he spoke Horse, and Pretzel came plodding over to him, his head halfway down as if to let Jeremiah know he'd go wherever the cowboy wanted him to. Whitney couldn't blame him.

Jeremiah reached over the top of the fence and stroked the horse. "Come on," he said, patting the side of Pretzel's neck. "Down to the gate."

"Are you the horse whisperer?" she asked. "He's just going to come?"

Jeremiah gave her a look she could only classify as flirty as he reached into his pocket. "He'll come." He pulled a piece of hard candy from his pocket, started walking, and sure enough, Pretzel turned and walked along the fence as well.

"Ah, I see," she said. "I used to do that with my nieces and nephews."

"Is that why Dalton would only sit by you at the parade?"

Whitney took a deep breath. "Ah, Dalton." She didn't want to say anything bad about her nephew. "He's going through a hard time right now."

"We all do," Jeremiah said. "From time to time."

Honest and wise. And he knew how to charm a horse into doing whatever he wanted. Whitney was starting to wonder if the man had any faults at all.

They reached the gate, and Jeremiah unlatched it, pulling a rope from around the post there. He looped it around Pretzel's neck and allowed the horse to leave the pasture. "It's just a little bit farther."

Walking again, the horse clopping along behind Jeremiah, he didn't take her hand again. She didn't know what else to say to him, and he wasn't asking another question either. She didn't wholly hate the silence, but it didn't comfort her either.

"There," he said after several minutes. He indicated

the fields to their right. "This is the cattle yard. Our large horse pasture is here, and I think with the trees in the distance, and the sun, and the animals...." Jeremiah exhaled, and it was clear he loved this spot.

"Horses or dogs?" she asked.

"What?"

"Which do you like better?"

"Is that not obvious? Horses." He kicked a grin in her direction and moved over to the gate. "Go on now," he said to Pretzel, pulling another candy from his pocket. He removed the rope and hung it on the post there, and Whitney started clicking before the cowboy could step out of the shot.

"Stay, stay, stay," she said when he turned at the sound of the clicking.

"Whitney," he said. "I don't want to be in the picture."

"But it's perfect," she said, not giving in on this. "Turn back around and look out into the pasture again." She didn't actually care what he looked at.

He sighed like she was insufferable, but he did what she said. He ducked his head, and Whitney's pulse went wild. That was the perfect shot—at least for her.

"All right," she said. "Come on out of the frame."

Jeremiah gave her a look that could've been categorized as a glare, and she just shook her head at him. "You invited me out here."

"I'm starting to regret it."

And there was his flaw—that mouth. He was so blunt,

which Whitney usually liked. She'd rather know than have to guess how a person was feeling. Guessing had never really worked out for her.

She chose not to respond as she started shooting the view he loved so much. She could see what he liked about it, from the distance from the homestead to the serenity of the horses dotting the horizon.

Pretzel wandered away once he realized Jeremiah wasn't going to give him any more candy, and Whitney moved up and down the fence, getting different shots. Her phone rang, and her heart skipped the way she imagined Pretzel's did when he heard that crinkly candy wrapper.

It was her Lake Winters ringtone, and she didn't want to ignore the call. But she didn't want to answer it in front of Jeremiah. She decided the lesser of two bad options was to let the call go to voicemail. She'd have some time in the car as she drove to town for dinner to check it and return a phone call.

Satisfied she had something Jeremiah would like for his brother, she turned back to him. "I think we're done here."

"Yeah?"

"Yeah."

"You don't want to get a shot of the silos? The windmill?"

"I don't think that's the shot you want to put on your brother's wall," she said. "But if you're asking if I want to come out here and shoot my next wedding, the answer is yes, absolutely."

Jeremiah grinned as he shook his head.

"Just think about it, would you?" she asked, not caring that a bit of a whine had entered her tone. "You could charge people a *ton* of money, and they'd pay it."

"I don't really care about the money," he said.

Of course he didn't. She'd heard the Walkers were independently wealthy, and his nonchalance about money proved it.

"Then *I'll* charge people a lot of money, and they'd pay it," she said, adding a laugh at the end so he'd know she wouldn't really do that. She peered at him, and he seemed absolutely closed off again. The man who'd held her hand and asked her what she liked to do in her spare time was not the same, tense cowboy standing in front of her at the moment.

Hoping she wasn't about to blow everything between them—especially the possibility of more hand-holding—Whitney stepped over to him and laced her arm through his. "Tell me what specifically you're worried about if I shoot out here."

"I dunno," he said automatically, not softening the slightest bit at her touch. Maybe Whitney had been imagining the fireworks between them. She sincerely hoped not, but he was difficult to read with all the walls up so high.

"Yes, you do," she said gently, the stroll they'd fallen into nice and easy.

Jeremiah took his sweet time answering, but he finally said, "I'm worried about you disrupting my peace," he said.

"We can schedule around that," Whitney said.

Jeremiah shook his head and chuckled. "You're never going to give up on this, are you?"

"Probably not," she said. "Maybe we could do a trial or something."

"Let's talk about it over dinner," he said. "Have you decided where you want to go? Are we doing that new steak place?"

"Yes," she said. "And I'll get my arguments for a trial shooting period ready on the way in. You want to follow me?"

"Sure," he said, and they fell into silence again. This time, Whitney rather liked it, her cells singing with the warmth of Jeremiah's body next to her. He had a very calm presence, despite the walls.

She sure hoped she could convince him to let her shoot out here—or at least ask her out again. She felt stupid praying for such a thing, but she'd been taught the Lord heard prayers of the heart, so it probably didn't matter.

What will be will be, she thought. *But another date would be nice.*

20

Wyatt Walker groaned as he got to his feet. "That's the last of it," he said to Orion. "You guys okay to haul this all out? I have to get over and sign the crop-dusting contract."

"You got it," Orion said, and Wyatt left him and Dicky to clean out the ripped up flooring in the cowboy cabin where they'd been working for a couple of hours.

Wyatt's back ached, and he was once again reminded why he'd left the rodeo circuit. He literally wouldn't have physically survived another season, but he masked the limp until he made it to the front porch. The wood here needed to be replaced in spots, but Wyatt wasn't going to be the one who did it. Thankfully.

He didn't have the heart to tell Liam he couldn't help at the Shining Star. The truth was, he could. He'd just need to ice his shoulder and take a fistful of pills every few hours. He'd also put an icy patch on his back last night before going to bed, though he wasn't technically supposed to wear them for that long.

His skin had been a bit blistered that morning, but his back had been pain-free. Now, though, after only a couple of hours of work, he felt like he'd been trampled all over again. His hip hurt, and his knee hurt, and he felt like a complete invalid as he made his way to his truck.

It was hard work pretending like he didn't live with constant pain. Hard work acting like he could walk normally, that some of the ranch chores Jeremiah had given him didn't make his fingers clench.

He'd been working out at Bowman's Breeds a lot more, which was easier work, though taming a stubborn horse wasn't always a picnic. His hands did hurt at the end of every shift, because after years of tying himself to a bucking horse or a mad bull could do that to a man.

He climbed into his truck, a long sigh coming from his mouth. Wyatt carried painkillers with him everywhere he went, and he reached over to the glove box and pulled out the bottle of pills. He swallowed them dry, because he was already late leaving to get over to Payne's Pest-free and sign their next contract.

Wyatt did a lot of driving, and he didn't mind the quick trip into town. He had his favorites around town, including the bakery and the coffee shop next door. But such luxuries would have to wait until after he'd inked the contract.

He drove past his favorite haunts, his stomach growling for more than a doughnut and coffee, and turned west. The nicer parts of town were the new north suburbs, and all the rolling estates on the east side. But Wyatt liked the smaller houses out this way, the more old-town feeling of Three Rivers.

Wyatt was still making himself at home in town, though he'd been here for a year. Out of all the brothers, he probably came to town the most. Sure, Jeremiah did the grocery shopping every week, and Rhett seemed to have a love affair with the pancake house. But Wyatt had a goal to eat his way through every restaurant, diner, coffee shop, and barbecue hut in town. And the surrounding towns.

He drove past the last convenience store on the west side of town, the highway before him leading to Amarillo. He turned off after another mile, using a dirt road that most people probably drove by without even seeing.

Another couple miles down the dusty road sat a huge building that sheltered airplanes. A couple dusters sat outside the building too, and Wyatt pulled next to the only other vehicle in the lot—another truck, this one much older than his.

The pills Wyatt had taken a half an hour ago had kicked in, and his back barely pinched as he got out of the truck. The office at Payne's Pest-free was small, but clean, and Wyatt glanced around as he'd never been here before.

A simple counter stood near the back, with a sign that said, *Ring the bell. We're around somewhere.*

He hit the bell a couple of times and fell back a step. Only one other door led out of the office and into the hangars, but Wyatt didn't want to go wandering around.

No one came, though, and Wyatt rang the bell again, this time stepping over to the door. "Hello?" he called as he entered the hangar. A plane sat there, and a scraping noise came from under the aircraft. "Anyone here?"

He'd gotten a call from Martin. Could he have forgotten?

"Martin?" He rounded the front propeller of the airplane, and a very feminine figure was bent over, examining the inner workings of the aircraft's engine.

Wyatt froze, because he hadn't been expecting that. He wanted to call to this woman again, but his throat had turned into a desert.

In the next moment, she started singing. The lyrics belonged to a popular country music song, and she knew every single one. She had a beautiful voice that filled the hangar as she sang at the top of her lungs.

Wyatt smiled then, because he didn't see a way out of this situation that didn't end in embarrassment for both of them.

He'd had a fair few girlfriends while he rode the circuit, but none of them lasted, and truth be told, Wyatt hadn't wanted any of them to last. It was fun to celebrate with a pretty cowgirl when he won though, and he had missed the feminine touch in his life over the course of the past year.

He liked the Foster sisters though, and Brynn and Ethan Greene had been good to him too. He liked the family atmosphere out at Three Rivers Ranch, and Wyatt had found a place to belong in Three Rivers.

The woman's singing quieted to a hum, and Wyatt got the gumption up to step over to the airplane and knock on it. "Ma'am?"

A startled yelp came from her mouth, and she straightened, her eyes wild as they landed on him. He held up both hands and said, "Sorry. Sorry."

She yanked out her earbuds, and Wyatt realized why she hadn't heard him calling or the bell. "Who are you?" She lifted the wrench in her hand as if she'd hit him with it.

Wyatt couldn't help grinning at her again. She had short, blonde hair that wisped around her face, which bore a bit of grease on her chin. Her bright blue eyes sparked with fear and then fury, and Wyatt backed up again.

"Sorry," he said again, because she could hear him with those earbuds out. "I rang the bell." He hooked his thumb over his shoulder, toward the little office space. "I'm supposed to meet Martin here?" Why he'd phrased it as a question, he wasn't sure.

He was sure that he wanted this woman's number, and that surprised him a little. Number one, she didn't seem like his type at all. She wore cargo pants instead of jeans, and heavy work boots instead of the cute cowgirl boots that usually got his pulse racing.

She visibly relaxed and lowered the wrench. "You must be Wyatt Walker."

"Guilty, ma'am." He tipped his hat at her, sure he'd win her over with his cowboy charm.

She barely reacted, other than to toss her wrench into the toolbox where it landed with an earsplitting clanging noise. "Whoops," she said as Wyatt flinched. She brought her gaze back to his. "I'm Marcy Payne. I have your paperwork over here."

"You do?"

Marcy's expression hardened, and she gave him a curt nod. "Follow me, please."

Oh, he would, and Wyatt wished he didn't let his thoughts rule his actions quite so much. He did follow her over to a workbench, where a pristine manila folder sat.

"You're with Seven Sons, right?"

"That's right, ma'am."

She flicked her gaze at him for a microsecond. "I have you down for a year-long contract, over four thousand acres. We'll do field-prep fertilizing in the winter and we move on to pest control through spring, summer, and fall. We've got you down for twice a month in the winter, and every week in the spring, at six-fifty per month." She glanced at him again, and she could've been telling him he'd need to give her his right kidney, and he would've agreed to it.

"Mm hm," he said.

"You get a five percent discount for signing for the full

year, and I just need your John Hancock right here." She tapped the paper.

"I wanted to ask you," he said. "Do you have a contract with the ranch next to mine?" Seven Sons so wasn't his ranch, but Marcy probably already knew that.

"The Shining Star?" Marcy looked confused. "No. They barely plant anything there."

"Well, they're going to this year," Wyatt said, because he knew Callie Foster had done the best she could. "And I want to pay for a year of their dusting too. Same terms as ours."

Marcy's eyebrows went up, and those electric blue eyes sent pulses through Wyatt's body. "Really?"

"Yes, ma'am." She didn't need to know the idea had been Jeremiah's. "I probably should've called. Then you could've had the paperwork ready."

"I can get it done quick," she said. "Let's go into my office." She collected the folder and headed away from what Wyatt had thought was the office. Down in the front corner sat another office, and Wyatt wasn't sure he'd fit inside.

Marcy ducked inside and sat at a metal desk, where a computer waited. She tapped and said, "Have a seat, Wyatt. It'll just take two shakes."

Wyatt surveyed the office. It was definitely tiny, and the scent of powder and flowers hung in the air. Wyatt entered, because he wanted to see if they could co-exist in such a tiny space.

"Shining Star," she muttered. "What's the number there?"

"I have no idea," Wyatt said.

"Whose name should I put this under."

"I don't know," Wyatt said.

Marcy peered around her computer. "What do you know, honey?"

He smiled at her, glad when she returned the gesture. "Put my brother's name on it. Jeremiah Walker. And I'll Google the number." He tapped and put in Seven Son's address. "We're thirty-four seven-eight-six. They're...."

"Thirty-five one-four-seven," she said. "Do you know how big the ranch is?"

"I do not," he said, grinning at her.

She giggled and wiped her bangs out of her eyes. "I can come talk to Callie."

"Oh, she's out of town."

Marcy leaned around the computer again. "She's what? Callie Foster? She hasn't left town in years."

Wyatt didn't know what to say about that, so he said nothing.

"Where is she?"

"Hawaii," he said.

Marcy scoffed, those eyes glittering at him. "Oh, you're not joking."

"Nope."

"Why—?"

"She married Liam," Wyatt said. "My brother. They're on their honeymoon."

Pure surprise moved across her face. "Oh. Wow. Good for them."

"I'll ask Simone or Evelyn," Wyatt said. "Can I just call you and let you know?"

"Yeah, that would work." She went back to the computer, and a moment later, a printer from somewhere he couldn't see whirred. "Here we go." She produced the paperwork. "I'll just have you sign it."

"Do we get the five percent discount?"

"Yep," she said. "And you'll get a fifty-dollar credit for a referral."

"Perfect," Wyatt said, as if fifty dollars mattered to him. But it didn't. He'd been a billionaire before his father had retired and sold his company. He supposed his bones had paid for his lifestyle in the rodeo.

"Sign here," Marcy said, and he signed both contracts. "Great, I'll fly you guys on the same day. Tuesdays still work for you?"

"Yes, ma'am." He reached up and touched his cowboy hat. "Now, should I just call your business line here after I talk to the Fosters? Or is there a...personal number I can use?" He grinned at her again, encouraged when a slow smile touched her mouth too.

21

Simone Foster climbed the steps of the cabin way down on the end of the row. She drew in a deep breath and opened the door to what would become her new home. Joy danced through her, and she once again knew she'd made the right decision.

True, the cabin was in shambles right now, but Simone's artistic mind started imagining where the new chair she'd found at a yard sale could go, and where her false flower arrangement would look best.

Putting little details in place made her so very happy, even if she had to walk across a bare plywood floor right now. She trailed her fingers down the wall to her left, the living room expanding to her right. In the back corner of this cabin sat a back door, which led out onto a small deck. From there, the ranch spread out into the horizon, and Simone loved standing there and taking in the view.

"I can't believe I get to live here," she said to herself, stepping into the kitchen. She was having the flooring guys put the vinyl throughout the cabin, so there wouldn't be a real line from living room to kitchen, but Simone knew when she entered the kitchen. The cupboards were all still in, as hers had just needed to be cleaned.

And that was what she was doing this morning. Down the hall sat a bathroom, and the water still ran in all the cabins. Across the hall was the hot water heater and a small linen closet, with two bedrooms, one in each of the remaining corner of the house.

Simone loved the small cabin with everything inside her. She wasn't sure she'd live out here alone, but Liam had hired twelve people to work the Shining Star, and all of them were going to live out here. Well, ten of them were. The other two had been assigned a cabin at Seven Sons, and Simone was excited to start meeting new people.

New men, if she were being honest with herself. New cowboys.

She hadn't been in the dating pool in a very long time. Those waters had been so dangerous for her health before, and she didn't have the right swimwear. But Evelyn had dove in, and now Callie, and Simone didn't really want to live alone with her reupholstery business for the rest of her life.

In the bathroom, she filled a bucket with hot water in the tub, adding a pine-tree-scented cleaner. She took it into the kitchen and started wiping everything down. The wood gleamed under the touch of her rag, and she started to sing as she worked. Daddy had always sang while he worked, and Simone's earliest memory of her father was one where she toddled after him as he went out onto the ranch to feed the cattle.

Of course, they didn't have many cattle anymore, and sadness slipped through Simone, making her change the song coursing from her mouth. It was okay; she liked more forlorn tales of love and faith too, and she knew a lot of hymns from her time in the church choir.

With the cabinets along the back wall shining and spotless, she turned her attention to the small island. By the time she finished that, her fingers ached, and the water was nearly black. She stood and stretched her back, finishing the hymn she'd been singing.

She needed to clean the bathroom today too, as well as scrub all the windowsills and windows. Then the cabin would be ready for new flooring, and once that was in, all Simone needed was furniture before she could move in. She could take dishes and utensils from the homestead, as Liam had ordered new pots and pans, new plates, bowls, cups, and china. New everything.

Simone sure did like Liam, and she hoped Callie wouldn't fillet him alive when they got back from Hawaii. If he was smart, he'd warn her before just bringing her back to a completely different ranch than the one she'd left. Simone loved Callie, but her sister had a hard time adjusting to changes, and Liam had made dozens of them.

She bent and picked up the bucket, a groan coming from her mouth.

"Was that you singing?" a man asked, and Simone cried out and dropped the bucket. It hit her foot, sending pain exploding through her bones and up her leg, and then tipped. Tears sprang to her eyes, and she spun toward the voice.

Micah Walker stood there, wearing that sexy cowboy hat and a look on his face she couldn't read before he sprang into motion. "I'm sorry," he said, his voice a deep baritone she wanted to hear sing. "I didn't mean to startle you." He righted the bucket with one hand while the other slid around her waist, holding her steady as she tried to balance on one foot.

Foolishness raced through her, and she swiped at the tear that had managed to escape. "It's fine."

"It sounded like an angel was out here," he said, that smile making her stomach vibrate in a strange way. A very good, very strange way. "You're a great singer."

"Thank you," she said, testing her weight on her toe. "I think I might have really injured my foot."

"I'd help you to a couch if there was one," he said, looking around the empty, floorless cabin. "So up you go."

Before she could figure out what he was talking about, he picked her up. "Oh," she squealed, the strength in his hands and arms making a flush move through her whole body.

He set her on the island and said, "Let me see." He used those large, strong hands to take off her tennis shoe in the most gentle way. She didn't even know a man with as many muscles as him could do something so soft.

"I don't think there's anything broken," he said, probing at her foot with two fingers. "I'm going to bend your toes, okay?"

"Mm hm," she said, because she wasn't sure she could form words. She'd met Micah at Christmastime, of course. He was gorgeous, just as all the Walker brothers were. But he'd been aloof and almost like he wasn't present for the meal. Simone had sat quite far from him, and she'd learned not to judge someone based on one meeting.

"I think it's just bruised," he said. "Want me to carry you to the homestead for some ice?"

"That actually sounds awful," Simone said, clapping one hand over her mouth the moment the words left her mouth. Her eyes widened and looked right into Micah's dark green ones.

He chuckled, the laughter building in his chest before he let it out. Pretty soon, they were both laughing, and Simone reached for her shoe. "I'm Simone Foster, though you probably know that already."

"I do remember." He tapped his chest. "Micah."

"Right." After pulling it back on, she got down from the counter, feeling too big and out of place next to Micah.

"Can I help you with something?" he asked.

Her eyes flew to his. "You want to help me?"

"Well." He leaned closer, a sparkle in his eyes. Simone's heart flopped around inside her chest, and while she'd thought for a moment that she might meet a cowboy in the row of cabins where she was moving, she didn't think she'd feel something for a Walker brother.

Evelyn and Callie had already done that.

"Jeremiah is in a snit about something, and I'd rather stay out of his line of sight." Micah pulled back, and Simone giggled. Actually giggled.

She cut the sound off when she realized how stupid she sounded and nodded to the bucket. "Well, I have windows to wash and a bathroom to clean. Baseboards, windowsills. Basically, no one's lived in this cabin for a long time, and I'm going to live here, so I need it cleaned up."

"You're going to live here?" He stooped for the bucket and picked it up with one hand when she'd barely been able to do it with two.

"Yeah," she said. "That way, Liam and Callie can have the homestead."

Micah nodded and took the bucket into the bathroom. Embarrassment pulled through her as he poured the dark water down the tub, though she wasn't sure why. It wasn't like she'd been living here, and the house was still filthy.

"All right," he said, rinsing out the bucket and setting it to fill again. "What are we putting in for the windows?"

"Uh." Simone turned and picked up the bottle of window cleaner she'd bought last night. "This said it could be used inside and out."

"Inside and out," he said. "I think I may have made a mistake walking through your door." He grinned at her, and Simone ducked her head. Actually ducked her head. She gathered herself together and handed him a clean rag.

They started in the living room, both of them working on the same window. "So, you don't live at the ranch yet? But you're coming." She remembered him saying something about it during Christmas dinner.

"That's right."

"Where do you live now?"

"Temple," he said. "I have a carpentry shop there I need to close and move."

"Oh, you're moving the shop too?"

"Honestly? I don't know." He could reach up to the top of the windows, and they settled into an easy rhythm of rinsing rags. She worked on the windowsills while he worked up high. "Jeremiah says I could have a building out here at the ranch to do carpentry, but he also said he wants to add more cattle and horses to the ranch, and he needs my help with that."

"Are you an actual cowboy? Or just a handsome man wearing the right hat?"

Micah chuckled, squeezed out his rag and stepped over to the other window. "You think I'm handsome?"

"Well, I mean, for a woman who likes that sort of broad-shouldered look."

"Are you that kind of woman?" he asked.

"Maybe," she said, feeling flirty at the moment. "But if you're a carpenter, then you're probably just wearing the hat."

"I'm decent with horses," he said.

"Decent," she teased. "Do you ride?"

"Honey, I'm Texan. Of course I ride." He flashed her a playful grin, and Simone found him so different than the other Walker boys.

"How old are you?" she asked.

"Thirty-three, ma'am."

"Oh, you *are* Texan," she said, her cells buzzing with more life than she'd experienced in a long time. And he was younger than her, which made her a bit self-conscious.

He didn't ask her how old she was, instead saying, "I heard you shop yard sales and restore old furniture. Is that right?"

"Yes, sir," she said, adding some twang to her voice as well. He returned to the bucket, rinsing his rag and straightening as she bent down. Some water splashed on her arms, and she pulled in a breath.

"That was an accident, I swear," he said, but he was chuckling.

"Oh, you're asking for it," she said, dipping her rag.

"Simone," he warned, plenty of playfulness and flirtation in his voice.

She rinsed out her rag but barely squeezed any water out of it before lifting it up.

"Oh," he said, eyeing the rag and then her. "Don't you dare."

Simone ran through her options quickly. The floor needed to be dry to lay down the new flooring, but everything would go in at the homestead first. She had at least two or three days before they'd show up at her cabin, and that meant she could have a little water fight with the handsome cowboy.

She jerked as a splash of water hit her face. Micah's laughter filled the house, and Simone gaped at him. "You're so dead."

She rushed toward him, slapping her sloppy, wet rag against his chest while he yelped. They laughed together, and Micah's arms came around her, pinning her hands against her chest so she couldn't splash him further.

Enjoying the feel of his arms around her, Simone wiggled to try to get away.

"Truce," Micah said.

"Only because you dropped your rag," Simone said through her giggles.

"Simone?"

She practically leapt away from Micah, panic covering every other emotion in her body. Evelyn stood in the doorway, and Simone felt like she'd been caught kissing a forbidden boyfriend by her father.

"Evvy," she said, dropping her rag in the bucket as she walked away from Micah. She glanced over her shoulder to find him bending to pick up his rag. "What do you need? Are you okay?"

"I'm fine," Evelyn said slowly. "I just wondered where you were, and Tripp said you'd asked Liam for a cabin?" She glanced around, definitely letting her gaze linger on Micah.

"Yeah," Simone said. "I'm going to live out here once Callie and Liam get back. That way, they have a house, and so do I."

"Simone," she said, lowering her voice. "Callie doesn't care if you live there."

"I care," Simone said. "Can we talk about this later?" She didn't want to glance over her shoulder to Micah, because she could still feel his presence.

Evelyn looked past her too. "Oh, sure. I'll let you get back to flirting."

"I was not flirting," Simone hissed, though she totally had been.

"Good to see you, Micah," Evelyn said in a loud voice, throwing Simone a smirk as she turned around.

"Ma'am," he said behind her, and Evelyn grinned.

"He's cute," she whispered. "Good luck with the windows." With that, she opened the door to leave. "Oh, and we need to go through the art and stuff and decide what to put back in the homestead."

"Okay," Simone said. "I'll be over in a little bit." The door closed, sealing her and Micah back in the cabin together. She pressed her eyes closed and drew in a deep breath. Then she turned around and got back to work, the handsome cowboy who'd heard her singing doing the exact same thing.

22

Callie stood on the balcony as the sun set into the ocean. "I can't believe tomorrow is our last day here," she said to Liam.

"Mm." He pressed his lips to her forehead. "More snorkeling?"

"It's what I love most," she said. "And coconut shrimp and another one of those shaved ices."

Liam chuckled. "And I'm going to give surfing another try."

"You almost had it yesterday." She laughed with him, because while Liam was very good at almost everything he did, surfing could not be counted among his talents.

"You're such a liar," Liam said. "Did you want to go to that dessert bar tonight?"

"Have you ever heard me say no to chocolate?"

"No, ma'am."

"Great, then put your cowboy hat back on, and let's go." She tugged on his hand to get him to come in off the balcony. Callie had enjoyed the island immensely, the sleeping in, the time on the beach, the swimming with sharks.

They'd gone sailing and parasailing and deep-sea fishing. Anything either of them wanted to do, they did. Liam's plans for their honeymoon had only included getting to Oahu and having a place to stay.

The activities for each day were wide open, and Callie had suggested anything that sounded remotely fun to her. And she'd enjoyed everything they'd done, even if she wasn't good at it.

"Are you coming?" Callie asked when she realized Liam still stood by the balcony, his focus on his phone.

"Yeah," he said, clearly distracted. He didn't look up, and he didn't come over immediately. Callie slipped on her sandals and picked up her own phone. She'd texted a little bit with Evelyn and Simone, but not much. She knew they didn't want to disturb her on her honeymoon, but she felt removed and left out for a reason she couldn't name.

With nothing to do on her phone, she sat down and waited for Liam to come back to reality. Several minutes passed before he did, saying, "Are you ready?"

"Yep." Callie stood up and headed for the door. Liam texted all the way to the elevator and all the way down to the street. Her irritation with him continued to grow as they stepped onto the busy streets of Waikiki, and he still had his head down.

"Is that work?" she asked.

"No," he said. "Jeremiah."

"Crisis at the ranch?" Callie tried to stuff her annoyance away. She didn't know what was going on at her ranch either, though Evelyn had said everything was fine. She'd worked through the thoughts that Liam had taken care of everything, and she'd tried to enjoy herself.

And she had.

"No," Liam said, finally glancing up. "Just getting caught up."

"Mm." Callie suddenly didn't want to be out. She just wanted to go to bed and look forward to another day of sun, sand, and snorkeling.

Down the block, the line for the dessert bar was out the door, and Callie stopped. "It's too busy," she said. "Let's just go back upstairs."

Liam didn't answer, and she turned to find that he hadn't come with her. She could see him standing down the sidewalk a little ways, his head bent over his phone again. Callie had half a mind to leave him there, the cowboy island in the stream of tourists.

She stepped out of the way, because people didn't flow around her the same way they did him. She'd get trampled while he got respected. Liam finally looked up, and she could see the confusion on his face. What? Did he think she'd just pause in the middle of the sidewalk and wait for him to finish his conversation with his brother?

In the end, she couldn't just leave him standing there, especially when he turned around as if he'd go back to the hotel alone. He hadn't taken a step in any direction when Callie lifted her hand to get his attention.

It took several seconds for him to see her, and then he came toward her. "Sorry," he said.

"I say we just go back," she said. "I'm not in the mood for dessert anymore."

"Not in the mood?"

"The line is out the door," She said. "And you're not present."

"I'm present."

"It's fine," she said, because she didn't want to fight with him. They'd done plenty of that in the past, and Callie wanted to enjoy her last day in paradise.

"I just have a lot going on at home," he said.

"It's fine," she said again. "I'm tired."

"Sweetheart," he said, taking her hand in his. "I'm sorry."

"Maybe we can order room service."

"I need to tell you something," he said, steering her off the sidewalk and down another path. This one had less people on it, but plenty of noise from the music coming off the beach and the busyness of a nearby restaurant.

"What is it?" Callie asked, but Liam didn't say anything. He led her to an outdoor bar, which didn't seem like a great place to have a conversation. "I can't even hear myself think," she said. "I don't want to be here."

Everyone around her was at least a decade younger than her, and she felt like everyone was staring at her. Or maybe they were staring at Liam, what with that cowboy hat and all.

"Two shaved ices," he said to the bartender anyway, and Callie looked away.

A few minutes later they got their drinks, and Liam did lead her out onto the sand then, away from the crowd and the noise. He sat down, a groan coming out of his mouth. "I think you're going to be mad."

Callie just scooped up another bite of shaved ice. "Just say it then. Blurt it out."

"I've been texting with Jeremiah a lot, because they're moving my computer stuff to your place. *Our* new place."

Callie's mind whirred through what he'd said. "That's good, though, right?" She looked at him, still trying to figure out what about what he'd said was catching in her mind.

"Yes," he said slowly. "But I have a lot of delicate equipment."

Our new place.

She nodded, finally realizing what he'd said and why it was a bit strange. "Our *new* place? We're just living on the ranch, right?"

"Yes," he said. "And Simone wanted to tell you herself, but with everything else, she'd been texting me too, and she's asked me to tell you." He took a bite of his shaved ice, but he was still distracted.

"Tell me what?"

"She's moving into one of the cabins," he said.

Callie opened her mouth to respond, but the air left her lungs. Simone was leaving the homestead?

"And that's only the beginning of the changes you'll find at the Shining Star when we get back."

Callie blinked at him, trying to wrap her head around having the house on the ranch to herself. Her and Liam. Alone.

Of course, they'd been alone for the past two weeks, and their time together had been wonderful. She'd been nervous about being in such close quarters with him, and now she wondered what it would be like to wake up alone again. She liked the warmth of his body next to hers, and she liked the way he held her close until they both fell asleep.

"What else am I going to find?" she asked, finally catching up to the situation. Simone had moved out so she wouldn't have to be across the hall from Callie and Liam. Simone had done that to give Callie her privacy, and Callie couldn't be too upset about it. She did like her private time with Liam.

"I, uh...." Instead of speaking, he just watched the waves continue to come ashore.

Callie wanted to tell him to spit it out, but she'd had plenty of things stuffed inside her mouth that she couldn't get out. Heck, she'd almost lost her ranch because she couldn't tell anyone about her problems.

"I've had everyone I know working around the ranch and the house," he said. "Everything is cleaned up and cleaned out, and all three thousand acres are ready for planting or cattle or whatever you want to do."

Whatever she wanted to do. She didn't know what she wanted to do.

"You cleaned up the ranch," she said.

"We gutted the house too. New carpet, new flooring, new furniture. All the cabins have been spruced up, and people are moving in there tomorrow. The barns are cleaned out. The stables were in great condition. The landscaping has been redone. You're hardly going to recognize the place, and Evelyn thought you might freak out if I didn't tell you."

"She's not wrong," Callie said. "Do you have pictures?"

"No."

She held out her hand. "Let me see your phone."

He didn't argue as he passed it over. She scrolled through the texts, and he'd been texting more than Jeremiah and Simone. But no one had sent him any pictures. Something boiled in Callie's gut, but she couldn't identify it.

"I want to remind you about our rules," he said gently, taking his phone back. "You were going to keep an open mind about what I choose to spend my money on."

"I don't need new couches," she bit out.

"No, but *we* needed new couches," he said.

Callie stared out at the ocean, her shaved ice forgotten. Twilight had fallen, and it would be full dark soon. She suddenly just wanted to get on the first flight back to Texas, see her ranch and find out what he'd disturbed.

"I have things—*precious* things—" she said. She shook her head. "My mother lived on that ranch. Certain aspects of it are important to me."

"I know that," Liam said. "We didn't change any of that."

Callie opened her mouth to retort, but she couldn't.

"Evelyn and Simone went through everything," he added. "They didn't throw away anything they thought you'd want or that they knew was important to you."

"I'm not even going to recognize my own home."

"Maybe not," he said. "Because it's *our* home now."

Callie wanted to ask him what would happen if they broke up. But the thought was ridiculous. His proposal might have started out as a way for her to keep her ranch, but they'd confessed their love for each other. They'd been sleeping together every night. She did love Liam, and she didn't want to lose him.

You want to share your life with him, she thought, some of her fury fading. Liam put his arm around her, and she leaned into him. She did love him, but she didn't like how he got to do what he wanted and then tell her to have an open mind.

"We fenced the family graveyard," he said. "It's all cleaned up and hasn't been disturbed."

Callie looked at him, trying to decide how she felt. "My mother is buried at the church. She said she'd barely lived on the ranch, and it was Daddy's family land." Quaking moved through her chest. She hadn't been out to her grandparents' graves in a long time. She probably wouldn't have even been able to find them among the overgrowth.

"Are you mad?" he asked.

"Yes," she said simply, though some of her anger had started to quiet. "We should've talked about it first. It's not fair to do whatever you want and then tell me I have to abide by the rules, when you didn't really follow them either."

"What rule did I break?"

"You said Simone could stay at the house."

"*She* came to *me* and asked for a cabin. We're housing two of your cowboys at Seven Sons so she can have that cabin."

"And why didn't you say anything to me about it?"

"She asked me not to."

Callie sighed, because this felt like an argument she couldn't win. Liam wouldn't see things from her side no matter what she said, and she stood up. "All right. I really am tired."

"That's it?" He scrambled to his feet too.

"You said we could talk about what you choose to

spend your money on," she said. "It was *your* rule. And you didn't discuss a complete ranch and home remodel with me. That doesn't just come together in a day."

He didn't deny it.

"So that means you spent a lot of time *before* we got married breaking your own rules." She turned away from him, something stinging in her chest. And Jeremiah had been in on it. Her sisters. Everyone. Callie felt like a complete and utter fool, and she started back up the beach toward the hotel.

"Callie," Liam said from behind her, but she kept going. She couldn't outrun him, and he stepped to her side a few seconds later. He didn't try to apologize, and Callie wasn't sure if that made her happier or angrier.

Back in the room, she grabbed her pajamas and went into the bathroom to change. She hadn't done that once since they'd arrived on the island, and she felt stupid standing in the bathroom while her husband waited in the room. She should be able to change in front of him, but she didn't even want to look at him right now.

And sleeping with him? Wasn't going to happen tonight.

23

"Careful, boys," Jeremiah said. "Liam's whole life is in that thing." He wasn't actually going to touch anything in Liam's computer setup. But he'd taken a dozen pictures and gotten his brother's instructions for moving everything and setting it all back up.

The Shining Star Ranch was beautiful, with every blade of grass in the exact right spot. All of the suppliers and deliveries and fixes that Liam had arranged for had come through, and all they needed to do was move and set up the office, and Jeremiah's work would be done.

Finally.

Evelyn and Simone should be finishing all the finishing touches on the décor by lunchtime, which Jeremiah wasn't serving at Seven Sons. No, he'd ordered pizza for everyone who'd been working like dogs for the past two weeks, with plenty of garlic knots and soda to go with it.

Orion and Dicky should be setting up the tables in a couple of hours, and if it took longer than that to get Liam's office set up, Jeremiah might scream.

"All right," Tripp said. "That cord goes here. I need that drawing tablet over here."

Jeremiah got out of the way as Tripp took over. He knew how to make a command center, though Liam's was bigger than Tripp's. The office here was smaller than the one at Seven Sons, and Jeremiah only wanted to be in charge of one thing—the photo Whitney had taken.

She'd sent him several choices a few days after the photo shoot and dinner. Jeremiah had thought that evening had gone so well, but Whitney had only communicated with him about the photos. No more fun, flirtiness from her.

Of course, he knew how to ask out a woman, and he hadn't done it. He hadn't seen her at Wilde & Organic, and once he'd chosen a picture, all she'd had to do was order it for him. He'd gone to town to pick up the huge canvas print, and he hadn't spoken to Whitney in a few days now.

Maybe that was why he was so surly.

No, it's not, he told himself. He was in a mood because he'd been working so hard for so long, and he was ready to just be back on his ranch, taking care of his own business, and making dinner so everyone could come gather at the homestead. Micah had gone back to Temple, and Wyatt seemed to leave the ranch earlier and earlier each morning, not returning until later and later.

With Skyler off to school in Amarillo now, he only came back to the ranch on the weekends, and Jeremiah had been alone in the homestead since the wedding.

He hated it. He didn't want to live in that huge house alone, and now Liam's computer was half a mile away, which meant his brother would be too.

First Rhett, then Tripp, and now Liam.

Micah will be back soon, he thought. And if he'd ask Whitney out, maybe he wouldn't have to spend his evenings alone, with only Rhett's cattle dog for company.

His phone chimed several times in quick succession, and he stepped out of the office while Tripp continued to instruct a couple of the cowboys Liam had hired to work the Shining Star on where to put screens so the sun didn't reflect off of them.

Liam had texted once—*Can you please take some pictures of the remodel and send them to me? Callie wants to see them.*

Callie had texted a whole lot more than once, and Jeremiah didn't like the anger he felt in her messages.

I need pictures of my ranch, Miah.

Why did you go along with this crazy plan?

That's my space, and you knew how much it meant to me.

He could feel her pain in the words, and Jeremiah

sighed. He hadn't meant to hurt her, and he knew that wasn't Liam's intention either.

He just wanted it to be a surprise, he tapped out and sent to her.

I don't need you siding with him, she sent back.

Jeremiah sighed. He wasn't siding with anyone. He'd been trapped between Liam and Callie for so long, and he'd hoped he'd never have to pick a side.

I'm taking a bunch of pictures, he texted. *Give me a few minutes.*

He glanced back toward Tripp, but his brother didn't need him. Jeremiah felt a keen sense that no one needed him, and he slipped out the front door, already trying to change his thought patterns.

All he could think about as he aimed his phone at the new flooring running down the hallway, at the new couches in the living room, at Simone and Evelyn as they hung new curtains over the back door, was Whitney.

Whitney should be here taking these pictures. She'd know how to get the best light and the right angles. Jeremiah went through the process clumsily, taking pictures of the newly planted shrubs outside, the new trees that had gone in along the line in the backyard where grass met ranch. He walked out to the cowboy cabins and took pictures of them from a distance, as they'd all been newly painted on the outside, each of the six doors a different color.

It would be impossible to go around the entire ranch

and show her everything, so he snapped a few pictures of a field that had been dormant that was now ready to be planted, and a barn that had been filled with old tools that had been cleaned out. He returned to the house and took pictures of the new driveway, with the new pebble gravel in it, and he walked down the lane to the gate he rarely saw, because he always came to the Shining Star through the gap in the fences between their properties.

But a bright, shiny, silver star had been added to their gate, with the name FOSTER imprinted on it. Jeremiah actually really liked it, though it didn't have the Texas colors on it. He stood in the January sunshine and texted picture after picture to Callie, some with explanations and some without.

It's been a labor of love, he concluded. *Everyone has been here for the past two weeks, working and doing their best to make this ranch what I know you want it to be. It's exactly what you want it to be, and it's now yours. So please don't be mad at me.*

He didn't want her to be mad at Liam either, but Jeremiah wasn't going to say that. Liam could deal with his wife. But Jeremiah couldn't lose her as a friend, and he once again felt stuck in a really awkward position.

Sighing, he looked up into the sky. "Now what?" He and God were still on shaky terms, that was for sure. But Jeremiah had been trying to open up to the possibility of having a girlfriend.

"Should I call Whitney?"

Before God could answer, Jeremiah's phone rang, and he swiped on the call from Callie, his heartbeat speeding the moment he saw her name. And not in the same way it would've accelerated had Whitney's name sat on the screen.

"Hey," he said.

"Miah," Callie said. "The ranch is beautiful. I—" Her voice cut off, but Jeremiah knew it wasn't because the line had gone staticky.

"You should thank Liam," Jeremiah said. "He made a billion phone calls and had everything arranged down to the minute the floors would go in to make sure everything would be ready when the new furniture came. I just orchestrated his plans."

Sniffling came through the line, and Jeremiah just waited. Crying didn't really affect him anymore, as his last conversation with Laura Ann had been filled with her blubbering about why she just couldn't marry him, and how sorry she was, and he deserved better than her.

In that moment, Jeremiah realized something huge—he did deserve better than Laura Ann. Why it had taken him over three years to realize that, he didn't know, but it felt like the Lord had turned a spotlight on from heaven and was shining it right into his mind.

"Thank you," Callie finally said, her emotions streaming through the line from so far away.

"Don't thank me, Cal," he said. "Thank Liam."

"I don't know where he is right now."

"You don't know where he is right now?"

"He got up early and said he was going to go running," she said. "He's not back yet. I've been so mean to him. What should I do?"

Jeremiah could only imagine the state Callie was in right now. He'd seen her distressed a few times over the last several months, but she'd just shutter everything away and keep going. He admired her strength in that regard, because he knew what it took to keep everything he felt and thought stuffed down his throat. Put his head down. Work the ranch. Make dinner. Stay up so late, he could barely function, only so he could finally sleep just a little bit.

Do it all again the next day.

"Have you called him?" he asked. "He texted me this morning too."

"I've tried," she said. "He texted back and said he needed some time to think."

Oh, boy, Jeremiah thought, but he'd had so much practice keeping quiet that the words didn't come out of his mouth. When Liam started thinking too hard about things, he could come to some pretty crazy conclusions.

"Well, call me back if you don't hear from him in an hour or two," Jeremiah said. "I can ask Tripp if he's heard anything from him. The twins talk a lot."

"Okay," Callie said, her voice breaking again. "Thanks, Miah."

"Callie," he said. "You know we all love you, right?"

"I know," she said. "I love you too." Then she hung up, and Jeremiah let his arm drop to his side.

Now what? ran through his mind again. Call Liam? Call Whitney? Go talk to Tripp? Let everything be and pray it would work out?

Jeremiah had spent a lot of months letting everything be, and he was tired of doing that. So he tapped out a quick text to Liam—*call your wife, Liam. She's upset*—and started toward the homestead to see if Tripp had heard from their brother.

"Liam?" Tripp asked, pulling his phone out of his back pocket. "Nope. Haven't heard from him." He went right back to stringing up the speakers on their brother's machines, completely unconcerned about Jeremiah's question.

Back on the front porch, he leaned against the post, his mind still whirring. Then he dialed Whitney's number, hoping it wasn't too early to be calling her.

24

Call your wife, Liam. She's upset.

Liam hated those words with the fire of a thousand suns. They meant Callie and Jeremiah had been talking. "Look who's breaking rules now," he muttered to himself. Maybe he'd run away from Callie—literally. Pounding the sand had been good for him, because exercise always helped him see a bit clearer.

And he could see clearly. Callie was mad—not that he'd spent his money, but that he'd changed her ranch and her house without her permission.

"You knew she was going to be mad," he said, hoping the people at the table next to his didn't think he was crazy, talking to himself through breakfast.

He hadn't been able to get himself to go back to the hotel yet. Yes, Callie had called a couple of times. Texted once. He'd responded that he just needed some time to think, and she'd gone silent.

And silence from Callie was never good.

He'd been about to call her when he'd gotten Jeremiah's text. But now he didn't want to until his own frustration and anger simmered down. He'd asked her to come to him with her troubles and problems, and at the very first sign of trouble, she'd run right to Miah.

You're not being fair, he thought, glad the words had just sounded in his mind. She had called him—twice.

Another text came in, and it took all of Liam's energy to glance at his phone and swipe past the lockscreen to see Jeremiah's next text. *I sent Callie a bunch of pictures. She doesn't seem that mad.*

Liam scoffed and practically slammed his phone down as he turned it over. He didn't want to find out from his brother that his wife wasn't that mad. That made *him* mad, and he reached for his coffee cup again. Just when he'd started to cool down, he had to get that blasted text.

He reached over and silenced his phone so he wouldn't have to see stupid texts like that one. His heart flailed in his chest, sending out irregular beats. Had he made a mistake in marrying Callie? Would she always run to Jeremiah when she needed to talk something through?

Liam had the strong desire to call Tripp and talk to him. Get his perspective. Being twins, Liam had never really done much on his own. He and Tripp had always been together, through growing up, through college, and even for the last twenty years as adults, as they worked in the same industry.

But he didn't call his brother. He needed to figure things out for himself.

And that started with calling his wife.

He took another sip of coffee, though he definitely didn't need the extra caffeine. Even the sound of the ocean couldn't soothe him, and he realized he only had one thing that could. One *person*.

Callie Foster.

He picked up his phone and tapped on her name in the text string. Then he tapped the phone icon and lifted his phone to his ear. Everything around him seemed to be happening in slow motion, except for his nerves and his pulse.

"Liam," Callie said, pure relief in her voice. "Where are you?"

"Sitting down the beach at a little coffee shop," he said. "You want to come down? I'll order you a cappuccino." He pressed his eyes closed. As if everything between them could be fixed with specialty coffees.

"Yes," she said. "What's the name of the place?"

"Uh." Liam glanced around, finally catching sight of the menu above the ordering counter. "Liahona Brew."

"All right," she said. "I'll be right there."

"I have a table outside," he said. "I'll go get your coffee." The call ended, and Liam stayed in his seat for an extra moment. He wanted to be with Callie, and maybe this was just a little road bump for the two of them.

He got up and joined the growing line of people. People took their morning coffee seriously, but he finally made it back to his table with a fresh cup of Hawaii's finest brew for him, and a cappuccino for Callie.

She slid into the seat across from him about two minutes later, and one look at her told him she'd been crying.

"I'm sorry," he blurted out, because he could not stand the sight of her red eyes and blotchy face. He couldn't be the reason she was upset. "I just wanted the ranch to be nice," he said. "And I can't help you with it any other way than paying for stuff. I have a very busy job when we get back, and I wanted everything to be perfect for you."

She nodded, her chin quivering slightly. "I know that."

Then why was her voice so high? Why did she look like she was about to fall apart, right there on this beach-side patio?

"I saw the gate," she said, making her voice strong. "It's beautiful. The shining star, and my last name...." She lifted her eyes to his. "You said I'd get to keep the ranch, and you weren't lying."

"I haven't lied to you," he said.

"Some would say keeping secrets is a form of lying."

"Surprises aren't secrets," he countered. He took a breath and pushed it out. "Whatever. I don't want to argue over semantics." He put both hands flat against the table.

"I'm sorry. I wanted to give you a beautiful space to live in and a functional, operational ranch to come home to."

"I know," she said. "Miah—"

He sucked in a breath so sharply that she cut off. "Oh," she said. "You're mad I talked to Jeremiah."

"Yes," he said plainly. "You said I broke a rule, but then you turn around and do the same thing."

"Is that why you left so early this morning?"

"No," he said, wishing he had a pastry to hide behind. But there was just him and Callie at this table, and he should probably just say what needed to be said. "My shoulders hurt from the couch, and I thought you'd like some privacy to get ready for the day. So I went jogging."

"And you ended up here, sipping sugary coffee."

"Life is about balance," he said, hoping she'd hear some playfulness in his voice, though he wasn't sure it had come through. "And I asked Jeremiah for the pictures too. You didn't have to call him and confide in him."

"How do you know what I said?"

"I just do," he said. "But I know you, and he said you were upset, and I needed to call you, and then he said he'd texted you a bunch of pictures." Liam lifted his eyebrows. "Tell me I'm wrong. That you didn't call him and ask him what to do."

She didn't say anything. In fact, she looked away from him, her shoulders sinking in such a way that told him he was exactly right.

The coffee he'd swallowed burned in his gut, and

everything inside him told him to get up and run again. Run away from this woman who had an emotional attachment to his brother. Run until he couldn't think anymore. Until everything hurt, because maybe then, the biggest pain wouldn't be inside his heart.

"Let's go to the beach," he said.

"You still want to?"

No, he didn't. He wanted to pack up and get an earlier flight home. "You love the beach," he said. "And it'll be a while before we can come back here. So let's just go."

Then she could go snorkeling, and he could take a surfing lesson and then a nap, and maybe he wouldn't have to talk to her much for the rest of the day.

"I'm sorry too," Callie said as they stood up. Liam tossed a couple of bills on the table for a tip and looked at her. "I guess I was worried your brothers would go through my stuff and throw away things that are important to me."

"I told you I'd enlisted the help of your sisters." He didn't mind if Callie had an emotional relationship with them. He wanted her to call her sisters and ask them what to do. The fact that it was Jeremiah really bothered him though. Really, really bothered him.

"I know," Callie said. She tentatively reached for his hand, and with her touch, Liam settled even more. "I should've trusted you—and them."

Yes, she should have. And maybe Liam should've run a few plans by her before ripping everything out and starting over. "What pictures did Jeremiah send?"

"You want to see them?"

"I haven't seen anything," he said. "Does it look nice?"

"Very," she said. "Which also makes me feel stupid, but I'm trying to accept the gift, like we agreed I would." She handed him her phone. "He texted them."

Liam took her phone, unsure if he wanted to see the texts between his brother and his wife. In the end, he tapped and scrolled, taking in the beauty of the new floors, the new carpet, the curtains her sisters were hanging. The cabins looked completely different, as did the ranch space, the fields, the yard. And yes, the gate was spectacular, that shining silver star gorgeous in the morning light.

"Wow," he said. "Everything is beautiful." He handed her the phone back without looking at any of the regular text messages. "Just as I hoped it would be."

They walked back to the hotel and gathered their beach things. Liam had hated sleeping on the couch, Callie so close and yet so far out of his reach. She still felt removed from him, though she smiled as they went back down in the elevator and got their rental car from the valet. He navigated the busy downtown area, finally breaking free of it and heading over to the east side of the island, to a snorkeling spot with pristine water, not as many people, and a fish shack right on the sand.

He could get his coconut shrimp. Take his surfing lesson. Enjoy the day.

The flight home tomorrow would be brutal, and Jeremiah had already arranged a big returning-home party for the newlyweds that included a tour of the new digs. Now that he and Callie had seen the pictures, Liam didn't see why he needed a tour.

But he wouldn't argue with Jeremiah. His brother—all of them, actually—had done a lot for him over the past two weeks, and he couldn't stay mad at him forever.

After all of that, Liam really had to get back to work on his CGI, as he had deadlines to meet if he wanted to keep the Marvel contract, which he did.

Callie spread her towel on the sand while Liam opened the low beach chair. He sighed as he sat down, and Callie glanced at him. "Are we okay?"

He reached over and took her hand in his, because he didn't want to be mad at her anymore either. "Yeah," he said, lifting her wrist to his lips. "We're okay."

And they were. Marriages took work, right? He couldn't expect everything to be perfect all the time, especially when they returned to Three Rivers and had to go back to normal life.

All he could do was pray that he and Callie would be able to find a way through the rocky times, so he did that while she got out her snorkeling gear.

25

Callie felt like an old pro at flying by the time she landed in Amarillo. They'd flown to Los Angeles overnight, but Liam had once again purchased first-class tickets, and the seats laid all the way down like a bed. She'd slept a lot, actually, as she hadn't slept much the night before.

Liam wrangled all of their baggage and got them out to his truck in the long-term parking lot. How he could do all of that, Callie wasn't sure. She was dragging, and hard, glad when Liam swung through a drive-through for coffee.

He'd told her that their families had planned a big brunch event for their return to the ranch, and that they wanted to take them on a tour. Callie had smiled and agreed, though the last thing she wanted was to see all the things Liam had done without talking to her first.

Yes, her anger had faded until it was almost gone. Her lungs hardly stung at all anymore, and her worry about what had been kept and what had been thrown away had lessened. But until she saw for herself, anxiety continued to blip through her.

The drive to Three Rivers seemed to pass quickly and slowly at the same time. Liam didn't have anything to say, and neither did Callie. He went through town and turned onto the highway leading south, and her heart really started to pound then.

Another turn onto the lane where Seven Sons welcomed everyone first, and then the Shining Star sat behind that. Even when Mason had owned the ranch, it had outclassed the Shining Star.

But as Liam turned to go down the driveway, a whole new world opened before Callie's eyes. "The gate," she said, because a picture didn't do it justice. She felt like the ranch had gotten a much-needed breath of fresh air, and it was suddenly vibrant and alive in a way it hadn't been in decades.

"Quinton Cooke did it," Liam said. "He's a master metalworker, and he engraved the name himself too."

Callie knew Quinton Cooke, and she knew that star had been pricey. Her first instinct was to ask how much it had cost, but she pushed against it. "It's beautiful," she said.

"You want me to take your picture by it?"

"Yes," she said immediately, unclipping her seatbelt and sliding out of the truck. She didn't care that she looked like she'd been flying all night, crammed into a tiny seat that wasn't quite big enough for her.

Joy moved through her as she breathed in the Texas air, and she was so glad to be home. No wonder she didn't travel much. She stood next to the gleaming star, running her fingers along the F in Foster.

"Look here," Liam said, and she turned toward him to find a smile on that handsome face. She smiled too, and Liam took the picture. He looked at it as she approached, and she took his phone from him.

Surprise danced across his face as Callie tipped up and kissed him. "I'm sorry," she said against his lips. Once, then twice. "I'm sorry," she said a third time. "Will you forgive me?"

"Yes," he breathed, taking her fully into his arms and kissing her again, this time with as much strength and passion as he did when he made love to her. "Will you forgive me?"

"I already have," she said.

"Yeah, I don't think that's true." He chuckled and glanced toward the house. "But I really think you're going to love it, so maybe you'll be able to forgive me faster because of that."

Callie tucked herself against his chest, a spot she fit so well. She liked listening to his heartbeat, liked the easy way his chest rose and fell, liked the safety and comfort she'd always been able to find in his arms.

"We better get up to the house," he said. "We're already a bit late, and Jeremiah said he made French toast sticks for brunch."

Callie smiled, because French toast sticks were so Jeremiah, and she hurried back to her side of the truck. Liam left the luggage and instead pointed to the front yard. "New bushes. New roses. Everything is trimmed and cut back the way it should be for good growth in the spring."

"The trees," she said, noticing that she wouldn't be hitting her head on the low-hanging branches when she mowed the lawn.

"Trimmed," he said. "The sprinkling system was fixed on the side, and we put in a bunch of trees in the backyard as sort of a wind-break between the ranch and the house."

"It's great," she said. "Really nice. I can probably keep it up."

Liam cleared his throat, and Callie almost rolled her eyes. "You paid for a landscaping service, didn't you?"

"Just for a year," he said. "We can re-evaluate after that."

Callie nodded, her jaw tight. Having someone come mow her lawn when she was perfectly capable made her feel weak, though she knew that wasn't Liam's intention.

"Talk to me," he said as they went up the steps.

Before she could say a word, the front door flew open and Evelyn yelled, "They're here!" She bustled out onto the porch, and Callie swore her stomach had grown to twice its size in just the past two weeks. Evelyn laughed as she embraced Callie, and then Simone joined them, also all smiles.

Callie wanted to ask Simone why she'd thought she had to move out, but that was another conversation for another time. She just basked in being reunited with her sisters, and she looked at all the right things as Evelyn started pointing them out.

New vinyl floors that looked like wood. Waterproof. *Isn't that nice?*

Yes, so nice.

Liam went into the office—his office now—with Tripp and Jeremiah, while Evelyn steered Callie toward the living room. New carpet. New couches. Huge TV. The cabinets in the kitchen had been stained a darker color, and Callie absolutely loved them against her lighter countertops. The appliances were all silver, and shiny, and new, and Evelyn filled a glass with ice and then water, right from the fridge.

Isn't this great?

Yeah, so great.

The guest bathroom was completely redone, with a shower curtain in green and gray. "This should be in a magazine," Callie said, awed as she ran her fingers along the brushed nickel faucet.

"Wait until you see the master," Evelyn said. "I've

always thought those three-day kitchen and bath people were a joke, but wow. They did a great job."

Callie walked on wooden legs as she followed her sisters down the hall. "We kept all the pictures," Evelyn said, indicating the wall. "And we reframed them and hung them here."

Callie slowed so she could see her family pictures from decades past. "Wow," she said. "These are so beautiful. And you added one of you and Rhett. I kept meaning to do that."

"I know," Evelyn said, opening a door. "Simone's room is a guest room now. So is mine." She bypassed them both, as if Callie didn't really care that two brand new beds had been brought in, with more of that luxurious carpet on the floor, and curtains in muted tones that made the rooms feel like a much-needed escape.

"So let's see the master." Evelyn entered Callie's room. She stepped onto the carpet, and sure enough, it was the best stuff Liam could buy in Three Rivers. She had a brand-new, king-sized bed, with a huge wooden headboard with a carved F in it.

Her breath stuck in her chest. That was custom furniture. How had he managed to get that made and delivered in such a short timeframe?

Money, she thought. He really could do anything with money.

The dresser and nightstands—his and hers—matched the bed frame and headboard, and Callie wanted to dive into the bed and go to sleep right now. The scent of syrup and cinnamon hung in the air though, and she knew a nap was a long ways off.

She turned to enter the bathroom, stunned at the scene before her. Everything was gray or white or glass, which was nothing like the old bathroom she'd had before.

"He did a tub and a standing shower," Simone said as if Callie had suddenly gone blind. "And the master closet has new shelving."

Callie just nodded at everything instead of walking through. "Wow," she said, her voice scratching on the way out.

"And the upstairs bedrooms all got the same carpet," Evelyn said, her voice starting to fall on Callie's deaf ears. Blah, blah, blah. The house was simply stunning now, and Callie was supposed to be happy about it.

She *was* happy about it. She was just overwhelmed, and everything she looked at that was shiny, clean, and new reminded her of how run-down, old, and dirty the house had been previously. And how embarrassing was that?

She followed Evelyn and Simone into the kitchen, where all of the Walker brothers were standing in the kitchen or sitting at the table, Liam included. He came toward her, anxiety plain in his eyes. "So?" he asked. "What do you think?"

She wrapped her arms around him and let him hold her upright. "I think it's great," she said, and she did. She honestly did. "Thank you so much." She touched her lips to his, and everyone started cheering.

Just get through the next hour, Callie told herself. Then she'd have time and space to process all the changes to her once-familiar safe-haven.

———

The next morning, Callie knocked on the cabin with the bright blue door. Her sister opened it a moment later, her face made of sunshine and smiles. "Heya, Cal." Simone hugged her and stepped back. "C'mon in. You're going to love these cabins."

Callie hadn't been able to finish the tour of the ranch yesterday. It had all simply been too much. Plus, she didn't want to go around with Miah, as he was the main source of contention between her and Liam.

But she'd promised Simone she'd bring her some of the leftover marbled peanut butter and banana bread Jeremiah had made for brunch yesterday, and to see her new house.

"Oh, it's wonderful," Callie said, looking around. She couldn't remember the last time she'd been in one of these cowboy cabins, but they hadn't looked like this. Natural light filled the area, and Simone had brought in a couple of her pieces that she'd restored. They gave the cabin a vintage-upscale feel and look that was so Simone.

The same flooring in the homestead ran through the

space, and Simone had taken a rug from the house and put it in the living room. "It's Grandma's rug," she said. "And Micah said he could build me some shelves for over here, but he had to go back to Temple first."

"Mm," Callie said. "Did you sew the curtains?"

"Yes." Simone beamed up at them, and Callie wished she had a crafty eye the way her sister did. She really could make any space beautiful, and she set an old-fashioned kettle on the stovetop. "Are you upset I moved out?"

"No," Callie said slowly. "I was a bit surprised. I didn't realize you wanted your own place."

"Well, when it was just me and you, I didn't. But I don't need to be in the homestead with you and Liam." Simone cut her a look out of the corner of her eye. "You love him, right?"

Callie nodded, unable to vocalize that yes, she loved Liam.

"Then you deserve your own space," Simone said.

"I can't have kids," Callie said. "I don't need a house with six bedrooms in it. You should've taken it. Liam and I could've lived out here."

"His computer station takes up a whole room," Simone said with a smile, getting down a pair of teacups.

"Yeah, and this cabin has two bedrooms, right?"

"You belong in the homestead," Simone said. "The ranch is yours."

"Yeah." And Callie was starting to wonder why she'd fought so hard to keep it. Who would she pass it on to?

"Do you like the changes?" Simone asked. Callie sighed, and her sister laughed. "Ah, I see you don't."

"I do," Callie said. "It's just a lot to take in all at once."

"I can see that," Simone said. "But I'm telling you, the Lord put those brothers next door to us for a reason."

"Oh?" Callie's eyebrows lifted. "So is there some truth to the rumor I heard?"

"Depends," Simone said, turning her back on Callie. "What did you hear?"

"That you and a certain Walker brother were flirting shamelessly while I was gone."

"Shamelessly?" Simone burst out laughing. "Just because Evelyn doesn't know how to flirt doesn't mean the rest of us do it shamelessly."

Callie grinned from ear to ear. "So it's true?"

"I mean, maybe?" Simone shrugged as the kettle started to whistle. "But he's back in Temple now, and I don't know. I sensed some hesitancy there."

"So maybe you'll go out with someone else," Callie said. "I mean, we don't all have to marry a Walker."

Simone poured the hot water over the tea bags and turned back to Callie. "You know what? You're right. I am going to find someone to go out with."

"Good for you," Callie said. "Maybe that guy who runs the flea market every month."

"Jonas?" Simone laughed and shook her head. "Nope."

"Why not?" Callie stirred her tea, waiting for it to cool.

Simone sipped hers, looking at Callie over the top of the cup. "Because I've asked him out before, and he said no."

"Ouch," Callie said with a giggle.

"Right?" Simone tossed her hair over her shoulders. "No, I think I'll try my luck at the Valentine's Day dance. That's always fun, and it brings in a lot of cowboys from the outlying farms and ranches."

Callie grinned at her sister, glad they'd had this chance to talk. She finished her tea and slid off the barstool. "Okay," she said. "I have to go meet Miah and Liam. Apparently, Jeremiah has another surprise and he wants both of us there." She rolled her eyes. "Honestly, I don't know how many more surprises I can take."

Simone watched her. "Cal, these are good things."

"I know they are." She waved as she walked away. "See you later, little sis." She left the cabin, glad for a breath of fresh air. She knew the changes were good, but wow, they were also hard. And for someone like Callie, who liked routine and enjoyed things just how they were, she'd been asked to tolerate a lot of change—and be happy about it—in a short amount of time.

"I'm not a bad person for needing time to adjust," she said out loud. "Am I?"

The wind picked up, as if telling her, *no, of course not. Take the time you need.*

And she decided right then that she would. After all, it

took time to have an open heart and an open mind. Liam couldn't expect her to transform overnight.

"I just don't want to fail," she whispered. "Please help us work everything out." Then she picked up her pace as her phone rang and Jeremiah's name sat on the screen.

"I'm coming," she said after answering the call. "I was at Simone's. Be there in a minute."

26

Liam waited in the kitchen at the Shining Star—his kitchen, he supposed—with Jeremiah. He wouldn't let Liam into his office, and he had work to do.

"She's on her way," Jeremiah said, hanging up after calling Callie.

"I told you she went out to Simone's," Liam said. "Thank you for everything you've done here."

"You've told me that like, twenty times." Jeremiah smiled at him.

"Well, I mean it." Liam finished his coffee, ready to be in front of his screens. He hadn't checked on his set-up at all yesterday, because by the time they'd finished the tours and the brunch, all he'd wanted to do was sleep.

The giant bed in the master suite was comfortable, and he and Callie had enjoyed a lazy afternoon in bed. She'd fried eggs for dinner and he'd made honey roasted peanut butter popcorn, and they'd watched a movie on the new TV.

But today, he needed to get back to business.

"Any more...human connections with Whitney?" Liam asked, watching his brother for any reaction. Jeremiah was very good at masking things, but Liam was very good at seeing them.

"Maybe," his brother said, his jaw clenching.

"So not good ones," Liam said.

Jeremiah deflated as if someone had stuck him with a pin. "I don't know, Liam. I honestly don't."

"I thought you two liked each other."

"So did I," Jeremiah said. "And she came out to the ranch, and I let her shoot, and—"

"Whoa," Liam said. "Wait. You let her shoot on the ranch?"

Jeremiah's eyes widened, almost like he'd given away a secret. "I'll tell you later."

"Why can't you tell me now?"

"Because." Jeremiah moved over to the back door and opened it, and Callie came in a moment later.

She looked back and forth between Jeremiah and Liam. "What did I miss?"

"Nothing," Jeremiah said, barely looking at her. "We're just waitin' on you."

"All right," Callie said. "Surprise us."

"It's in the office." Jeremiah started that way, and Liam

got up from the table. The sooner he got this surprise over with, the sooner he could get to work.

"What are you going to do today?" he asked Callie. "Now that we've got ranch hands taking over with the horses and cattle, you should have some free time."

"Yeah," Callie said. "Honestly? I don't know."

"You wanted to do beehives," Liam said, remembering a conversation they'd had on their tour of the pineapple plantation during their honeymoon. "I bet Jeremiah could help you with that."

"I sure could," Jeremiah said, pausing at the office door.

Liam couldn't believe he'd just suggested Callie spend more time with Jeremiah, but neither of them seemed to have a strange vibe. Liam was probably just being oversensitive about their relationship.

"But not today," he said. "I have a ton of work to do at Seven Sons. Might have to wait a week or two."

"I can do some research about them," Callie said. "And I want to talk to Evelyn about helping set up her nursery."

"All right," Liam said. He knew Evelyn wasn't due until summer, but maybe women set up their baby's room six months early. He had no idea. He wanted to ask Callie about what she wanted to do about having kids, but he didn't want to do it in front of Jeremiah.

He filed the conversation topic away for later and

looked at his brother. "Are we going in, or what? I have a ton of work to do too."

Jeremiah simply put a big smile on his face. "Okay, I got you each a wedding gift."

"More gifts?" Callie asked, looking at Liam. "Do you know about this?"

"I know nothing," he said. "But Jeremiah is a *really* good gift-giver." Another wave of appreciation for his brother ran through him.

Jeremiah pulled an envelope out of his back pocket. "For you, Cal."

She took it, her eyes narrowed. "You Walkers are going to be the death of me."

Jeremiah just burst out laughing, but Liam didn't. He watched as Callie opened the envelope, wondering what he hadn't covered for her. Her eyes scanned the single sheet of paper she'd pulled out, and she finally looked up. "Crop-dusting and fertilization?"

"You'll need it," Jeremiah said. "There are a ton of pests here in the late summer." He grinned at her and drew her into a hug.

"Thanks, Miah," she said, stepping back quickly. She showed the paper to Liam, who nodded.

"Yeah, thanks, Miah," he echoed.

"Okay," Jeremiah said, reaching for the handle on the barn door that slid back and forth to close off the office. "Liam, your gift is in here." He opened the door and stepped inside.

Liam followed, his hand tightening around Callie's as he scanned the office. Computers looked normal. He sucked in a breath at the huge, beautiful canvas print on the wall behind his screens.

"Jeremiah."

"It's Pretzel," Jeremiah said. "On Seven Sons Ranch."

Liam could hear the pride in his brother's voice, but he couldn't look away from the gorgeous landscape, the glorious sunset, the absolute perfection of this photo. Emotion choked in his throat, because this was the view he wanted while he worked. And Jeremiah had filled the wall with it, so every time Liam needed a moment to lean back in his ergonomic chair, he could see the ranch he loved.

"Thank you." He turned quickly and enveloped Jeremiah in a hug. "I love this. I love it."

"Love you, brother," Jeremiah said, clapping him on the back. "I'm going to miss you at the homestead."

"I'll still come drink your coffee and eat your bacon in the morning," Liam promised.

"I hope so," Jeremiah said, his voice a bit on the emotional side too.

"Miah, it's spectacular," Callie said. "Who did you have take it?"

Jeremiah stepped back from Liam, who already knew the answer to that question. He glanced at his brother, who clearly didn't want to say.

"Maybe he can get you one of the Shining Star," Liam said, stepping between the two of them. "Now, everyone out. I have so much work to do." And he wasn't just saying that. He had a deadline looming at the end of the month and dozens of scenes to perfect.

"All right, all right," Jeremiah said. "You two come by later if you're looking for something to eat."

"Will do," Liam said, watching Jeremiah turn right to exit the house and Callie turn left to go further into it. He followed her to get more coffee, sweeping his arm around her waist and pulling her in for a kiss. "I love you, sweetheart," he said.

Callie's eyes met his, and they softened instantly. "I love you too."

He ducked his head and kissed her, finally feeling like he and Callie were on the same page. "I really do have a ton to do," he whispered. "I'll be on the computer almost constantly this week."

"You do what you need to," Callie said. "I'll bring in lunch later, if you want?"

"Sure," he said. "I'm starting the day out right with peanut popcorn and coffee." He chuckled and grabbed the bag with the leftover popcorn before pouring himself another cup of coffee.

With everything in place, Liam looked up at his beloved horse and the ranch he'd come to love, and then he got to work.

———

"Done," Liam said to himself several days later. He leaned back in his chair, his fingers aching and his shoulders so tense. A quick glance at the clock told him it was almost four, and he quickly reached for his phone. *Too late to go riding?*

Nope, Jeremiah answered almost immediately. *I'll start saddling.*

On my way.

"Sweetheart?" Liam called as he got up from his desk. Callie didn't answer, and he decided to call her on his way over to the stables at Seven Sons.

"Heya," Callie said, answering after the second ring.

"I'm heading over to ride with Jeremiah and Tripp," he said. At least he hoped his twin would be there. "Where you at?"

"Out in Simone's shop."

"Okay, I'm sure Jeremiah will have dinner on. Y'all want to come over later?"

"Sure."

"Okay, see you then." Liam hung up and hurried to the stables, where he did find Tripp finishing up with his horse, Lightfoot.

"Hey, man." Liam embraced his brother, chuckling. "How's married life?"

"I could ask you the same thing." Tripp shot him a look, but Liam wasn't going to talk about it. He and Callie were still navigating a lot of unchartered ground, but he knew they were going to make it.

"Jeremiah has Pretzel ready around the side there," he said. "He's just finishing up with Stony, and we can go." Tripp checked his saddle while Liam went to get his horse.

"Hey, boy," he said, stepping over to Pretzel. He stroked the horse's nose, so glad he'd been able to make this deadline and spend this time outside, with his horse and his brothers.

"Liam!"

He turned just in time to catch Oliver as he launched himself at Liam. They laughed together, and Liam set Oliver on his feet again. "What are you doin' out here?"

"Ridin'," Oliver said, picking up his child-sized cowboy hat. "Tripp said I could come this time."

"Yeah?" Liam unlooped the reins from around the post where Jeremiah had put them, and Pretzel came closer to him. "Who are you riding?"

"Rodman?" Oliver asked, and Tripp whistled from around the side of the stables.

"Comin'!" Oliver yelled, dashing off toward his step-dad. Liam sure did love that kid, and he was once again reminded that he wanted to talk to Callie about having kids.

He took Pretzel around the stables too and paused to watch Tripp help Oliver into the saddle. He started talking to the boy about how to hold the reins and how to stay in the saddle. Liam wanted to have a son to do the same thing with, and soon.

"Ready?" Jeremiah asked, bringing his horse out of the stables.

Oliver cheered, and Liam swung into the saddle. With everyone ready to go, Liam let Jeremiah lead them out onto the ranch. They didn't follow a path, and Liam knew his horse would be able to get him back to the ranch should they get lost. But Jeremiah never went very far during their rides.

Tripp hung back with Oliver, Rodman an older horse that didn't care about keeping up with his friends. Liam glanced over his shoulder, finding quite a bit of distance between him and Jeremiah and Tripp and Oliver.

"Talk about Whitney for five minutes," Liam said, employing one of their mother's conversation techniques.

"Okay, *Mom*," Jeremiah said, heavy sarcasm in the words.

"Seriously," Liam said. "Five minutes. You let her shoot on the ranch, and...."

Jeremiah drew in a deep breath. "And she's kind of disappeared."

"Really? Were you nice while she was here?"

"Liam."

"Come on, Jeremiah. Five minutes."

"I was nice," Jeremiah said. "We held hands, and I even took her to dinner afterward. I had a great time, and she acted like she did too."

"Kissing?"

"No," Jeremiah practically barked. "That's a great big

no." He shook his head. "I'm not ready for that." He swallowed, and Liam's heart went out to him.

"What are you ready for?"

"You know, I thought I was ready to start dating a little," he said. "And I thought I wanted to date her."

"And you don't?"

"I don't know," Jeremiah said. "She disappeared, and I just can't help thinking that she's going to be exactly like Laura Ann."

"Ah." Liam nodded, because that was pure honesty right there. "Have you called her?"

"Yes," Jeremiah said. "It goes to voicemail. She texted me when the print was ready, and I went and picked it up. We texted a little bit then."

Liam watched the sun start to sink, his brain moving through ideas. "Here's a thought. She called you over and over about shooting at the ranch, right?"

"Yes," he said. "For months."

"Then maybe you do the same."

"Badger her?"

"Yeah," Liam said. "Remind her you're here, and you're interested."

"Maybe she was only interested in the ranch," Jeremiah said. "And I'm not sure I want to know that for certain." He looked at Liam, and so much anxiety lived in his brother's eyes.

"Think about it," Liam said. "I think your five minutes are up."

"Thank the Lord," Jeremiah said with a sigh, and Liam chuckled.

"I needed this," he said. "Thanks for inviting me."

"Anytime, brother," Jeremiah said. "Honestly, come over anytime."

Liam thought he heard something new in Jeremiah's voice, but he wasn't sure what. Before he could ask, Tripp whistled again, and Liam swung around in his saddle.

"Oh, Oliver's down," Jeremiah said, swinging his horse around. Liam did the same thing, getting back to help as quickly as he could. Because that was what the Walkers did. They helped and loved each other, and Liam was glad he was part of such a great legacy.

27

Jeremiah couldn't let go of Liam's suggestion that he call and text Whitney the way she had him. He thought about it while he laid in bed that night, and he thought about it the moment he woke up only a few hours later. He thought about it while he did a crossword puzzle, made the morning brew, and watched Wyatt leave with only a thermos of coffee.

The silence in the homestead ate him alive, and he pulled out his phone and called Whitney. She didn't answer, though she had to be at the store by now.

"Hey," he said in the brightest voice he could muster. "It's Jeremiah Walker. Wondering what veggies you have for that chicken bake we talked about. Maybe call me?" Instant humiliation flowed through him and he added, "Okay, bye," and hung up as quickly as possible.

"Maybe call me? Why was that a question?"

The real question was why had she gone cold? Their dinner had been fun, with easy conversation and good food. Whitney hadn't answered his last phone call, though she had responded to his texts about the pictures.

He sighed, set some bread in the toaster, and cracked eggs into a hot pan. He mucked out horse stalls, fed the goats, and spent a couple of hours in the office, reviewing their plans for planting in a few months.

That afternoon, he drove to Wilde & Organic to get the vegetables he'd use in a chicken bake. He didn't think he'd run into Whitney, as she stocked the produce section in the mornings.

Back at the ranch—still alone—he put together the spices, chicken, and vegetables and slid the pan into the oven. An hour later, he took a picture and sent it to Whitney with the caption *Wish you were here to share this with me.*

He felt like a complete fool, like he was pursuing a woman who didn't want him. The same thing had happened with Laura Ann, and he hadn't known it until he was wearing a tuxedo and a boutonniere.

He couldn't do what Liam had suggested, especially because he couldn't handle the rejection. Already he felt his heart cracking open and bleeding, and it didn't feel good.

His phone chimed, and he looked down at it. *Looks good*, Whitney had texted. Nothing more.

Jeremiah didn't know what to do with the message. Respond? Delete? Invite her out?

He paused and listened, hoping the Lord would nudge him in one direction more than another. But Jeremiah couldn't hear anything. Couldn't feel much.

He sighed and looked around the empty kitchen, hating the silence and the fact that he'd just cooked a meal, but he didn't have anyone to share it with.

But Whitney had texted.

"So that's good, right?" he asked. He honestly didn't know, and his brain hurt from trying to figure things out.

Another message came in, this one from Callie. *Want to help me with the beehives next week?*

Yes, he sent back quickly. *Name the day.* At this point, he'd do anything to be able to spend his evenings with someone he knew cared about him.

28

Callie fell into a new routine, and she didn't much like it. Well, she liked waking up next to Liam, but that was about all she saw of him. He made coffee and disappeared into his office. He kept that new barn door open, but he wore headphones and seemed to have a singular focus on his screens while he was in there.

Callie couldn't blame him. He had work to do. The problem was...she didn't. Cayden had quickly emerged as the cowboy designated to come ask her questions, but she had no idea what to tell him.

She didn't know how to run a ranch, and while she'd known it before, the truth of it stared her in the face every morning now.

Monday dawned after a week of Liam's insane work schedule. He'd still managed to find time to go horseback riding with his brothers, and Callie had asked Miah for his help with the beehives. Maybe if she had something to do every day, she wouldn't feel so useless. So neglected. So humiliated that she couldn't even answer simple questions.

"Mornin', ma'am," Cayden said as he came in the back door. "You wanted to see me?"

"Yes, sir," she said, reaching for another mug. "How would you like to be the foreman here at the Shining Star?" She didn't need to beat around the bush. Maybe if Cayden was the one giving orders, the ranch wouldn't fall into disrepair again.

"Ma'am?"

She poured him a cup of coffee and set it on the counter. "Cream? Sugar?" They had plenty of both now that Liam was bankrolling everything in Callie's life. She expected the annoyance she'd experienced in the past to flood her. Only a tiny pinch started in her lungs, and it disappeared quickly.

Pushing the sugar bowl closer to his coffee mug, Callie said, "I think it's pretty obvious I don't know how to take care of a ranch this size." She poured a healthy splash of cream into her own coffee. "And you do."

"I'm flattered," he said, scooping sugar into his cup. "And yeah, I can do that."

Relief filled Callie from top to bottom. "Great," she said. "I'm meeting with Jeremiah Walker this week to find out what to do here." She swallowed, and she knew how hard it was to get that pride to go back down her throat. "But what are you thinking?"

"Honestly?"

"I think you'd better be honest with me," she said. "My husband went to a lot of trouble to get this ranch back on its feet, and I don't want to disappoint him." Or herself. Her father. Her mother. Her sisters. Or God.

She'd been given a huge gift, and she needed to make sure she did the right thing with it.

"Well, you have a ton of land here," he said. "And twelve cowboys. I'd make teams of people and get their tasks solidified. That way, every morning, everyone knows what to do without any wasted time."

"Solid plan," Callie said, her mind racing. "What kind of teams? Like agriculture, livestock, feeding...?" She let her words hang there, because she honestly wasn't sure what else there was to do. Those were the things she did, but she could only do so much. She'd been able to work about one-tenth of the ranch, and she couldn't even imagine what this place would be at full capacity.

"Sure," Cayden said. "Maintenance, for now, would be huge. So would agriculture. We cleaned up a lot, but your land isn't ready to be planted. Not really. So we could have a large team on that right now. If we're going to be working out in the fields on the edge of the property, we need cabins."

"I have a cabin out there," she said. "But it might have

been blown over by now." She gave him a smile, though she felt like crying.

Cayden smiled right on back. "See? Maintenance. And we need to go through the equipment shed and make sure we have what we need to plant, fertilize, and harvest all the land that's been wild for awhile. I know Jarrod's a decent mechanic, and he'd be a great maintenance manager."

"Oh, sure," Callie said, taking a long moment to sip her coffee again. "So...do we have managers over those things?"

"Yep," Cayden said. "And you might consider investing in more cattle. You have *plenty* of room for them here, and that can be a huge source of income. With all the fields being planted, you'd have enough to feed them right here, without having to outsource that, which is *so* expensive."

Callie knew how expensive. She just nodded, because she knew she needed more cattle. More fields planted. Better equipment.

"So I'd have a maintenance manager. Jarrod would be that. And an agriculture manager. I think Soren would be good for that. She has a great eye for details, and land rotation has to be managed right. She could be over groundskeepers too."

Callie must've worn a blank look on her face, because Cayden continued with, "You know, someone to make sure the paths are clean and clear and in good repair.

Someone to dispatch maintenance to fences if they're breaking down. That kind of stuff."

"Soren," Callie said. "Sure." She didn't know the woman well, but Liam had hired two cowgirls to work the ranch.

Cayden lifted his cowboy hat and pushed his hair back. "Maintenance and agriculture. You'd need a live-stock manager. And a sales manager."

"Livestock over the animals," Callie said, finding somewhere else to look. "Sales over buying and selling cattle."

"And crops," he said. "If you have excess, you get to charge the high prices to other ranchers who don't have enough."

Callie had so much to think about, and she couldn't wait to meet with Miah that afternoon. "Okay," she said. "Do you have people in mind for those positions?"

"I don't know them all real well yet," he said. "Maybe Liam—"

"No," Callie said, shaking her head. "Liam is very busy with his computer work. You and I will deal with this."

Surprise darted across Cayden's face, but he just ducked his head. "All right, ma'am."

"Do we interview for manager positions?"

"We can."

"Great," she said. "Let's do it right after morning feed-ings are done."

Cayden drained the last of his coffee and nodded. "Yes, ma'am. Here?"

"Yes," she said. "I'll make lunch."

He nodded and left the way he'd come in, and Callie finally had a purpose for that day. She pulled open the fridge to see what she had that could feed twelve people and reached for the ground beef.

Her cheese-stuffed burger bombs would do the trick, and she had the soft, sweet rolls that went with them in the freezer.

Maybe Miah could come for lunch too. She set the hamburger on the counter and reached for her phone. "Heya," he said after only the first ring. "We're still on for tonight, right?"

"Yes," she said, sensing his anxiety that she might cancel. He definitely had something going on he hadn't told her about. "Are you okay?"

"Fine," he said.

"Okay," she said, heavy doubt in her voice. But Miah didn't volunteer anything else, and Callie knew him well enough to know he wouldn't. And if she asked, she could get the growly, grumpy, grouchy version of Miah she'd rather avoid.

"Listen," she said. "I'm wondering if you could come here for lunch today. I asked Cayden to be the foreman here, and we're going to start assigning ranch hands to specific tasks." She turned away from the windows that showed her the expanse of the Shining Star, her feelings of being overwhelmed almost crushing the life from her heart. "And I need your help with that. I—well, I have no idea what I'm doing. I don't know how to run a ranch. I don't know how to talk to cowboys. I don't know what tasks need to be done and—"

"Callie," Miah interrupted.

She paused, taking a deep breath.

"I can come for lunch," he said. "It's all going to be fine. You can figure this out."

She nodded, a storm swirling inside her. "Okay."

"Noon?"

"Yes, please."

"Great, I'll see you then."

"Okay." She hung up, glad she'd made it through the last few words of the conversation without breaking down. And she wasn't going to break down now either. She believed Miah when he said she could figure this out—and that was exactly what she was going to do.

A few hours later, her burger bombs sizzled in the frying pan. She'd had a bit of an adjustment as she learned how to cook with gas instead of electric heat, but burgers were supposed to have a bit of char on them, weren't they?

She tore lettuce leaves as the front door opened, and she turned at the sound of Miah's boots coming into the kitchen. Their eyes met, and while Callie didn't and had never felt sparks between her and this particular Walker brother, she was glad to see him.

He gave her a hug and held her tight. "You okay?"

"Yes," she said into his shoulder. "I'm just—" She cleared her throat and stepped back. "Embarrassed." She picked up the head of lettuce and got back to work.

"Nothin' to be embarrassed about," he said.

Callie didn't argue, though she thought there was plenty to be embarrassed about. "Cayden just texted to say they were on their way in." Her nerves picked up speed, zinging around inside her chest.

"He's a good choice for foreman," Miah said, looking out the windows along the back of the house. Callie got out a serrated knife and started cutting tomatoes. She barely had the ketchup, mayo, and mustard on the counter before the back door opened and all of her hired help entered the house.

"Something smells good," Soren said, and Callie smiled at the blonde woman.

"Burger bombs," Callie said. "Oh, and potato chips." She spun to grab the bags of chips off the counter behind her, placing them next to the toppings for the hamburgers. She realized then that everyone was looking at her, waiting for her to say something.

She wiped her hands on a kitchen towel and faced them, lifting her chin. She'd done hard things before, including showing Liam that foreclosure notice and then marrying him a couple of weeks later.

"Thanks for coming," she said. "I'm planning to make lunch for you guys a few times a week, and I wanted to start to get some administrative things established." That sounded professional enough. "I've asked Cayden to be the foreman, and he's accepted the job." She nodded at him and he came to stand beside her, looking out at the other ranch hands.

"And I've asked Jeremiah Walker to come, because he's been running Seven Sons fairly well these past few years, and I think his expertise will be valuable."

"Fairly well," Miah said with a chuckle.

Callie's face softened into a smile too, as did several others. "But let's eat first. We can talk while we do that."

"Can I say something?" Cayden asked.

"Of course." Callie fell back a step, feeling foolish for not asking him if he had something he'd like to contribute.

"Callie has several managerial positions she'd like to fill, and anyone who wants to be considered should plan to stay after lunch and talk to us both." He glanced at her. "Right?"

"Right," she said.

"We talked about maintenance, agriculture, livestock, and sales," Cayden said, now switching his gaze to Miah. "What else do we need to consider?"

"Groundskeeping," he said.

"I thought that could go under agriculture."

"Not if you're going to plant two thousand acres of crops," Miah said. "You need a manager for that, and a co-manager. And at least half of these people for this year." He surveyed the cowboys and cowgirls who still hovered near the table.

"All right," Cayden said easily, though Callie's heartbeat fired in her chest. "Groundskeeping, which includes the homestead and the cabin common areas. Land around the barns, pastures, stables, and all pathways." He looked at Miah, who nodded.

"That's five managers," Callie said. "And Cayden is the foreman, which only leaves six of you for crews."

"They're all full-time, paid positions," Miah said. "Cabins included." He smiled at them and then Callie. "This is a good set-up."

"It sure is," Cayden said. "And I'm grateful for the work, ma'am."

Callie did not need their gratitude, though several of the others nodded too. She knew it wasn't because of her that they had jobs. No, that was all Liam's doing. She was surprised the scent of cooking beef hadn't brought him out of his cave, but he did have a lot of work to do.

And so did she.

"All right," she said. "Are we ready to eat now?"

"Yes, ma'am," Cayden said, and Callie nodded toward the food.

"Come and get it then." She stood out of the way while her ranch hands—and who she hoped would become her friends—came forward and picked up plates, dressed their burgers, and took chips.

She joined them last, content to listen to them talk to one another. She and Cayden and Miah talked to every one of them individually in the formal living room across the hall from Liam's office.

He'd closed the door at some point, and Callie felt a bit guilty for disturbing him.

"So, what are you thinking?" Miah asked, and Cayden proceeded to tell him his thoughts on who should be the managers. Callie listened, trying to learn the qualities and attributes of the people they wanted in the leadership roles for the ranch.

"Jarrod at maintenance," Cayden said. "Soren for agriculture. Blaine for livestock—he has a real way with horses. Shawn for sales. He was the sales manager at an auction a few years ago, and that seems like a good fit."

Even Callie could've put Shawn at sales, and she started to feel a bit more confidence in herself. She simply hadn't known which questions to ask. But she did now.

"Mm," Miah said. "I agree with all of those. I think Anita should be on the livestock crew. She has some experience with veterinary medicine."

"Yes," Cayden said, making a note on the piece of paper he'd asked for. "Mike and Tanner live together and would be great hands for Jarrod."

"I agree," Miah said. "Cal, who are you thinking for groundskeeping?"

"Wilson," she said. "He has an eye for detail."

"And he could do it himself," Cayden said. "I could help him in the heavier months in the spring and fall."

"So everyone else on Soren's agriculture team," Miah

said. "That's Louis, Joel, and Roger." He looked at the other two. "How are we feeling about that?"

"Where's Trey?" Cayden asked.

"Oh, I thought he'd do sales with Shawn," Miah said. "They're brothers, and they'd work great together. And Callie might not need two men there all the time, but this year, I think she does if she wants to expand her herd." He looked at her, and all Callie could do was nod.

Cayden studied his paper and nodded. "I like this plan."

"I do too," Miah said. "Cal?"

"Fine," she said. "Great."

Cayden grinned and said, "I'll have a meeting at my place tonight, and we'll get everything sorted."

"Thank you, Cayden," Callie said, keeping her perfect smile in place as the cowboy left. She deflated the moment the sound of his footsteps faded. She faced Miah, and she was so tired. She reached for him, and he gathered her into his arms.

"You can do this," he whispered, stroking her hair.

"Thank you," she said. "I hate feeling weak."

"Oh, I know the feeling."

Callie pulled back. "You do?"

"It's something I fight every day," he said. "But it's not weakness to admit you don't know something. That's actually a sign of strength."

Callie grinned up at him. "I appreciate your help Miah."

"You're not alone," he said. "We all love you, Cal."

"I love you too, Miah," she said, hugging him again. Her eyes drifted closed.

"Jeremiah," Liam barked, and Callie's eyes shot open again at the same time her pulse ricocheted into the top of her skull. She jumped away from Miah, who turned toward his very angry brother.

"Hey, Liam," Miah said as if nothing had just happened.

"What's goin' on here?" Liam asked.

"Nothing." Jeremiah's phone rang, and he pulled it out of his pocket. "I have to take this. See y'all later." He took a few steps, slipped past Liam, and was out the front door before Callie could blink.

Then she was left to face her husband.

"I think that broke the rules," he said evenly. "Did you really just tell him you loved him?"

Callie opened her mouth to defend herself, but only a squeak came out.

29

Liam stood in the hallway between his office and the formal living room, waiting for Callie to say something.

Anything.

"He was just helping me with the ranch," she said. "I was just...telling him...I appreciated it?"

Yeah, that wasn't what Liam had heard. He'd distinctly heard *I love you too, Miah,* and he'd seen Callie gripping his brother in a tight embrace.

Jealousy surged through Liam, and the room spun around him. He shouldn't have skipped breakfast and lunch, but he'd had a ton of work to finish before his meeting that afternoon.

"Was that a question?" he asked. "You appreciated it?"

"He was just helping me—*us*, Liam." She glared at

him and stepped past him. "There's leftover burgers if you want one. I'm not making dinner."

"Right," Liam said. Callie never made dinner, because Jeremiah did that next door. He swung around and followed her into the kitchen. "What was he helping with?"

"Ranch assignments," she said. "I made Cayden the foreman, and we interviewed everyone today and assigned managers."

Liam didn't know what to do with the terrible emotions streaming through him. "And what?"

"And what?" she repeated. "We made some decisions, and Cayden is going to talk to everyone tonight and give out their assignments. And then I was just saying good-bye to Miah."

"Yeah, that's what it looked like."

"Liam."

"What?" he asked.

"You don't trust us?"

"You broke the rules," he said.

"I didn't know we still had those rules."

"Are you kidding?" He glared at her and folded his arms. "And I trust you guys."

"Do you?"

"I trust my brother."

Callie fell back at step, and Liam realized what he'd said. "I mean—"

"You don't trust *me*."

"You said you *loved* him," Liam said, aware his voice had gone up in volume. He worked to calm himself. "I have work to do."

"Yeah, you always have work to do."

He spun back at her sarcastic tone, his temper rising. "Yes, Callie, because I have a full-time job. I've told you all about the Marvel contract, and I've taken a ton of time off during the holidays. You can't blame—"

"I can," Callie said. "You said you'd help with the ranch, and I don't know what I'm doing."

"Obviously," he said, and Callie shut down completely, right in front of him. "Cal," he tried, but she shook her head and stalked out of the kitchen and down the hall. "Wait."

Only the slamming door answered him, and the fight left Liam's whole body. "Idiot," he muttered. "Why did you say you trusted Jeremiah and not Callie?"

He stomped back toward his office, but he didn't go inside. He yanked open the front door and found Jeremiah standing there, his fist about to knock. "Oh," he said, stepping back. "You're angry."

"Dang right I'm angry," Liam said. "You're over here, hugging my wife and, and, and...." He wasn't sure what else to say. He hadn't heard what Jeremiah had said.

"Liam," Jeremiah said. "It was nothing."

"It didn't look like nothing," Liam said. "And she said she loves you, and we had *rules*."

Confusion crossed Jeremiah's face. "I don't know what

you're talking about with the rules, but yeah, she said she loved me. We're good friends."

"Too good of friends." Liam lifted his chin. "I don't want you two to see each other anymore."

"That's insane," Jeremiah said, a panicked look crossing his face. "You can't take her from me too. She's all I have left."

"She's all you have left?" Liam laughed, but it wasn't happy. "What does that mean? Why didn't *you* just marry her?"

Jeremiah swallowed, obviously working through something in his head. "I would *never* do anything to hurt you," he said, his voice calm. Freakishly calm. "*Ever.* And I can't lose either of you right now. Please, don't make me choose you or her." He lifted his chin too, and Liam saw the Walker stubbornness mirrored right in front of him.

"Wyatt's gone all the time," Jeremiah said. "Rhett, you, and Tripp are happily married."

Liam scoffed. What was going on at his house was not happy.

"Skyler lives in Amarillo full time now. Micah's not here," Jeremiah said as if he hadn't heard Liam. "It's just me and that huge ranch and that massive house, and I can*not* keep living like this. So yes, when Callie called, I came over. I'd die if you two didn't come for dinner. I can't get Whitney to talk to me anymore, and I have no idea what I did, and I just—please. You can't be mad at me too."

He held Liam's eye for another moment, and then he turned away with a huge sigh.

"I'm sorry," Liam said, knowing this apology would be a hundred times easier than the one he needed to say to Callie. "I guess calling and texting didn't work."

"No." Jeremiah paced to the end of the porch and stayed there, leaning against the railing.

Liam took slow, tentative steps toward him, stopping a few feet away and facing the front driveway. "Where's Wyatt been?"

"I don't know," Jeremiah said. "I haven't asked him, because I literally see him for five minutes in the mornings, and then he's gone."

"Micah will be here soon."

"Yeah."

"And me and Callie are right here."

Jeremiah let several seconds of silence go by, before he said, "I do love her like a sister, and she loves me like a brother. Not like she loves you."

Liam nodded, though Jeremiah wasn't looking at him. He wanted to believe his brother. When he made love with Callie, he believed it. Why couldn't he believe it now?

"You should go make sure things are okay with her," Jeremiah said. "Tell her we'll have to do the beehives another day."

"It's fine," Liam said, turning as Jeremiah started to leave. "You guys go do the beehives. I'll go to town and get us something to eat and meet you guys at the homestead afterward."

Their eyes met, and a heavy dose of foolishness hit Liam smack dab in the chest. Of course Jeremiah and Callie weren't doing anything wrong.

"Liam," Jeremiah said.

"No, seriously. Go." He needed another few hours in the hotseat in front of his screens, but he could stay up late tonight. He knew he wouldn't be crawling into bed with Callie, chuckling with her while he kissed her, while she ran her fingers through his hair, because he knew it would take more than a single apology to convince her that he did trust her.

"I'm heading out for food," Liam said. He opened the front door and darted into his office, grabbing his truck keys and hurrying right back outside. "What are you feeling like? Chinese? Pizza?"

"Whatever I don't have to make," Jeremiah said, and Liam knew then that his brother was in a very bad way. He grabbed onto him and hugged him. Neither of them said anything, but Liam could feel the negativity pouring off of his brother.

He wanted to fix things for Jeremiah too. But all he could do was step back and look at him. "I'll be back soon." Liam tipped his hat and hurried down the front steps, hoping he could find a way to make things right with Callie.

———

He took a very long time in town, buying out the last of the doughnuts at Heidi Ackerman's bakery, and allowing himself to get drawn into a conversation about horses and ranches with Frank.

The man had been there, serving coffee and wiping tables, and Liam liked the older man. Plus, the news was out about Liam and Callie's marriage, and Frank wanted to know how things were going at the Shining Star Ranch.

"Y'all get the right help," Frank said. "You'll be fine. And stick together. That's important too." He knocked on the table and glanced around, but no one else had come into the bakery. "My wife sacrificed for a long time before her dream of this bakery came true," he said. "And now here I am, supporting her." He smiled like there was nowhere he'd rather be than wiping tables in a bakery.

He sighed and shook his head. "Plus, I get out to the ranch every few days to ride. That makes my cowboy spirit happy."

"Yeah." Liam chuckled with Frank. "I like to ride with my brothers too."

"Anyway, Heidi will be wondering why I'm not home yet." He stood up and groaned. "We closed twenty minutes ago."

"I'm sorry," Liam said, jumping to his feet too. He hadn't even gone anywhere for real food yet, and he wondered how long it took to learn about how to keep bees. Neither Callie nor Jeremiah had called or texted yet, and Liam wondered where they were and what they were doing.

Can't think like that, he told himself as he shook Frank's hand and headed out the front door. Frank locked it behind him, already whistling as he got back to his closing tasks. Liam faced Main Street, wondering if there was anything else he could do to waste an hour.

The town hosted summer dances, but it was January. Cars steadily moved up and down the street, as it was dinnertime and a lot of restaurants in Three Rivers offered free meals to kids on Monday night.

Liam stood on the sidewalk, wishing he had the happy wife and smiling toddler to take for dinner. He'd been so busy with his projects that he hadn't said anything to Callie about having children.

Now, he wondered if he'd be saying anything to Callie about anything serious ever again. He wanted to, and he had to do something about their situation.

A truck pulled up to the curb, and Liam looked over at the same time Tripp called his name. Liam stepped over to the truck, where Ivory sat, her son between her and Tripp.

"What are you doin' here?" Tripp asked.

"Getting dinner," he said.

"Where?"

"I don't know." He glanced down the street. "Pizza maybe? I'm taking it back to the ranch for us and Jeremiah."

"It's an hour wait for pizza tonight," Tripp said. "We just left there."

Liam groaned. "What should I do instead?"

"Jeremiah likes those Philly cheesesteaks," Tripp said. "And salsa from that salsa bar."

"Salsa is not a meal," Ivory said.

"Can't argue there," Liam said. "Well, I'll try somewhere fast. There's that Mexican place Callie likes."

"Good luck," Tripp said. "It's a bad time if you want something fast."

"Liam," Oliver said, leaning forward. "Tripp says I can come out and try riding again soon."

"Yeah, real soon," Liam said, smiling at the boy. Oliver waved, and Liam waved back as Tripp pulled out onto the street. He did end up going to Callie's favorite place, and he ordered her favorite pulled pork enchiladas and plenty of the beans and rice he knew she loved.

His phone chimed just as he was accepting his to-go bag of food, and he saw a text from Jeremiah. *Not sure what you ended up getting or where you are. Callie says we can just eat. She's going to Simone's to try something, I guess.*

"Of course," Liam said. She wouldn't want to be stuck with Jeremiah and Liam, trying to eat while the three of them stared at one another in awkward silence. And it would be silent, as Jeremiah was hurting, and Callie retreated without words when things got hard.

Liam pulled up to Seven Sons a while later, calling,

"Jeremiah, food," when he walked in. The empty office to his right stared back at him, and he suddenly knew why Jeremiah was having a hard time. Not long ago, this homestead was full of brothers, and laughter, and family meals.

Tonight, it was quiet except for Jeremiah saying, "Come on into the kitchen," as if Liam would take the food anywhere else. Jeremiah stood at the counter, stirring a huge pitcher of sweet tea.

"Mexican," Liam said, putting the bag of food on the counter.

"Great," Jeremiah said, leaving the tea to get plates.

"How did things go with Callie?"

"Fine."

Liam sighed and started unpacking the bag. "I got you the steak burrito."

"I'm starving," he said.

"Are we not going to talk about Callie?"

"Nope," Jeremiah said. "If you want to do anything about her, you need to talk to her. Not me."

"I just...." Liam shook his head and pulled his steak and cheese nachos closer. "I said some awful things to her."

"I know."

"So she said something? You two can talk about me, but we can't talk about her?"

"She wouldn't say anything," Jeremiah said. "And I didn't ask anyway. She took a bunch of notes on her phone about bees and honey, and she made a list of all the equipment she needs to buy. She seemed excited about it."

"She is," Liam said, because Callie had been talking about an apiary and being a beekeeper all week. No, he hadn't seen her a ton since they'd returned from Hawaii, but they saw each other a few times a day for a few minutes, and they slept together every night.

Liam had been happy with his marriage until that stupid declaration of love. *Better to know now, though, right?* he asked himself.

And a more rational part of himself asked, *Know what, exactly?*

He didn't know the answer to either question, and he stayed at the homestead until long past dark. He and Jeremiah had always had a good relationship, and they talked about easy things. Nothing to do with the women in their lives. Liam made scones and honey butter, and he'd been yawning for an hour before Jeremiah said, "You better get on home, cowboy."

"I'm going to stay here," he said without meeting his brother's eye. "Or did you turn my bedroom into a yoga studio?"

Jeremiah burst out laughing, and Liam felt a temporary slip of happiness move through him too.

"I'm not into that cowboy yoga," Jeremiah said.

"Yeah, well, I heard Soren and Anita are, and since they're livin' over here, they might rope you in."

"Doubtful," Jeremiah said. "Stay if you want, but I think it's a mistake."

"Do you think Callie will be at the house? Hundred bucks says she sleeps at Simone's."

"Oh, I'm not a betting man." He grinned and got up just as the front door opened. Wyatt entered, and Liam stood up too.

"There you are," he said. "Where have you been? Do you know what time it is?"

Wyatt paused and looked at him, then shook his head as he walked down the hall. "Thanks for getting my heartrate going the way it did when Daddy would catch me sneaking in the house."

Liam chuckled, noticed that Jeremiah threw Wyatt a quick look and then went down the hall, and indicated the couch. "Seriously, bro. Where have you been?"

"Oh, you know," Wyatt said, taking off his cowboy hat and stroking his hand down his face. He looked exhausted, and Jeremiah's report of him getting up super early, leaving the homestead, and coming home late seemed spot on.

"No, I don't know," Liam said. "And Jeremiah doesn't know. And we're worried."

"Nothin' to worry about," Wyatt said. "I'm going to work and all of that."

"So you're seeing someone."

"Yes," Wyatt said.

"Who?"

"Not telling yet," he said with a smile.

"Okay, fair enough," Liam said. "But could you come home a bit earlier? Jeremiah is going nuts here by himself, and he feels abandoned."

Wyatt leaned forward, the playfulness slipping from his face. "Yeah, I can do that. Sorry, I forget how he is sometimes."

"How is he?"

"Broken," Wyatt said, turning to look toward the mouth of the hallway.

"He's not broken," Liam said. "He's so much better than before. Just...come home a few times a week. Bring your lady friend. He just doesn't like being alone."

"Yeah, I know." Wyatt leveled his gaze at Liam. "And I know you're married and all that now, but never say 'lady friend' again."

They both laughed, and Liam decided that tonight was exactly what he'd needed, even if he had been avoiding Callie for hours.

Tomorrow, he thought. Tomorrow, he'd fix everything.

Help me to know how, he prayed, but he fell asleep before any good ideas occurred to him.

30

Jeremiah couldn't sleep, Wyatt's words bouncing through his brain. Not even more than one word. Just one.

Broken.

He was not broken.

Sure, maybe he had been when he'd first come to Seven Sons, but Wyatt hadn't been here then. He hadn't seen anything if he thought the man Jeremiah was now was the broken one.

He'd done everything he could think of short of becoming a stalker. He'd called Whitney—she never picked up. He'd texted her, and she'd responded once. *Looks good.*

He'd ended up throwing the chicken bake in the trashcan without eating a single bite. He'd felt guilty for a couple of days after that, and he'd called the local food bank and donated a bunch of money to make himself feel better for throwing away perfectly good food.

He'd ordered another print of Seven Sons, this one the glorious sunset over the land, without any horses. He tapped on his phone, looking through the pictures Whitney had put into an online gallery for him. He could feel her hand in his as he did, almost smell her perfume, hear that voice....

"What did I do wrong?" he asked for probably the fiftieth time. God, of course, had never been one to give Jeremiah really loud answers, and all he felt was frustration. "Am I broken?"

He didn't feel broken, and he was embarrassed Liam had told Wyatt to come home earlier. Humiliated he'd eavesdropped on their conversation. So many negative things swirled through his mind, along with that word— *broken*—that he'd only been able to sleep for a few hours.

He hoped that by getting on his phone for a few minutes, he'd be reminded of how exhausted he was and be able to fall back asleep. Nothing he'd done to help him sleep had worked. Not melatonin. Not lavender oil. Not medication or massage therapy. He'd thought about calling a doctor and getting some sleeping pills, but he hadn't done it yet. He supposed he didn't want to admit, on any level, that he wasn't functioning the way he should.

Broken.

Maybe he was broken. He knew his relationship with

Whitney was, and he hated that he wanted to fix it. No, he hated that there was a relationship in the first place.

He closed the online gallery and set his phone on the nightstand. He just needed to sleep. Everything would be fine if he could just sleep. In the morning, Liam would go talk to Callie, and they'd make up. Whitney would call him, and Jeremiah would ask her to dinner. They'd go, and it would be romantic and perfect and he'd kiss her afterward....

He woke sometime later, purely relieved that he'd been able to get some shut-eye. The scent of maple syrup hung in the air, and he padded down the hall to find Liam and Wyatt in the kitchen, a stack of pancakes on the counter between them.

"There he is," Wyatt said. "I just told Liam we better go make sure you were still alive, that you never sleep this late."

Jeremiah glanced at the clock, startled to see it was almost eight o'clock. "Yeah," he said. "Been stressed lately."

Liam kicked Wyatt's barstool, causing Wyatt to glare at him. Jeremiah didn't like the exchange, but he said nothing.

"Want to get barbecue tonight?" Wyatt asked. "I recently found this place that has the best brisket in the state of Texas. Maybe in the country."

"Oh, wow," Jeremiah said with a laugh. "And if you

think so, it must be good, what with you being a world-traveler and all of that."

"Yep." Wyatt just grinned like he could rope the sun. And he probably could. Jeremiah wondered what it would be like to have that much confidence, but he didn't have the world champion title nor the belt buckles to back it up.

No, all he had was the very clear mental image of himself standing at the altar while Laura Ann's father walked toward him, no daughter on his arm. Of Liam and Tripp's backs as they blocked him from the gossipy eyes of everyone he'd known in Austin. Of his unanswered texts to Whitney Wilde.

"I can barbecue tonight," Jeremiah said, turning away from his brothers and wishing he could turn away from his thoughts just as easily.

"Great," Wyatt said.

"Where've you been at night?" Jeremiah asked, though Liam had last night. But he'd take the fact that he'd eaves-dropped on his brothers to the grave with him.

"Just...out," Wyatt said.

"Right." Jeremiah turned around, his coffee poured and his stomach growling for pancakes. "What's her name?"

"He's not telling," Liam said.

"She doesn't seem that interested," Wyatt said.

"Oh, just put on your bull riding belt buckle," Liam said. "She'll come around."

"Nah." Wyatt shook his head as he chuckled. "She doesn't seem impressed by that."

"She sounds smart," Jeremiah said.

Wyatt rolled his eyes as he stood up, a flicker of pain stealing across his face. Jeremiah saw it, but he pretended not to. He knew the rodeo could beat up a man, but Wyatt hadn't said two words about being hurt or experiencing any pain. "I do have to get to work this morning," he said. "Ethan's down a cutting trainer, and he's convinced I can do it."

"Can you?" Jeremiah asked. "Because cutting. Wow. That's a lot of time on horseback."

"I'm going to try it," Wyatt said, still not saying a thing about himself. He never really did, and Jeremiah was starting to think he'd imagined that look of pain. He'd seen it before though....

"All right. Well, good luck," Jeremiah said, and Wyatt raised his hand as he left.

Jeremiah took another pancake and looked at Liam. "And you? What are you doin' today?"

"I have another deadline on Friday," he said. "So I'm going to work."

"Do you buy for a second that whoever Wyatt's been spending the last couple of weeks with isn't interested?"

Liam chuckled. "No, sir, I do not."

"Me either." Jeremiah poured more syrup over his pancake. "You gonna talk to Callie?"

"If she's home, which I highly doubt."

Jeremiah nodded. "Then I'll say good luck to you too."

"And to you," he said. "You gonna try Whitney again?"

"No," Jeremiah said, deciding on the spot. "She knows how to find me if she wants to. She clearly doesn't want to." The words hurt, slicing open old wounds. But if there was one thing Jeremiah knew, it was that the heart as an actual organ didn't stop beating just because it broke.

31

Callie woke the next morning, the homestead utterly silent. Still. Unscented.

She hated it.

She'd stayed at Simone's last night until well after dark, sure Liam would beat her home. But all the windows had sat in darkness, and she'd opened the back door to an empty house. She known it was empty, because it had no spirit.

It still didn't.

Liam hadn't come home. He hadn't called or texted her either, and Callie felt the ground disappear beneath her feet the same way it had when he'd said he trusted his brother. It was as if he'd heated a blade and then stabbed it right between her ribs. She reached out and steadied herself against the new nightstand he'd bought.

"Is that it?" she asked. "How could he really think I'm

in love with Miah?" It made no sense, and Callie's desperation and despair felt endless. She showered though, and she went into the kitchen to make coffee. She'd operated under duress plenty of times over the course of the last couple of years, and life would go on. That much she knew.

But she now also knew the joy and peace of waking up without a heavy burden hanging over her. She now knew how amazing it was to have a man at her side—and not just any man. Liam Walker. Strong, sexy, and soft all at the same time. He could make her feel cherished just by looking at her, and he made her feel sexy and strong while they made love, though she knew she wasn't sexy or strong.

She gathered her hair on top of her head and took her coffee out onto the back deck. The ranch had a new spirit about it, despite Liam's absence. Of course, it was because of Liam that she saw a couple of cowboys walking along a well-kept path and entering a barn that used to sit idle.

After her morning coffee, she'd go to town and get everything she needed to keep bees—minus the bees. She'd figure out how to do that once she had the proper facilities for her new winged friends.

She liked that she didn't have cowboys asking her what to do. She got a couple of texts from Cayden about the office he'd established in the biggest barn, along with the whiteboard of chores. She thought about that huge administration building out at Three Rivers, and she wondered if she needed something like that.

"Three Rivers has thirty thousand head of cattle," she muttered to herself. "You have five hundred." But both Cayden and Miah thought she could grow that to three thousand this year, and six thousand next year. She had the land to do it, and now she had the money and the manpower.

Extreme gratitude overcame her, and tears sprang to her eyes. "I can't believe this is my life now."

And yet, money hadn't fixed everything. But if there was someone she wanted to work through things with, it was Liam. So she pulled out her phone and texted him. *I'm running to town for beekeeping supplies. Do you need anything?*

No, he answered.

You're not going to stay away all day, are you?

No.

Hope filled Callie's heart, and she thought about her grandmother's homemade barbecue sauce and the chicken and onion pizza she could make with it.

Dinner tonight then? she typed. *Just the two of us, here at our house.*

She stared at the words, wondering why it was so hard to send them. She knew she was the one who initiated the silence between her and Liam, and things had always turned out well when she broke it. But he still felt cold, unreachable.

Deciding not to wait for him to answer with a text, she called him.

"Hey," he said, his voice definitely guarded.

"Dinner tonight?" she asked. "Here at the house."

"All right," he said. "I'll be at the house, working all day too."

"I'll stay out of your hair."

"Callie," he said, a heavy dose of annoyance in his voice. "You're not in my hair."

"I know," she said lightly. "Dinner tonight. We'll talk it all out. Make new rules. Whatever you want." She pulled back any other words she might have said, because she didn't want him to think her weak after sleeping in the house alone for one night. She used to like sleeping alone, but now it felt like a chore she didn't want to do.

"I don't need new rules," Liam said.

"All right." Callie didn't know what else to say. Something buzzed in her chest, but she didn't know what to do about it. "Liam, I—I love you."

"I love you too, sweetheart." And he sounded like he did.

Callie pressed her eyes closed and nodded. "See you tonight." With a solid plan that hopefully wouldn't have her sleeping alone again tonight, she headed into town. She pulled into the farm supply store, feeling a bit out of place. Of course, she'd bought plenty of things from this store in the past, but she'd never felt like she belonged.

The first person she saw when she stepped inside was

Morris Fennigan, and she grinned at him. "Morris, it's good to see you."

"Callie Foster," the man said, his face splitting into a smile too. "Although, I hear congratulations are in order. You got married."

"That I did." She liked Morris, who co-owned the store with his brother. "I'm looking to introduce bees at the Shining Star." She pulled out her phone and navigated to the supply list she'd made the previous evening with Miah. "And I was told you would have everything I needed."

"Of course we do," he said. "Let me get you Harrison. He's the apiary specialist." He picked up the phone on the counter and paged the man, who turned out to be more of a boy. Callie went with him to get the supplies, taking more notes as he told her about different kinds of trays and different kinds of bees.

"What kind of flowers are you going to plant?" Harrison asked.

"Uh." Callie had no idea. "Is there a certain kind?"

"Nope," he said, picking up a strainer and putting it on the flatbed cart he'd brought with him. "But the flowers can flavor the honey. If you've got normal flowers, they'll be happy with those. I think grape vines and raspberry canes are awesome for bees. Loads of flowers, all the time."

"Okay," she said, typing the fruits into her phone.

"I love lavender honey," he said. "And it's easy to grow here. I like having spring flowers like crocus and bluebonnets. Hyacinths are good. Then others that flower all summer, like hosta, foxglove, snapdragon."

Callie's mind buzzed like she hoped her bees would as she took notes. "So I need to make like a bee garden."

"Bees will go anywhere," he said. "But yeah, if you have things for them close by, they'll be happy. If you have a big space, they love sunflowers."

"I have a big space," she said.

"Let's start you off with this," he said. "Do you need me to come out and help you assemble it? We've got a ninety-nine-dollar assembly fee."

"Yes," she said without hesitation. Anything with any kind of fee would've put her off before. But not now, and another rush of gratitude and appreciation for Liam filled her.

"And you can either come back once we're set up, or even later today if you want to go through our nursery. It's not a great time to plant, but we can do some drawings, help you map out where things will be, all of that."

"Okay," she said.

"If you take pictures of your space, it's even better." He smiled at her, and Callie wished she had even a portion of his passion for beekeeping and could apply it to anything.

"Thank you, Harrison."

"Anytime, ma'am. And we can get the bees for you too. They're organically sourced honeybees from right here in

Texas, and we deliver and help you introduce them to your hives starting in April."

"Perfect," she said. "I definitely need help with all of that." Excitement built inside her, and she realized it was the first time she'd been excited about anything in a long, long time. Between now and when she got her bees, she'd read everything she could about beekeeping, learn how to feed her ranch hands, and work on her marriage with Liam.

A few hours later, she'd stopped for breakfast at the pancake house and watched Harrison unload all of the equipment she'd bought for her beehives. She'd watched him assemble it all, taking notes on her phone as he said things she thought she'd want to know later.

She tried to burst into Simone's she-shed to tell her about her exciting morning, but the door was locked. "Simone?" She knocked and tried the door again. Her sister often kept the shed locked while she wasn't working inside, but she'd told Callie last night that she'd gotten a lot of "amazing items" at a huge estate sale over the weekend and she'd probably be living in the shed for the next couple of weeks.

Callie looked over her shoulder, but the row of cabins couldn't be seen from here. Maybe her sister had gone home for lunch, or—

The door whipped open, and Simone stood there, her face slightly redder than usual. She leaned into the opening between the doorjamb and the door and said, "Hey, Cal."

"Hey." She tried to see past her sister, but she couldn't. "What's going on?"

"Nothing. What's going on with you?"

"The door was locked."

"Yeah, I was working on something secret."

Callie's eyebrows went up. "Secret? Can I come in?"

"I'm about to go to lunch." Simone wasn't moving from her spot, and she was completely blocking Callie from entering the shed.

"I got the beehives," Callie said, a smile filling her soul and her face. "And Liam is coming for dinner."

"That's great, Cal." And Simone sounded genuine. But she still wasn't moving.

"Okay," Callie said. "I was just going to sit with you while you worked, and maybe talk your ear off about the beehives. But I can see you're busy."

"Oh, I'm just going to finish one thing and go to lunch."

Callie thought of Liam at the homestead, in his office. She didn't have much to do now that she'd taken care of the beehive purchase, and she wondered if she could spend the afternoon with her sister.

Not if you're going to make homemade barbecue sauce.

"Okay," she said. "Well, we can talk about bees later. I have to get home and start dinner."

"What are you making?"

"Barbecue chicken pizza."

"Oh, pulling out the family recipes." Simone smiled, her grip on the door just a little too tight.

"Yeah," Callie said. "Can't wait to see your secret project." She gave Simone a knowing look, but her sister just gazed evenly back at her. Callie left and went back to the homestead, and she knew instantly that Liam was there.

The whole house seemed to hold more life and laughter when he was around, and Callie basked in the warm feeling of it. Then she got to work on that barbecue sauce. After all, she really wanted to impress him and hopefully make everything right between them in just a few short hours.

32

Simone closed the door on her art studio and leaned into it, sighing. A general feeling of excitement moved through her, and a smile decorated her face.

"She's gone."

A cowboy stepped around a tall cabinet in the back of the shed Simone had never really gotten around to refurbishing. He likewise wore a grin, and with that sexy black hat, Simone definitely had no defenses against the rugged, handsome man—who now lived next-door to her.

"So we're not tellin' anyone about us," Jarrod Rust said.

"Nothing to tell," Simone said, looking away from the man she'd just met a few weeks ago. *Same as Micah.*

But Micah wasn't there, and she honestly had no idea when he'd be back. She wasn't going to ask one of his brothers, and she hadn't gotten his number.

And Jarrod was cute, and available, and Simone was ready to stop being the recluse who worked out of a shed and only went to town a few times a year.

"Nothing yet," Jarrod said, catching her hand as she sat down at the table she'd been varnishing. He touched his lips to the back of her hand. "Dinner at my place later? Seems like your sister won't interrupt us tonight."

Callie had come over quite suddenly last night, but Simone had been able to explain away the pizza casserole as her just wanting to try out her new stove. She'd felt bad for distracting Callie so Jarrod could sneak out the back door, but he'd worn a look of delight and playfulness then, the same as now.

"Yes," she said, letting him tug on her arm until she stood up.

"Great," he said. "Shawn is at his folks' until the weekend, at least in the evenings."

"Yeah." Simone looked into Jarrod's light blue eyes, something sizzling between them. "I hope his mom is feeling better."

"I'll ask him this afternoon," Jarrod said, his gaze dropping to Simone's mouth. She wouldn't push him away if he kissed her, but the moment lengthened, and he still didn't move.

Simone was tired of waiting, as it seemed like that was all she did. She waited for people to come to her booth and buy her antiques and treasures. She waited for Evelyn and Callie to figure things out.

In fact, she had no idea where the past ten years of her life had gone, and she was ready to seize every day by the horns.

So she tipped up onto her toes, her forehead bumping against Jarrod's hat. She giggled and reached up to remove it. "Are you going to kiss me, cowboy?"

"Do you want me to kiss you?"

If he moved at all, Simone would fall flat on her face. "Yes," she whispered, and Jarrod finally lowered his head and touched his lips to hers.

Simone felt wild and completely unlike herself. She normally didn't let anyone in her she-shed at all. Just her sisters, and Rhett, had come inside a few times.

But this kiss felt stolen. Forbidden. And absolutely wonderful. He let her set the pace, and Simone felt drunk on the touch of this man. She hadn't had a boyfriend for a long, long time, and she wondered why she'd isolated herself so completely out at the Shining Star.

Because kissing was fun.

Jarrod broke the kiss and ducked his head as he pulled in a long breath. "All right," he said. "Dinner at my place tonight."

"See you then." She stepped away from him then, her bones feeling a bit like pudding. She smiled him out of the building, and then she sank back into her chair. But she wasn't going to varnish. Oh, no, not after a kiss like that.

Plucking her phone from a pocket in her apron, she tapped and dialed her best friend, Kara Adrian.

"Hello, Miss Simone," Kara said, which meant her boss was nearby. Didn't matter. Simone didn't even need Kara to say anything else.

"We just hired ten new dreamy cowboys at the ranch," she said. "And I just kissed one of them." She sighed and then giggled.

"Wow," Kara said. "Yes, I can get you in tomorrow."

"Tomorrow," Simone said, and she could definitely get to the salon tomorrow. She didn't need anything done with her hair though. "What time?"

"Uh, let's see." Kara took a few seconds, as she was probably trying to see when Glenda would be out of the salon. Then the rumor mill wouldn't be as loud, and Simone might actually be able to tell her the story of how she and Jarrod had gone from neighbors to neighbors-who-kissed in just a few days.

"When can you come out to the ranch?" Simone asked. "We should schedule that too."

"Oh, I'm off on Thursday," Kara said. "But I can get you in tomorrow at three-fifteen."

Simone squealed and said, "See you then."

She sighed as she sat back in her chair. She didn't even have to worry about hiding her newfound giddiness from Callie, because she had her own place now. Simone adored her little cabin, and she was glad she'd decided to break out of the mold she'd been in for so long.

Of course, she knew why and how she'd gotten into that mold, and it had served her well for a while.

But now...now Simone was ready to broaden her horizons. Expand her world. See what else was out there beyond the borders of the Shining Star Ranch. And she had never been happier about the possibilities.

———

THAT AFTERNOON, her phone rang just as she stepped out of the shower. She still had hours before it could be considered dinnertime, but she hadn't been feeling particularly creative after that kiss.

Her head actually felt like it was bobbing up in the blue Texas sky with the clouds. But she had enough awareness to see her gran's name on the phone, and she swiped on the call, surprised her elderly grandmother could use her cellphone.

"Gran?"

"Simone, dear," she said, her voice shaking more than usual. "Your father is ill, and I'm wondering if you can come in and help me get him to the hospital."

"Ill?" Alarms rang through Simone's head. "What's wrong?" She couldn't go racing into town wearing just a towel, and she hurried into her bedroom to get dressed.

"He's had a fever for a few days," Gran said. "And just now he started complaining of chest pains."

"Gran," Simone said, straightening. "You need to hang up with me and call nine-one-one."

"Oh, I don't—"

"Gran," she said louder. "I mean it. Hang up with me and call nine-one-one. I'm getting dressed, because I just got out of the shower, and I'll come get you and we'll meet him at the hospital."

"Oh."

"He doesn't have time for me to drive in,' Simone said. "Do I need to call?"

"Could you?"

Simone smothered a sigh, because this wasn't the time. "Yes," she said. "I'm hanging up now." She did, and in the few seconds it took for the call to truly end, she felt like a lifetime had passed. Her heart pounded in an irregular way, and she couldn't even imagine how her world would be flipped upside down by her father's death.

She'd never known her mother, and she couldn't stand the thought of not having a parent in the world.

"What's your emergency?" someone asked.

"My father's been having chest pains," Simone said. "He's at his home in town, while I'm out on our ranch. I'm too far to get to him quickly. Can you send an ambulance to five-seventeen Lumberjack immediately?"

"Is he conscious?"

"Yes," Simone said, though she honestly didn't know. "I'm on my way. Should I meet you there or at the hospital?" It didn't really matter, because she had to go pick up Gran anyway. They wouldn't let her ride in the ambulance, Simone knew that much.

Flashes of her fiancé's body made her vision go black.

They wouldn't let her ride in the back of the ambulance with him, and she leaned over, sure she was about to be sick

"Ma'am?" a voice asked, but Simone didn't answer it.

She needed to get to her father.

Now.

33

Liam still had no good ideas for how to get back into Callie's good graces. He didn't have time to go to town and buy something, and she wouldn't have appreciated the gesture anyway.

He thought about simpler times, when he used to go out to the garden at Seven Sons and pull up microscopic weeds in an attempt to see her. She'd wander out to the fence sometimes, and they'd talk. She didn't know it, but those easy conversations had meant the world to him. They'd given him hope in a landscape that didn't have much of that, and they'd encouraged him to finally get to know her, ask her out, offer his help.

But their marriage was about so much more than him helping her now. He had spoken true when he'd said he didn't need rules. He didn't. Not really.

"What do you need?" he asked himself, the scent of

barbecue sauce almost a slow, silent torture device. It had been simmering all afternoon, and Liam couldn't wait to finish this last scene and go eat with his wife.

Problem was, he didn't know what he needed. Maybe just for her not to tell his brother that she loved him. Which was stupid, because of course Callie could love Jeremiah. Liam loved Evelyn and Simone as if they were his sisters.

Everything felt confused and muddled in his mind. He pushed it all away by cranking up the volume in his headphones, which forced him to focus on the computer screens in front of him. He generated fire and explosions, made them move in beautiful ways, and set it all against the backdrop of the caped superhero sprinting away from certain death.

With that done, Liam stood and stretched, removed the headphones, and took a moment to appreciate the silence. Before he could think too hard, he knelt down at his desk chair, balancing his elbows against the cushioned seat. He bowed his head and poured out his whole soul to God, begging Him for a solution that would end with both him and Callie happy and thriving.

And for me, Lord, that's right here at the Shining Star, with her. I love her, and I want to be with her. Give me the words to say. Help me have courage to say them. Provide her with a forgiving heart.

He needed one of those as well, and he actually felt his

soften the longer he prayed. For some reason, his brother popped into his head.

Help Jeremiah, he prayed. *With whatever he needs. He's a good man, and he just wants to do the right thing.*

Liam knew, because that was what Liam wanted too. He didn't know or understand everything Jeremiah was going through—or had gone through—but he knew he wanted happiness for his brother too. For all of them.

He got up, his knees not as young as they'd once been. A groan pulled through his throat, and he took a moment to stretch his back really well and readjust his cowboy hat. Drawing in a deep breath and employing as much bravery as he had, he slid open the barn door that separated his office from the rest of the house.

Soft music played down the hall in the kitchen, and he turned that way. He paused to watch his wife, needing a moment to discover how he truly felt.

Callie worked at the stove, sprinkling something over a pan before she bent and slid it into the oven. She wore jeans and boots and a pink blouse that made her seem younger than she was. Over that, an apron covered her clothes, and she wiped her hands on it as she exhaled.

An overwhelming sense of love descended upon Liam, and he knew he didn't need fancy speeches or extravagant gifts. Not for Callie.

He strode toward her, glad when she turned at the sound of him coming. "I love you." He cradled her face in his hands and looked right into her eyes. "I'm sorry about yesterday. I trust you, and I love you."

Tears filled those eyes, and she said, "I love you too."

Liam bent down and kissed her, a sweet touch of his lips against hers. "Something smells amazing."

"It's Gran's barbecue sauce," she said. "Secret family recipe."

"I'm starving."

"It's almost done."

Liam stepped back and started getting out plates and napkins. "So, did you want to talk rules?"

A few seconds passed, and then the timer on the oven went off. Callie reached for the oven mitts and pulled a glorious pizza out of the oven. The crust was golden brown and crisp, with melty cheese and bright dots of green onion among the dark red barbecue sauce and chunks of chicken.

Liam's mouth watered, and he retreated around the island and sat at the bar. Callie pulled a bagged salad out of the fridge, still not speaking.

"Silence is never good with you, Cal," he said. "What's goin' on?"

She poured the salad into a bowl and opened a drawer. "Will you cut the pizza while I get out the sweet tea?"

He took the pizza cutter from her, giving her back some of that same silence. He'd made the first, long cut across the pie when she said, "I don't need rules, Liam."

"No?"

"No. I know the ranch belongs to us, and even if we did split up, you wouldn't try to take it from me."

He had to work to keep his hand steady as he made the second cut.

"Simone will find some amazing man to marry, and she'll leave the ranch, just like Evelyn did."

"Probably," Liam said.

"I like sleeping with you," she said, and that got Liam to look away from the pizza. Her face reddened slightly, and she shrugged. "So that's not really a rule anymore. And those were all of mine."

She'd clearly tossed him the ball, and Liam put the pizza cutter in the sink and stepped to her side. "I like sleeping with you too," he whispered. "Last night was torture."

Callie leaned her head against his bicep, and Liam swept his arm around her. "You haven't fought with me about money and what we choose to spend it on. The affection thing isn't a problem."

"It's just Miah."

"Yeah," Liam said. "And honestly, Cal, it's *my* problem. Not yours, or his, even."

"Did you talk to him about it?"

"Yes, a little."

"And?"

"And it's...my problem."

She looked up at him. "And that's it?"

"I get a little bit too far into my head sometimes," he

said. "But when I stop and think about it, I know you'd never cheat on me. I trust you, and I trust him. I have nothing to be jealous of."

"You really don't."

"I know that." He touched his lips to her forehead. "I really do. So I just need to re-center my thoughts, and I'm okay."

"I don't want this to happen again while you're re-centering."

"It won't," he said.

Callie's beautiful eyes smiled at him, and he felt such love for her. He'd never seen her look at Jeremiah like that, and all the jealousy he'd felt over Jeremiah and Callie's relationship evaporated.

"Let's eat," she said.

"Are you as hungry as I am?"

"Yes," she said. "And the sooner we eat, the sooner we can go to bed."

"Callie," Liam said, laughing. Still, it was nice to know she loved him and wanted to be with him.

She served him pizza and salad, and he glanced at her. "I've been meaning to talk to you about something."

"Oh, yeah? What's that?"

"Kids," he said.

Alarm pulled across her face for a brief moment. She relaxed, but before she could say anything, her phone rang. He saw Simone's name on the screen as Callie reached for the device.

"Hold that thought." She swiped on the call and said, "Hey, sissy." Only seconds later, her eyes widened, and her face paled. "What? When?"

Liam set down his fork, because he had a feeling it was going to be quite a bit longer until he led Callie down the hallway to their bedroom.

"We'll be right there." She hung up and sprang from the barstool. "My dad's in the hospital. He's had a heart attack." Her eyes met Liam's, and he felt her pure panic and fear. Tears streamed down her face, and he gathered her into his arms.

"It's okay," he said. "Let's grab my keys on the way out."

34

Callie thought her heart might burst from her chest before Liam got them to the hospital. Simone had answered all of her texts, and their father seemed to be stable now.

He's okay, Simone said. *He's awake. He wants more dinner than they gave him. Gran is asleep in the only chair in the room. You won't want to stay long.*

Callie had asked if Simone had called Evelyn, and she had. In fact, her younger sister had done everything Callie would've done.

She was glad she didn't have to do things alone anymore, and she squeezed Liam's hand as he pulled into the Three Rivers Hospital. "He's okay," she said. "He's going to be okay."

"What's Simone saying?" he asked.

Callie told him as he parked, and they both got out of

the truck. He met her at the front, his touch so soothing and so familiar. They walked in hand-in-hand, and Callie paused, the antiseptic scent of the hospital knocking her back thirty-five years.

"Oh, wow," she said, her stomach heaving. And she'd been so careful not to eat too much pizza. The first time she'd been here, her hand had been laced through her father's. There had been plenty of tears and drawn down faces as her mother kissed each of her daughters, and Callie barely went to the doctor after that.

She'd associated the hospital with death, and she didn't want to revisit those emotions. When she'd come for her hysterectomy, Evelyn had held one hand while Simone clutched the other. They'd been there when she'd gone in, and they were both waiting for her when she came out.

This time, with her hand locked in Liam's, she knew she wanted to always have him at her side. Always and forever.

"This way," he said gently, tugging her away from the information desk. She hadn't even heard him ask for her father's room number. But he obviously had, as he led them into the maze of long, sterile hospital hallways, taking her up to the fourth floor where patient rooms were.

"Do you want to go in alone?" Liam asked, pausing outside a room with all the curtains drawn.

"No," she said, her throat dry. "Absolutely not." She stepped toward the door at the same time Simone came out, and the relief in her younger sister's face triggered Callie's tears again. "Heya, sissy." She let go of Liam so she could hug Simone. "How is he?"

"He's ready to go home, of course." Simone gave a laugh mixed with half a sob. "The doctor will be here in a few minutes to talk to us about what happened and what he needs to do going forward."

Callie pulled in a deep breath. "Okay, good." She went into the room while Liam gathered Simone into a hug, her eyes adjusting to the darkness of the room quickly. "Daddy." She hurried to his side, hating how frail and old he looked lying in that bed.

He'd always been the tall, tough rancher who didn't spoil his daughters. Who expected them to work as hard as he did. He worked from dawn to dusk, made dinner for the girls, and learned how to braid their hair so he could send them to school looking like they had someone who cared for them at home.

He bought them cowgirl boots for their birthdays, and he'd paid for haircuts and manicures even when he didn't want to.

Callie loved him with a fierceness she couldn't put into words. She wept as she leaned over and touched her lips to his cheek, and that was all she had to do for him to know. His weathered hand covered hers, and she put her other hand on top. "How are you feeling?"

"I'm a little tired," he admitted.

"Yeah, you had a heart attack, Daddy," Callie said.

"I feel okay now, though." His gaze moved from her face as Liam joined Callie bedside. "Liam."

"Sir," he said.

Callie wasn't sure what else to say, and Evelyn came in with drinks at that moment. "Callie," she said. "Hey." She handed the drinks to Simone and enveloped Callie and Liam in a hug. "The doctor should be here in a minute."

"Simone told us," Callie said. She stood back away from her father's bed, and sure enough, Gran had snoozed through the whole exchange in the only chair in the room. Callie leaned against the counter and accepted the paper cup of water her sister handed her.

Of course, when a doctor said "a few minutes" that meant a half an hour, and Callie's patience for standing in a dark hospital room had reached its limit by that point. But she snapped to attention when the man wearing the dark blue scrubs entered. He looked like he could be her son if she'd started having children when her mother did, in her early twenties.

"I'm Doctor Bellamisi," he said, smiling like they were about to attend a fabulous holiday party. He shook hands with everyone, and Callie looked at him eagerly. "So your father had a CAS, a coronary artery spasm, what we some-times call a silent heart attack."

He looked around like Callie or her sisters would know what any of that meant. She sure didn't, and by Evelyn and Simone's silence, they didn't either.

"Basically, there's no blockage in any of his arteries," Dr. Bellamisi said. "Which is good. It's also bad, because it means we don't know why he had the heart attack and don't have anything to really fix." He pulled his stethoscope from around his neck and fixed it on his ears, starting to press the listening pad against her father's chest. "His heart sounds normal, and our scans and blood work does indicate the attack." He pulled back, that annoying smile on his face again. "I'm going to monitor him for the night, but he should be able to go home in the morning."

"That's it?" Callie asked. "What do we do...with him?"

Dr. Bellamisi glanced at Daddy and back to Callie. "I'm going to put him on a low-dose aspirin and some post-heart attack medication just to be safe. He should follow-up with his regular doctor immediately, and every couple of weeks for the first few months." He looked down the row of sisters. "Can I talk to you outside?"

"I'm not a child," Daddy said. "You can say what needs to be said right here."

Gran snorted, but she didn't wake up. Callie honestly couldn't believe she could sleep through such ruckus, and she shook her head while Simone giggled.

Callie laced her fingers through Liam's again and said, "It's okay to just tell us, Doctor."

"Your father was lucky," he said. "A lot of people who have silent heart attacks never come in and they never know it. Then, the next attack is huge, and they then don't have a chance to come in." He held up his hands quickly. "I'm not saying that's going to happen, but your father needs to be careful, and he needs to come to the emergency room the moment he feels anything abnormal." He looked at Daddy. "A lot of the pain you described as indigestion or a pulled muscle in your back was the silent heart attack. Those pains can't be ignored."

"All right," Daddy said. "I won't ignore them."

The doctor looked back at Callie, Evelyn, and Simone. "It's my understanding he lives with his mother."

"No, she's my mother's mother," Callie said, her voice tight.

"He says she sleeps a lot," Dr. Bellamisi said.

"I'm sure she does," Evelyn said. "She's ninety-two years old."

"Ladies," the doctor said. "The Good Lord must need your father here on the Earth a bit longer, then. Because it's double lucky he had this attack while your grandmother was awake and could call the paramedics."

"I called emergency," Simone said, her voice deathly quiet.

"What?" Callie asked in tandem with everyone else.

"Gran called." Simone looked around, her eyes wide. "And she didn't know what to do, and she wanted me to come take Daddy to the hospital. When she finally told me he had chest pains, I told her to call nine-one-one, but she didn't want to. So I did."

Callie knew at that moment what the doctor was

saying. "So they'll come live at the ranch with me and Liam." She turned to him. "Right, baby?"

"Of course," he said instantly, and Callie loved him even more for that. "We have plenty of room on the main floor."

"Right across the hall from your bedroom," Evelyn said, her point silent but there.

"It's fine," Callie said. "I'm not working the ranch anymore, and I can keep an eye on Daddy and make sure someone is there if he has another heart attack." She switched her gaze back to the doctor and then Daddy. "Daddy, did you hear that?"

"I'm not movin' back to the ranch," he said, his voice set on stubborn.

No wonder the doctor wanted to talk to them in private. Her father could be a bit crotchety sometimes. Callie stepped over to him and covered his hand again. "Dad, yes you are. Gran can't take care of you, and you might have another heart attack."

"We live about twenty minutes from the hospital," Callie said. "They're much closer here in town. Maybe they should just stay in the farmhouse."

"Ma'am," the doctor said. "If your father has an attack that goes undetected for a few hours, he could suffer major damage."

Helplessness filled Callie. Gran definitely slept for a few hours every day. But Callie couldn't be chained to the homestead either. And what if he had an attack in the middle of the night? She'd never know then.

"There are options for in-home care, or even an assisted-living facility."

"Oh, boy," Liam muttered at the same time Daddy nearly shot out of the bed.

"I'm not goin' into an old folks home," he practically bellowed. "I'm only sixty-seven, for crying out loud."

"All right," Callie said, putting one hand on his shoulder and pressing him back into the bed. "Do we have to talk about this right now?"

"No." The doctor backed up. "No, we don't. I'll have the nurse bring you some literature, and I'll be back in a couple of hours to check on you again, Mister Foster."

Her father looked like he could make the young doctor poof into a cloud of smoke with just his eyes, and the awkwardness in the room didn't lessen after the doctor left. Callie looked at her sisters, and then back to her dad.

None of them were going to be the decision-makers. They'd always looked to Callie for such things.

Yeah, and look how you ran the Shining Star into the ground.

She hated the thought, and she did her best to silence it.

"Okay," she said, trying to find her confidence. "Evelyn, you need to get home to Rhett."

"Oh, he's just outside on the phone. Something about a new case."

"Fine, whatever," Callie said. "I think you should take Gran and your family home. There's nothing any of you can do here."

Evelyn stepped next to Callie. "We're fine."

"I know," Callie said, smiling at her. "But you've been on your feet for a while, and I can see the exhaustion in your face. Go home. Take Gran with you. Make sure she's okay."

Her sister nodded and moved around the bed to wake Gran.

"Simone," Callie started, but Simone silenced her with a glare. Callie's thoughts switched quickly. "Will you stay with Daddy tonight? I'll come spell you in the morning."

"Yes," Simone said, nodding as her expression softened. "Y'all go on back to the ranch. I didn't mean to interrupt."

"You didn't," Liam said, stepping next to Simone. "If you need something, call me. I have a million brothers who can bring you whatever you need. And Jeremiah never sleeps." He grinned, and Simone smiled back at him.

Callie looked at her father. "Okay, Daddy. Simone is going to stay with you tonight. We'll all be back in the morning to see what the doctor says about going home."

Her father looked up at her, worry in his face. "I don't want to make life harder for you, buggy."

"Daddy." She pressed her forehead to his. "You aren't. But you really need to think about coming back to the ranch, at least for a little while."

"I'll think about it," he said, and Callie straightened. She met Liam's eye, and they left Simone in the room with Callie's father.

Rhett had just joined Evelyn and was helping Gran shuffle along. He waved over his shoulder to Callie and Liam, and a measure of gratitude for the good neighbors the Lord had blessed her with filled Callie from head to toe.

"Ready, sweetheart?" Liam asked.

"Yes," she said, looking at the man who had literally saved her life. Maybe his proposal had been convenient. Maybe their I-do had been invented in the beginning. But it sure wasn't now—not for her. And she knew it never had been for Liam.

She tucked herself into his side, hoping he knew she was as committed to him as he was to her. "Let's go home." She could show him then, and they could finish their conversation about having a family and building a life together.

And the things that used to scare Callie suddenly held so much potential, so much hope.

35

"All right," Liam said. "That's the last of it." He looked around at the farmhouse where Callie's father had been living for the last twelve years. It would need a good scrubbing from floor to ceiling, but Liam wasn't going to let his wife lift a single sponge. She was already going to have her hands full with her father and grandmother, and Liam still had miles to go on his current leg of the movie he'd been working on steadily for the past month.

But Simone lived on the ranch too, and Evelyn wasn't due for another four months. Callie wasn't alone, and that was the important thing. Her bees wouldn't be here for a while either, and she'd spent the last month learning as much as she could about ranch operations—and how to adopt a baby.

Liam's heart sped every time he thought about

building a family with her, of becoming a father. They were still very early in the process, but the hope they both had seemed to double with each passing day.

"Ready?"

He blinked his way out of his thoughts to find Callie standing in front of him. Just like the first time he'd met her, she took his breath away. Her spirit was so full and so kind, and he wanted to do whatever he had to in order to be the best man he could be...for her. Because she deserved the best.

"Yes," he said, moving toward her.

"Good, because Daddy is already complaining about how hot the homestead is." She shook her head, though a smile graced her face. "I keep telling him I've upgraded the air conditioner since he left."

He reached her and gathered her into a hug. "Whatever happens, it'll be fine." They swayed together, and he adored the way Callie clung to him like she needed him. The way she pressed her face to his chest like she wanted to hear his heart beating.

"I'm sorry about this," she whispered, and it wasn't the first time she'd apologized.

"Baby." He stepped back. "It's going to be great."

"You don't know my father all that well," she said.

"Cal." He swallowed and put a smile on his face. "I'd do anything for you. It doesn't matter if it's easy or hard. Because me and you, we belong together. And we're stronger together than we are apart. So whatever happens, it'll be okay. Because we'll still be together."

Her chin wobbled. "Do you really believe that?"

"Absolutely I do." And there was nothing invented about those two words. For him, there never had been.

She nodded and tipped her faced back so Liam could kiss her, which he did. "I love you," she whispered. "So much."

"And I love you, Callie, with my whole heart." He kissed her again. "Now, did you order pizza on your app so we can pick it up on our way out?"

She smiled at him. "I sure did. It'll be ready in five minutes."

"Great." Liam turned her toward the door. "Let's hope my brothers don't give your father another heart attack."

She giggled and snuggled into his side. "I'll text Miah and tell him to tell everyone to take themselves down a notch."

"Do you think that's possible?" Liam asked, and Callie shrugged as she continued laughing. "Because I'm not sure we Walkers know what quiet means."

"Hey, I've seen the lot of you be quiet...in church."

He chuckled and led her outside, thanking the Lord above for everything this woman had brought into his life —and that there was absolutely nothing invented between them.

———

Liam

Keep reading to find out if another Walker brother can get his happily-ever-after in Three Rivers! Why has Whitney Wilde gone cold? And will Jeremiah actually do anything about it? Chapter one and two of **JEREMIAH** are next! Keep reading!

345

Sneak Peek! Jeremiah - Chapter One

J eremiah Walker ignored Stony's snuffle of displeasure as he strode past. "I have to get to town, Stony," he said over his shoulder, wondering when his life had been reduced to talking to horses.

Oh, that was right. When Whitney had gone completely cold and silent on him. When Liam and moved in with his wife next-door. When Micah had gone back to Temple and was still tying up loose ends.

"Skyler's coming home in a couple of days," Jeremiah yelled to the horse, happier about his brother returning to Seven Sons than he dared to admit. Wyatt had gone back to normal, and he still hadn't told anyone who he'd been sneaking off to see in the evenings. Jeremiah, of course, didn't ask. He was just glad he didn't have to spend his evenings alone anymore. Those couple of weeks in January had been dark, dark days for him.

But with Skyler home, and Wyatt, Jeremiah had something to look forward to again. Rhett and Evelyn had taken a springtime trip to the Texas Hill Country to see the wildflowers bloom, and they'd be home by the time Skyler was too.

Jeremiah had been planning a feast for the past week, and he needed to get to town to get the groceries. Orion and Dicky, Simon and Wallace, would handle all the chores on Wednesday, and Jeremiah would spend the day in the kitchen.

Excitement ran through him—another indicator that his life had reached a low point. Who was actually excited to spend the day laboring in the kitchen?

It wasn't his lowest point ever, and for that, he was grateful.

He showered quickly and swiped his truck keys from the peg by the door leading to the garage. He was the only one who parked in the garage, as he seemed to be the only permanent resident at the homestead. Wyatt had been there for a year and a half now, though. Jeremiah wondered if he'd spend the rest of his life alone. When Laura Ann had left, he'd thought he would.

But now, with some time and distance between where he was now and that terrible moment when he realized his fiancée wasn't going to come out and become his wife, he'd changed. Healed. Well, at least a little bit.

His thoughts automatically betrayed him and went to Whitney Wilde. He may have put the truck into gear a little bit too hard with that woman in his mind, and he pressed his teeth together to get her to leave.

Four months. That was how long it had been since he'd heard from her. And her sudden disappearance from his life made no sense. She'd called him for a solid six months before he'd allowed her onto the ranch to shoot.

"She was using you," he told himself for probably the hundredth time. But she hadn't ever brought one of her brides. Or a family. Or anyone. She'd merely wandered the ranch with him, taking a picture for Liam, and poof. Disappeared.

Jeremiah was still trying to figure out what he'd done wrong. He'd held her hand that night. Bought her dinner. Been a perfect gentleman, with great conversation, and laughter, and he'd even thought about kissing her.

A scoff came out of his mouth, and he really wished he could get Whitney out of his mind. Funnily enough, when she'd been harassing him about shooting at the ranch, he never gave her a second thought. Even after he'd hung up on her.

But now?

Now she tormented him in his quiet moments and haunted him at other times. Even after four months, Jeremiah was still hung up on her.

"That's because you fall too hard, too fast," he told himself as he caught sight of the outskirts of Three Rivers. He'd just get to Wilde & Organic before they closed, get everything he needed for the feast, and get back to the ranch.

He went to town quite a bit, actually. Besides Wyatt, he was probably considered the most social. He was the public face of the ranch, and he went to ranch ownership meetings every other week. He attended church, though he still felt somewhat removed from the Lord. He did the shopping. He went to all the town celebrations. In fact, attending them had become somewhat of a family tradition.

No, he didn't go to the summer dances, which would be starting up again in about a month.

"Maybe you should," he told himself. But he couldn't imagine finding someone his age at a dance in the park. That felt more like something people in their twenties did, and Jeremiah would be forty-three in August.

Nope, he wasn't going to go to the summer dances.

He pulled into the parking lot at Wilde & Organic, thinking it would be darker than it was. He reminded himself that May had dawned last week, and maybe he hadn't had to rush into town so quickly.

Wilde & Organic was only open until eight o'clock, though, and he'd taken to shopping in the late afternoon or evenings to make sure he wouldn't run into Whitney. She'd told him once that she worked in the morning, stocking the produce before the store opened, so he wouldn't see her if he shopped later in the day.

Plus, he knew this was the perfect light she liked for

shoots. "Golden hour," he muttered to himself, sick of talking to horses or thin air.

Determined not to say another word unless it was to a human, he headed for the store. He had a long list that included premium cuts of meat and at least twenty produce items. He loved everything about Wilde & Organic, and he wasn't surprised to see Molly working the only register open. She didn't look toward Jeremiah, but she'd chat him up as she rang him out.

He liked Molly a lot, and she hadn't acted differently toward Jeremiah in the last four months. Of course, no one had known about their relationship, if it could even be classified as such.

He selected his honey whole wheat bread, a round of sourdough, plenty of cheese and lunch meat, a huge rack of lamb, pounds and pounds of organic chicken and ground beef, and then moved over to the produce section.

"Shoppers, Wilde & Organic will be closing in fifteen minutes. Please make your final selections and make your way to check out four."

Jeremiah glanced up at the sound of the female voice, and he wondered how many people were still in the store. He hadn't seen many people, and he was the only one left in the produce section.

Working quickly now, he finished up his list, adding a bottle of mayonnaise last, and heading for the check out.

"Jeremiah," Molly said, that warm smile on her face. "How are you, darlin'?"

"Just fine, ma'am." To his surprise, he found himself smiling. He supposed Pasty couldn't control her daughter any more than Jeremiah could.

"Looks like you're planning a big meal."

"Yeah," Jeremiah said. "Skyler's coming home from college on Wednesday. Everyone's coming for dinner."

"I hear you're a good cook," she said.

"I'm decent," he said, though he knew he was a good cook. Movement caught his eye near the customer service desk. A dark-haired woman came out the door there, and it took Jeremiah less than a blink to realize it was Whitney.

He sucked in a breath. Molly said something, but he had no idea what. White noise sounded in his ears, and all he could do was stare.

As if in slow motion, Whitney glanced in his direction. She didn't look long enough to truly see him, and she turned away a moment later, clearly not recognizing him. She set a basket on the ground and reached for a poster on the bulletin board near the exit.

Somehow, without even knowing it, Jeremiah had walked away from Molly and toward Whitney. He breathed, and he got a nose full of Whitney's perfume. "Hey," he said.

Whitney turned, barely looking at him. She jerked back to him, her eyes widening. "Jeremiah."

Even with the shock in her tone, he wanted to hear her say his name over and over again. "What are you doing?"

She just stared at him, almost like he was the one who'd gone silent four months ago.

"Jeremiah?" Molly said, and he turned back to her mother. She'd finished with his groceries, and he wanted to pull out his wallet and toss it at her. Instead, he looked back at Whitney.

"Don't disappear, okay?" He backed up a couple of steps, just making sure she didn't bolt for the door the moment he'd finished talking. She didn't, and he returned to the check out counter to pay for his cart full of groceries. "Thank you, Molly," he said as she flipped off the light on her check out station.

Jeremiah pushed his cart toward Whitney and watched as she stapled a new poster to the board. This one was the usual newborn picture. A darling, sleeping baby, probably only five or six days old, this one nestled among bright flowers—tulips, crocus, and bluebonnets—and tons of greenery. Vegetable greenery—kale, cabbage, and butter lettuce.

"Do you know Lake Winters?" he asked, indicating the poster.

"Not well," she said evasively.

"Why would anyone want a picture like that?"

Whitney stood back and looked at the poster. She stepped down the bulletin board a few feet and took down a flyer for a cooking class that had happened last weekend. If Jeremiah had known she'd be there, cleaning up the bulletin board, he wouldn't have come. Or maybe he would've made sure to come tonight.

He honestly didn't know.

"I think they're sweet," she said. "The baby photos."

"I guess," Jeremiah said. "I think they're weird." He wished he could bite back the words. He didn't want to argue with her. Or even disagree. He had so many questions for her, but he couldn't ask any of them, with her mother only a few feet away, and the store about to close.

He pushed his cart behind her and leaned closer to her. "If I called, would you answer?"

Before she could answer, the main lights in the store went out, leaving only the glowing light of emergency lights. "You should go," she said, which wasn't the answer he wanted.

He had so much more to say, but he simply did what she wanted. He left the store, holding his head high as he marched away from her.

Every step tore at him a little more, but he clenched the pain tightly inside him. Cinched it close to his heart as a reminder that he couldn't trust women and that he would be just fine with only ranching and cooking in his life.

He would.

Sneak Peek! Jeremiah - Chapter Two

Whitney Wilde's heart pounded in her chest for several long minutes after Jeremiah had walked out the door. Not only did she not like being in the store by herself, but that man was her biggest regret.

Would you answer if I called?

Whitney had wanted to blurt *yes. Yes, I'd answer.*

But then she'd have to tell him why she'd *stopped* answering. Humiliation burned through her. She just wanted to forget about Blake Thurston, the man that was like a recurring nightmare in her life.

He'd come into her life years ago and swept her right off her feet. That relationship had only lasted eight months. Then he'd broken up with her to go to farrier training. But he'd dropped out of that and worked as a loper for a horse farm in Oklahoma instead of returning to Three Rivers—and Whitney.

When he'd come back to Three Rivers, Whitney had fallen for his charms again. This time for only five months. Then Blake was off again, this time to Florida for some other job. And he'd come back just after the New Year, after a nine-month absence.

And Whitney had been sucked into his charms again. She had a horrible weakness for the man, who made her feel beautiful and sexy and like she was the only woman for him. Maybe she was—but only until he got bored of his job, bored of this town, bored with her.

Her heart wailed as it continued to pump, and she looked up at the new poster she'd just tacked up of her latest spring newborn shoot. Jeremiah's words spiraled through her mind, and she seemed to be able to remember every single thing the man had said to her.

So he didn't like the baby photography. He wasn't the only one. But somehow, his opinion carried more weight than anyone else's, and she could never tell him she was Lake Winters now.

Carrying the pseudonym was getting tiresome, and Whitney just wanted to put her own name on the cards and stop maintaining two websites, two phone numbers, two of everything. She wasn't sure why she'd wanted to keep the baby photography separate from her regular stuff in the first place.

Oh, wait, yes, she was. Blake had suggested it, and Whitney seemed to think everything the man said was made of pure magic. Whitney had done what he said. She wore what he liked. She laughed at everything he said. When he called, she answered.

She hated the person she was when she was with Blake, and she was glad his time in Three Rivers had only lasted eleven weeks.

Embarrassment and humiliation had kept her from texting Jeremiah, though she had a wedding that would be *perfect* if it were out at Seven Sons. But she didn't want him to think she was using him, because well, if a man did to her what she'd done to Jeremiah and then called about using the ranch...she'd think they were using her.

And Jeremiah was a smart man. A very smart, very handsome, very sexy man. Scratch that. Better than a man. A cowboy.

Whitney's breath whooshed out of her lungs, and she started piling everything into her basket. Her mother had left when she'd turned off the lights, and Whitney didn't normally like being in the huge supermarket alone. She went up the stairs with her supplies and into the office on the second floor.

With another sigh, she collapsed into the office chair there and looked out the one-way window that showed her the store below. Eerie shadows draped across the ends of aisles and mounds of oranges and other produce.

She simply sat, trying to figure out what she wanted her life to be. In Jeremiah's absence, she'd turned thirty-six, and her mother had spent the entirety of Whitney's birthday dinner talking about boyfriends and marriage and babies.

Things Whitney wanted, sure. Of course. She simply didn't have anyone knocking down her door.

"But you do," she muttered to herself. "Kind of."

If Jeremiah called, Whitney would answer. The problem was, he wasn't going to call. Whitney could feel it way down deep in her soul. *You have his number*, she thought, her gaze sweeping across the meat department.

Her stomach grumbled, but she made no move to get up and feed it. She didn't want to order another meal to be eaten alone. And she certainly wasn't going to cook tonight. She'd most likely drive through somewhere in town and eat it in her car, tossing the bag into the outside trashcan on her way into the house.

She'd sit in front of her computer and edit the senior pictures she'd done yesterday. Exhaustion moved through her body, because she'd booked six more seniors for that week alone. Tonight was the only night she didn't have anyone to shoot, and she had one in the morning on Saturday and one in the evening too.

She loved March, April, and most of May because she was so busy, but she hated them at the same time. Senior pictures and weddings paid her bills, though, and she didn't want to be ungrateful for the business the Good Lord sent her.

After all, if her photography couldn't pay the bills,

she'd have to work at Wilde & Organic full-time. While she loved her family, she sure didn't want to be here with her parents, her older sister, and one of her older brothers.

No, thank you, Whitney thought. She liked getting together for Sunday lunches and holidays. She went and saw her sister a couple times a week, but that was more for Dalton than Patsy.

Whitney opened the desk drawer in front of her, because Michael kept his favorite chocolate candy bars there for when he had a full day of paperwork ahead of him. He'd never miss one among the dozens he kept there, and Whitney wondered how he managed to eat them and stay trim and fit.

All she had to do was look at a bowl of macaroni and cheese or a plate of ribs and she'd gain ten pounds. Since Blake had left, Whitney had been eating potato chips or chocolate and counting them as meals, so she did carry a few extra pounds.

Her mind didn't seem to be able to settle onto any one thought, and she finally got to her feet. She moved her basket to the top of a filing cabinet, so Michael wouldn't get irritated when he arrived in the morning.

Whitney herself needed to be here in less than twelve hours, so she checked her pockets for her keys and headed downstairs. She hadn't parked out front, and she had to walk through the shadows to the back exit.

Her skin caught a chill as she hurried through the frozen section, and by the time she made it to the black, plastic door that led into the warehouse behind the store-front, she was almost running.

The exit lay directly in front of her, and Whitney exploded through it, though the darkness beyond wasn't much more comforting.

She'd parked right beneath the bright outside light on the building, and relief spread through her as the heavy, metal door slammed behind her. Whatever phantoms that had been chasing her through the store had been sealed inside. She turned back to make sure that door was locked, because if she didn't, and a robbery happened, she'd never be trusted in the store again. Her siblings already gave her sideways looks for how little she was involved in the family business, but Whitney had never minded.

With the door locked, Whitney turned back to her truck.

A man stood there.

Whitney sucked in a breath and screamed as loud as she could, spilling backward toward the door she'd just checked.

Her eyes didn't leave the man standing next to her driver's door, his cowboy hat bathing his face in darkness. He lifted both hands and said, "Whoa, it's fine. It's just me."

Even through her distress and the echoes of the screams, Whitney's brain connected the dots and "Jeremiah?" came out of her mouth.

"Sorry," he said. "Sorry." A nervous chuckle came out

of his mouth. "You have no idea how long I sat in my truck, trying to decide if I should go on home or wait to talk to you."

She pressed her palm against her chest and sagged against the door behind her. "Jeremiah," she said again as if she needed to convince herself that it was him and not someone else.

He hadn't taken a single step away from her truck, and a healthy distance remained between them. "I'm so sorry," he said. "I...." He closed his mouth and ducked his head in that adorable way he had, and Whitney straightened as a smile touched her mouth. Maybe her first smile in a long time, actually.

"I'll let you get on home," he said. "I know you're busy right now."

"How do you know I'm busy right now?" She took a step closer to him, then another one. It wasn't particularly cold outside, but she fought against a shiver.

"Uh, maybe I spend too much time on social media." He raised his head and looked right at her.

A thrill shot through her bloodstream with the sight of those beautiful, intense, dark eyes holding onto hers. "You're right. I'm shooting a lot right now."

"So if I maybe called during the day, it would be better?"

"Did you circle the store and pull behind my truck to wait for me to ask me when you could call?" Whitney teased, glad when the ghost of a smile touched his lips. She'd never had the privilege of kissing that mouth, but oh, she wanted to.

Thank goodness it was dark and the overhead light there threw shadows around, because her face heated to a dangerous level.

"You still stockin' shelves here in the morning?"

"I do the produce section," she said, stopping just out of reach from Jeremiah. Their whole relationship had been like that. He was always just out of her reach.

But closer than he's been in a while, she thought.

"I've told you that so many times," she said, shaking her head.

"That's what I meant," he said. "What time do you finish filling up the produce section?"

"Before we open," she said. "Daddy wanted everything pristine for the very first customer. Michael has adopted that stance." With only a couple of other grocery stores in town, Wilde & Organic didn't have a lot of competition, but her family wanted to provide the best experience. "I usually have to work in the back a little bit before I'm really done."

"So ten-thirty?"

"Closer to eleven before I leave here."

Jeremiah leaned against her truck like he wasn't going anywhere. "Do you always come tearing out the back door like the devil himself is chasing you?"

Whitney heard all the flirtation in his voice, and if she could see those eyes more clearly, they'd be sparkling like pure diamonds. "Yes," she said simply.

"Mm hm," Jeremiah said. "Well, maybe I'll call tomorrow then." He straightened and held her gaze for one more moment before circling toward the hood of her truck.

"Maybe?" she asked when he'd reached the far corner. She could barely see the light glinting off the chrome on his big, black truck. It seemed to melt right into the night, and Whitney promised herself in that moment that she'd never come to the store after dark and stay alone again.

Jeremiah looked over his shoulder at her. "You have my number, too, you know."

"Yeah, well, maybe I'll use it tomorrow then."

He grinned, tipped his hat, and continued to his truck. It purred as he started it, and he backed away from her vehicle. He didn't leave though, and Whitney hurried to get behind her own steering wheel and get the engine turned over.

She preceded him out of the parking lot, warmth moving through her like her momma had just pulled her favorite blanket out of the dryer and draped it over her shoulders.

"Please let him call tomorrow," she whispered to the sleepy town before her. She tilted her head back and added, "Please, Dear God. Give him the courage to me call tomorrow."

And if the Good Lord could do that, then Whitney would somehow find the strength to answer the phone when Jeremiah called.

———

Read **Jeremiah** in paperback today! Get it here by scanning this QR code with the camera on your phone.

Seven Sons Ranch in Three Rivers Romance™ Series

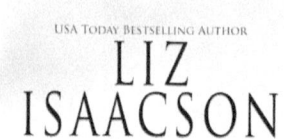

Rhett (Book 1): To save her business, she'll have to risk her heart. She needs a husband to be credible as a matchmaker. He wants to help a neighbor. **Will their fake marriage take them out of the friend zone?**

Tripp (Book 2): She needs a husband to keep her son. He's wanted to take their relationship to the next level, but she's always pushing him away. Will their trivial tie take them all the way to happily-ever-after?

Liam (Book 3): She's desperate to save her ranch. He wants to help her any way he can. Will their invented I-Do open doors that have previously been closed and lead to a happily-ever-after for both of them?

Jeremiah (Book 4): He wants to prove to his brothers that he's not broken. She just wants him. Will a fake marriage heal him or push her further away?

Wyatt (Book 5): To get her inheritance, she needs a husband. He's wanted to fly with her for ages. Can their pretend pledge turn into something real?

Skyler (Book 6): She needs a new last name to stay in school. He's willing to help a fellow student. Can this wanna-be wife show the playboy that some things should be taken seriously?

Micah (Book 7): They were just actors auditioning for a play. The marriage was just for the audition – until a clerical error results in a legal marriage. Can these two ex-lovers negotiate this new ground between them and achieve new roles in each other's lives?

Gideon (Book 8): It's 1971, and Gideon Walker is on the cutting edge of all the technology coming out of Texas. He has big dreams and wants to make something of himself. Then he meets Penny Aarons, and everything changes. He only has eyes for her, but she's got plans and dreams of her own...

Read this origin romance for Momma and Daddy from the Seven Sons series today!

Ivory Peaks Romance Series

Experience true Rocky Mountain life in the Ivory Peaks Romance series! You'll get more Hammond family romance, second chance romance, and all the heartwarming and uplifting family fiction you're craving. Ivory Peaks is the perfect escape for anyone looking to feel loved, cherished, and like they belong. You belong right here in Ivory Peaks!

His First Love (Book 1): She broke up with him a decade ago. He's back in town after finishing a degree at MIT, ready to start his job at the family company. **Can Hunter and Molly find their way through their pasts to build a future together?**

Brush Creek Cowboys Romance Series

Go up the canyon to Brush Creek Ranch, where a community of retired rodeo cowboys are looking for love...

Brush Creek Cowboy (Book 1): Former rodeo champion and cowboy Walker Thompson trains horses at Brush Creek Horse Ranch, where he lives a simple life in his cabin with his ten-year-old son. A widower of six years, he's worked with Tess Wagner, a widow who came to Brush Creek to escape the turmoil of her life to give her seven-year-old son a slower pace of life. But Tess's breast cancer is back...

Walker will have to decide if he'd rather spend even a short time with Tess than not have her in his life at all. Tess wants to feel God's love and power, **but can she discover and accept God's will in order to find her happy ending?**

Fuller Family in Brush Creek Romance Series

Join the Fuller Family in Brush Creek for heartwarming and inspirational romance series set in a picturesque small town.

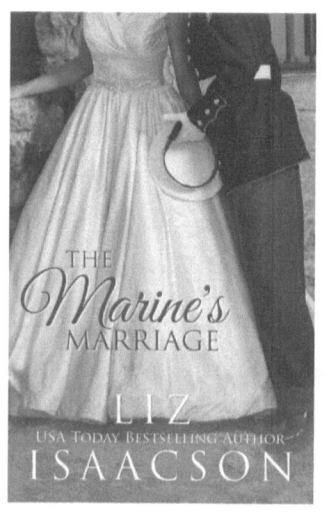

The Marine's Marriage: (Book 1): Tate Benson can't believe he's come to Nowhere, Utah, to fix up a house that hasn't been inhabited in years. But he has. Because he's retired from the Marines and looking to start a life as a police officer in small-town Brush Creek. Wren Fuller has her hands full most days running her family's company. When Tate calls and demands a maid for that morning, she decides to have the calls forwarded to her cell and go help him out. She didn't know he was moving in next door, and she's completely unprepared for his handsomeness, his kind heart, and his wounded soul. **Can Tate and Wren weather a relationship when they're also next-door neighbors?**

About Liz

Liz Isaacson writes inspirational romance, usually set in Texas, or Wyoming, or anywhere else horses and cowboys exist. She lives in Utah, where she writes full-time, takes her two dogs to the park everyday, and eats a lot of veggies while writing. Find her on her website, along with all of her pen names, at authorelanajohnson.com

www.ingramcontent.com/pod-product-compliance
Lightning Source LLC
Chambersburg PA
CBHW020716130726
47899CB00012B/1335